THE TURQUOISE/YELLOW CASE

by

P. K. Palmer

PINNACLE BOOKS * NEW YORK CITY

KILLINGER: THE TURQUOISE/YELLOW CASE

An original Pinnacle Books edition, published for the first time anywhere.

ISBN: 0-523-00299-8

First printing, January 1974

Printed in the United States of America

PINNACLE BOOKS, INC.
275 Madison Avenue
New York, N.Y. 10016

THE TURQUOISE/YELLOW CASE

Time
walks slowly
as it runs
in circles.

Yet,
Time
never moves.
For
it is always
Now.

a tale of four days

the
first
day . . .

Chapter One

The storm was born in the Pacific, off the coast of Baja California, child of a wild and passionate mating. Strange and violent winds met and danced together and spun and battled and wrapped their limbs around each other as they screamed in climax at the heavens above them.

The storm ran north, past San Diego and Los Angeles, on its way to Santa Barbara, piling up the waves before it. Beach sands were washed away. Pilings were torn out. Homes crumbled.

Strong winds multiplied the strength of the waves so that they tore forty tons of barge from its moorings, snapping the chains like pieces of kelp. The sound of thunder was a deep-throated, evil laughter.

The barge floated less than two feet high in the water, most of its waterlogged structure dangerously concealed below the surface, like a terrible wood and steel iceberg. It had become a weapon. A booby trap waiting for a careless ship.

Sails trimmed, the schooner moved with easy grace through the ocean's foamy hills and troughs. A lovely lady, her name and home port painted on the stern: *Katja* she was, and from Skagen, Denmark, she came. A beautifully formed and arrogant Scandinavian wench, skipping happily, carefree, and full of the love of life.

Strong hands held the wheel. They belonged to a sixty-eight-year-old Viking with white hair and a weathered

11

and well-lived-in face topping a body that might have belonged to an active man in his forties. A contest was his joy, and the foaming green waters had never defeated him. Nor had anyone or anything else.

A young Viking sea goddess came up behind him and gave him a big, thick, steaming blue mug of hot coffee half-and-half with thick Dutch chocolate, the whole lifted and richened with a great slug of twenty-year-old Spanish brandy. They drank together and toasted the raving sea.

She might have been the Danish Goddess Nerthus, worshiped by the bloodspattered tribes of the southern Baltic. Her long red hair was a glowing wet mane flung behind her. The gusts and eddies outlined her body, at once slim and fully rounded. The fine, strong, wide shoulders supported a proud and beautiful head.

As they looked at their world through the explosions of rain, the sea god and goddess knew that they owned the good things of the world.

Forever.

The barge was invisible beneath the waves which broke over it, covering it with foam. It was impervious to the swells which tilted it, pointing its sharp corners and aiming them carelessly.

From out of the gloom, the schooner moved into an oddly clear area in the midst of the turmoil. Instinct made the Viking spin the wheel. *Katja's* response was slow. She slid down the side of a big swell and onto the barge. . . .

The shock was hard and terrible. The rudder section was torn away. The main mast quivered from the vibration before it split off at deck level and fell slowly and heavily across the cockpit.

The barge slid away.

The Viking Gods had fallen. Ejnar Mylius lay on the deck, his scalp ripped and bleeding. Katja, his granddaughter, for whom the schooner had been christened, had fallen. Sobbing for breath, she moved tearfully to the side of the unconscious old man.

The mugs lay in the scuppers, shattered. Their warm and fragrant contents were now part of the sea.

An ambulance was waiting at the Peninsula Yacht Harbor in Oxnard. So too were the reporters. Whatever happened to Ejnar Mylius was News. He was a Power. Ejnar Mylius owned one of the world's great shipping and tanker fleets. . . . .

Within the hour, ticker-tape machines on the other side of the world were telling the story in their measured and staccato chatter.

And some very peculiar people were interested.

Chapter Two

The *Singapore Guardian-News* carried the story on page three, column one.

As soon as each edition of the paper hit the streets, the wrinkled little Malay news vendor rushed his first copy to Mr. K. Y. Smith. For this, he received a generous extra weekly bonus. Never would he entrust the paper to the Sikh doorman. He always brought it up to the penthouse himself and gave it to the beautiful lady.

She was Miss Smith, K. Y. Smith's daughter. Never had he seen a more wondrous body than hers in her Thai silk *cheong-sam*, each day a different color. And so skintight that if she wore anything beneath, the lines would show. Her long black hair was usually worn twisted and hanging over her left shoulder, coming forward to fall into the lush valley of her breasts. The Malay news vendor would have offered her the paper every day, without pay. In worship.

Her name was Talya.

She took the paper and gave it to her father. As though guided, he went directly to the story about Ejnar Mylius. His eyes swallowed the news item and tucked it into the computer of his mind. Without turning to her, he said: "Reserve space for two to Los Angeles. First flight." He spoke with a strong Australian accent.

"By way of the Philippines and Japan? Or Australia through Tahita?"

"The requisite is speed. Not comfort."

"I shall call Paya Lebar Airport."

She flowed to the telephone with liquid grace and spoke in low tones.

K. Y. Smith gazed into space, unblinking. His eyes were a

cold turquoise blue, and they belonged with the Aussie twang and the name Smith; but his yellow skin went with the initials K. Y. They stood for Kuan Yang. He was half Chinese.

K. Y. Smith wore beautifully tailored clothes, and he was a headache to his shirtmakers, his bootmakers, and his tailors. Fitting him required great skill. He was six feet one-and-a-half inches tall, and he weighed two hundred and eighty-seven pounds. His scalp shone through his close brush haircut, and he looked like a cross between a Japanese Sumo wrestler and a football lineman for a pro team. His movements were deft and hard and quick, as are those of men who practise Judo. His father had been a gambler who had hit it big digging for opals in a tiny Australian flyspeck of a city called Andamookay. He had bought himself a lovely lady from North China, tall and slim and feminine. When Kuan Yang was born, he had married her.

Smith's mind was a smooth, efficient computer, tough and precise. His laugh was a loud rumbling roar. And although he laughed often, the human wiring that controlled his laugh was not connected to his eyes.

Talya finished her phone conversation and smoothed the wrinkles in her golden *cheong-sam* which fitted her as closely as her ivory skin. It was evident that she wore nothing else except a very expensive musky perfume. She crossed her long, shapely legs which showed to the tops of her thighs through the high slits of the silken garment.

K. Y. Smith heard her hang up. "Call the Raffles Bank and tell Duva Margesh I shall see him before boarding the plane. Have him ready my cash balance."

She dialed the number from memory. Her voice was soft but firm.

The chill turquoise eyes examined inner space as the abacus within his head silently ran off various sums.

In Calcutta, the story about Ejnar Mylius was on page two of the *Calcutta Times-Journal*. It lay open on the desk of Count Vaclav Risponyi. As he leaned forward to read, the light was reflected from his shaven head. His fingers stroked his moustache, thick and black in the style of the English Guard regiments. When he had finished he looked up at the ceiling, digesting what he had just read. His black eyes glittered like onyx under his heavy eyebrows which met over the bridge of his nose, making a long and crooked line across the top of his face.

Risponyi picked up his telephone and got through to the Royal Bank of West Bengal, where he asked for the managing director, Mr. David Ochterlony. "Ochterlony? Count Vaclav Risponyi here." He spoke in a bullfrog's croak with clipped accents that had been honed and polished at Oxford's Balliol College. "I shall be going to the United States immediately. Have a letter of credit drawn in my name in the amount of two hundred and fifty thousand dollars, American."

When Ochterlony left the phone to check the records and do whatever it is that bankers do, Risponyi buzzed for his secretary. She entered immediately with her dictation pad and pen, came to his side and waited.

Without looking at her, he said, "Book me on the first flight to Los Angeles, California. In the United States of America."

He took his monocle from his breast pocket and began polishing it, a matter of nervous habit. He looked then at the superb Hindu girl and smiled. He reached to her and stroked the silken smoothness of her red sari. She moved closer. Suddenly his smile vanished. His voice was filled with a false honeyed friendship. "Of course, my dear David. I understand what you mean by relative liquidity." He forced himself to smile. "One hundred and seventy-five thousand will have to do. Yes, yes. I shall give you my warehouse stocks as collateral."

He slammed down the phone and croaked at it in anger. "Buggering banker! Telling me that I'm cash short!" Then he laughed, a mercurial change. "I didn't think he'd allow me that much." His left hand was admiring the roundness of her buttocks. "Remember, always ask for twice what you need."

She stood tall and straight as she made notes of his instructions. "Cable the Beverly Hills Hotel . . ."

"In Beverly Hills, California," she finished for him.

He rose and stood next to her. ". . . and have them reserve a bungalow for me. Also, tell them to arrange for a Rolls-Royce and chauffeur to meet me at the airport." With her heels, she was almost seven inches taller than he. Count Risponyi liked tall women. He was five feet two. His eyes and bearing gave the impression of power. His disproportionately long arms hung at his sides like those of a chimpanzee—and with the great strength of that ape.

He ran his fingers over the front of her sari to her breasts, and he toyed with her nipples. They hardened. She sighed as her eyes closed. "After you have made the arrangements, come back." He squeezed gently. Her breath was a sharp intake. "And lock the door behind you."

Risponyi watched her supple hip movements when she left the room. He smiled to himself and walked to the couch, unknotting his regimental silk necktie before he removed his black Milan silk suit.

Fond farewells leave warm memories.

Chapter Three

Burke's Peerage appeared in England in 1826, edited by a certain John Burke. It was an accurate account of the Peers and Lords of the Realm and their families. It was very useful in determining the use of proper pews during coronations. John's son, John Bernard Burke, made it an annual publication in 1847. For this he became Sir John Bernard Burke in 1854, when he was knighted. Thus, he was in a position to write wondrous things about himself.

Almanach de Gotha was a bastard child of *Burke's Peerage,* born in 1863 in Germany, in the district of Erfurt, in the town of Gotha. It was an almanac of the royal and princely families of Europe. Its editor, Johann Georg Justus Perthes, found it such a success at social affairs that he started a French edition in 1871.

Jedediah Killinger III appears in neither book.

The first Jedediah Killinger was found at the front door of St. Aidan's Episcopal Church in Nantucket, Massachusetts, in 1880. There was a note pinned to him. It said, "Introducing Jedediah Killinger. Conceived in passion. Born in poverty." The name might have originated in the Scottish town of Killin, on Lochtay, not far from the city of Dundee on the Firth of Tay.

Killinger the First ran away from the orphanage where he had been put. He headed west, where, with Colt .45 in hand, he was present when the Old West passed away. He married a lovely girl from the Chiricahua tribe of the Apache Indians. In her native tongue, she was called "Fawn who rises with the sun." Her mother was a princess, daughter of a Chiricahua war chief. Her father was an escaped slave from Mississippi who fought the White Man as an Apache warrior and became a

18

subchief. When he was shot in battle, a white soldier scalped him, proving that there had indeed been a black Apache.

"Fawn who rises with the sun" died two years after she had been wed, in childbirth. Her son was Jedediah Killinger II. Killinger the Second was put in a fine Boston school while Killinger the First was building a small shipping empire which specialized in trade with the Orient.

Killinger the Second married a beautiful Polynesian girl who walked in serene grace. In her blood was the lineage of the Kings of the South Seas, mixed with the genes of a rousting Portuguese sailor who was a Sephardic Jew.

... All this is Jedediah Killinger III.

The barefoot man was running along the ocean edge, in the wet sand. He wore sunfaded swim trunks which had been cut to his measure, high on the thigh and low at the waist, with a small slit at the side for freedom of motion. His longish hair jounced with each stride. The patch of blue tissue over his lip covered a small shaving nick that had stopped bleeding.

A stop-motion shows, as in a movie frame, wavy brown hair with sun-bleached streaks, hazel eyes wide apart, a fairly straight nose dented across the bridge during a rough water polo game. Character lines show strengths within the man, but not true age. The body of a well-conditioned twenty-eight-year-old athlete, hard and flat with ridged stomach muscles and pectorals which look as though they have been slapped on with a trowel. Looking at least five years younger than the forty-one years he has spent examining the world.

The frame is unfrozen, and Jedediah Killinger III sprints the last quarter-mile of his daily two-mile run. Two dogs cavort, crisscrossing in their running play. They are Vizslas, Hungarian pointers the color of copper and gold, their short hair shining in the sun, their copper-gold eyes laughing their joy, their long ears flapping.

Killinger had named them after the color of their coats when they had been born, brothers from the same litter. The slim one he called Copper. The larger one he called Auric, which the dictionary defines: *of or containing gold.*

19

Killinger finished his sprint by turning to the ocean, running and diving in. The blue tissue floated away. Fifty yards out with a fast butterfly stroke. A deep breath and a twenty-five-foot dive to the bottom to grab a handful of sand and pebbles. A few crawl strokes to loosen up. And then to the shore with a racing backstroke. The shorebreak was too small for a decent body-surf ride. So, across the beach to where his car was parked.

He had to walk carefully around the debris from the big storm of a few hours ago. A few of the nearby houses had had their windows smashed and the sand supporting their pilings torn away by the big waves and high winds.

When Killinger reached his classic old '57 T-Bird, both dogs were seated on the red upholstery, grinning at him. He grinned back and started the motor.

It had been a full and busy seven hours since the schooner *Katja* had smashed against the barge. Ejnar Mylius had been taken to St. John's Hospital. A famous neurosurgeon had caught a plane from Boston to fly to Oxnard and treat the broken skull. A tentative operation time had been set for thirty-six hours hence.

Katja had been cleated to a hundred-and-fifty-foot dock at the anchorage, stern-to-stern with a sixty-seven-foot Chinese junk with red sails and brightly painted hand-carved wood-work. The schooner, alongside such gay brightness, looked sad and broken. However, inside the schooner, living quarters habitable. Miraculously, she had shipped no water. So the red-maned Katja decided to live aboard her namesake, at the dock. A guard had been sent up from the Los Angeles office of the Mylius Shipping Lines to take care of what remained. The guard's name was Cornelius.

He did not know what was aboard.

Nor did Katja.

The beat-up Volkswagon camper parked at the dock. It was painted a violent yellow and covered with brilliantly colored flower decals. Twin surfboards were lashed to the top of the camper, and a sticker on the left side of the front bumper said that the parking place at the University of California, Santa Barbara, was paid for. A smiling Japanese boy of twenty-three hopped out, his arms full of supermarket bags. He started for the dock where the schooner and the Chinese junk were tied up, moving quietly in his thonged rubber zori sandals. His straight black hair fell neatly to his shoulders, topping off his wild shirt and his ripped-off Levi's. His name was Kimo, and up until a year ago, he had lived with his parents on their farm outside Boise, Idaho. When he decided that his goal in education was a Master's Degree in Underwater Sciences, he moved to California. He worked for Killinger and had his own cabin aboard the junk, which was named *Sybaris*.

Cornelius stood self-importantly at the gangway to the *Katja*, watching the Japanese boy approach. He hitched up his gunbelt and its heavy .45 and waited until Kimo's feet hit the floating dock. Then he walked over.

"Hey, fella! Private property!"

Kimo looked at him without expression. "Sure is."

"That means you don't belong."

Kimo started toward the junk. "Whatever's fair."

Cornelius moved to stand in front of Kimo. "Get your ass outta here."

Innocently. "I left my donkey up on the parking lot."

Cornelius grabbed Kimo by the shoulder to spin him. "One thing I can't stand is a fuckin' hippie."

One of the sacks fell, and Kimo looked down at it. Soft and cool. "I hope that's not the one with the eggs."

"C'mon. Pick up your garbage and get outta here, like I said. Or you got troubles." Cornelius grabbed Kimo's arm that still held a sack. Without effort, Kimo used a Karate chop known as *shuto*. The edge of his hand hit Cornelius' forearm, immobilizing it and freeing Kimo's arm.

Killinger had arrived about a minute earlier, and he watched the scene from the parking lot with approval. He couldn't hear what was said, but he approved of the way Kimo seemed to be handling things: his hundred and fifty-seven

21

pounds against the beefy guard. He trotted down to the dock, followed by Copper and Auric. He stopped near Cornelius. "What's the problem?"

Cornelius was shaking his arm to get the feeling back. "Just what we need. Dumb questions." His fingers moved easily. The arm worked. He faced Killinger. "Get those damn mutts offa the dock. An' you get outta here, too."

Kimo was picking up the things that had fallen from the shopping bag. He knew that Cornelius was heading for trouble, and he wanted to see how it went.

Killinger indicated the food on the dock. "Don't you think it would be nice if you helped him?"

"Whyn't you go fuck yourself?"

Killinger let out a deep and sad sigh. "Your manners are atrocious."

"Okay. That's enough outta you." Cornelius put his hand against Killinger's chest to push him away.

Killinger grabbed the wrist, turned it so that he could look at the guard's hand. Reprovingly: "Your hands are dirty. And so are your fingernails." He threw the hand aside. To Kimo. "Let's go aboard."

As Killinger turned to Kimo, ignoring Cornelius, the guard swung a heavy fist at Killinger's head. Killinger ducked beneath it. The guard's swing made him pivot away. Killinger helped Cornelius move along by spinning him with a yank on the guard's wrist.

Off balance, the guard moved in the direction Killinger had aimed him. With a splash, he fell off the dock and into the water.

Copper and Auric looked down at the guard and barked their laughter.

Cornelius began some very unimaginative swearing.

Killinger called to the Vizslas: "C'mon, pups. You're too young for that kind of talk."

They all went aboard the *Sybaris,* that Chinese junk named after a long-gone Greek city.

Chapter Four

The full name of the unhappy Norse Goddess was Katja O'Reilly.

After she had arranged for the neurosurgeon to be flown from Boston to Oxnard to operate on her grandfather, she had phoned the Dutch group of underwriters in Amsterdam which handled the insurance for the Mylius Shipping Lines. The company was The Association for the Improvement of Marine Insurance, and the Director who handled the Mylius insurance business was Mynheer van der Helft. He assured Mrs. O'Reilly that all would be taken care of. He asked about his dear friend, Ejnar Mylius. He clucked sympathetically, and said his representative in that section of the United States would soon be in touch with her.

When Katja returned to the schooner, she was in time to see the guard, Cornelius, climb from the water. "Did you fall in?"

He tried to squeeze his clothes dry.

"Two beach bums jumped me."

"How did it happen?"

He avoided the direct question by pointing to the *Sybaris*. "They come offa that big Chinese junk over there."

Katja looked up at the stern of the *Sybaris*. She saw she was being observed by Copper and Auric, who were standing with their forepaws on the rail, grinning at her with their tongues hanging out. Suddenly a large calico cat hopped up on the rail between the Vizslas. Her name was Coco Chanel and she spoke a small meow of greeting. Auric licked her. Then Killinger appeared, still dressed in his wet trunks, looking down at Katja without a change of expression.

Cornelius pointed. "That's one of 'em."

Katja stared at Killinger coldly as she spoke to Cornelius. "After you change to something dry, perhaps we'll call the police."

"Good idea."

Killinger picked up Coco Chanel and walked away, out of her sight.

Katja went aboard the schooner hating the man she'd just seen with the animals. She knew he was a terrible person.

It was night in Amsterdam, Holland. In California, it was not yet noon. An eight hour time difference.

Mynheer van der Helft had been trying to contact a man to represent The Association for the Improvement of Marine Insurance. It was important that his representative be the best money could buy. A diplomat who would not offend the Mylius interests. He had kept the long-distance phone busy, but so far he hadn't spoken to the one he wanted. He'd been ringing through to Oxnard for a marine insurance adjustor who would fit the qualifications. An expert.

Experts are a specialized breed. In insurance, the more expensive the possible claim, the more specialized the expert. And the more specialized the expert, the higher is his rate of pay. Top adjustors are normally in business for themselves. That is, they are free-lance operators working from job to job, much in the same pattern of private eyes. In the tight little world of ocean liners, gigantic oil tankers, and intercontinental freighters, insurance claims can and do run into the tens of millions of dollars. An adjustor's responsibilities are enormous. His character must be impeccable. He must know, among so many other things, metallurgy, oil drilling, ship construction, habits of the ocean, and the basic motivations of the individuals with whom he must deal. Finally, and most importantly, he must know International Law.

Van der Helft asked the operator to try the number again. She said the circuits were busy. Philosophically, he lit up a long, thin, quite green-looking cigar and looked around his elegantly casual office as he pondered his present problem. He leafed almost absent-mindedly through one of the Mylius

Shipping Lines' file folders which lay open before him on his vast cherrywood desk. The phone rang. The operator said that the party was on the line.

"Killinger here."

Van der Helft had his man. "Van der Helft here." He exhaled cigar smoke. "How is everything in Oxnard?"

Killinger laughed. "At twelve dollars a minute, that's a very expensive question."

"Right you are. Let's get down to business. I have a job for you."

Killinger was speaking on the yellow telephone from the large living room he had had constructed on the rear deck of the *Sybaris*. He was on an extra long phone cord, and he walked around as he talked with van der Helft. "I'm not looking for work." Killinger was standing at the bar, and with his free hand, he took a chilled beer mug from the special refrigerator. He moved to the side where a large, big-bellied Ho-Tai sat, legs crossed, laughing at life.

"You are a very difficult person, Killinger. Let us say, rather, that I am about to ask you for a favor." If money couldn't hook Killinger, perhaps friendship would. He tapped the cigar into the ornate ashtray. He repeated, to make his point, "A very important *personal* favor."

Killinger pulled the Ho-Tai's raised right arm toward him and down, holding his mug under the Japanese god's mouth. Cold Pilsener beer foamed to the top. Ho-Tai held a beer keg where his heart and soul normally lived. To Amsterdam he said, "You're using unfair tactics." He sipped the chill brew.

"Killinger, naturally we expect to pay you a reasonable fee for your time."

"My fees are never reasonable."

"That's what my auditors have been saying."

The long cord permitted Killinger to wander to all parts of the twenty-three-foot-square living room. He leaned against the bar, running his fingers over the carvings in the mahogany. "I haven't heard any complaints." He looked down at the figures which had been conceived and executed by a lecherous old Siamese craftsman and smiled at them. They were entwined nude figures of males and females in all of the imaginable positions of love-making.

"Killinger, this is a special situation. It concerns one of our largest clients." Impressively, he elaborated: "The Mylius Shipping Lines." Van der Helft began a full explanation of the whole situation as Katja O'Reilly had told it to him an hour ago.

As Amsterdam spoke, Killinger walked restlessly about, looking out the wall of windows which surrounded the unusually shaped deck cabin. Sections of the side of the junk were hinged and swung up, like gun ports of a man-o'-war. He was walking to the stern and looking out when he asked van der Helft to repeat. "What did you say was the name of the schooner?"

"The *Katja* . . ."

"Home port Skagen, Denmark?"

Greatly surprised: "How did you know?"

"I'm looking at her." He walked closer to the stern windows. "What did you want to know?"

"Is she badly damaged?"

"Not really." Killinger sipped his beer. "I can give you a refitting and repair price without moving from here." He squinted at the schooner. "Within five hundred dollars."

"Unbelievable."

Killinger grinned at the phone. "And it won't cost you one penny."

"As an American friend once said, The price is right." He puffed at his cigar, moistening the tip. "However, what I need is personal relations and diplomacy. You must keep Mrs. O'Reilly happy. She's Ejnar Mylius' granddaughter. Eventually, she will run Mylius shipping."

"I don't like ladies who are businessmen."

Van der Helft admired the moon in the Holland night. "I understand she is quite beautiful."

"Married ladies who are businessmen are even worse."

"This lady is divorced." Perhaps a clever bribe might turn the trick. "Do you yet possess a headboard for that gigantic bed?"

"Not really."

"We have in our warehouse several rare examples of Tenth Century Khmer art. Bas-reliefs and carvings."

"That type of thing belongs in museums."

"Quite true. Would you trust my judgement to choose for you a bas-relief for the wall behind your bed?"

Killinger knew that Khmer art was wholly concerned with fornication and love-making, with full-bosomed women and clean-limbed men in wondrous pairings. "You are a connoisseur. Of course I trust your judgement."

Van der Helft pursued his advantage and made Killinger promise to phone Mrs. O'Reilly for an appointment, after he had had his lunch. They said their good-bye's and ended the conversation.

Killinger remembered the striking redhead who had stared up at him from the dock. He knew that she was just too much to be Ejnar Mylius' granddaughter. Then he looked down at his right hand and laughed.

He was clutching a spread-legged female mahogany figure on the bar.

Chapter Five

Killinger worked on his Karate before lunch.

Kimo was his partner and pupil, and was improving rapidly. Soon, Killinger would take him to the Shinto Temple in Oxnard so that the priest, a Karate Master, who was Black Belt, Eighth grade, could give Kimo his tests for his first brown belt. Killinger was Black Belt, Sixth grade. To go further, he would have to make it his full-time religion.

Before starting their preliminary warm-up exercises, they dropped to their knees and touched their foreheads to the mat.

To the west, two very different men were flying over the Pacific, headed for Ejnar Mylius' schooner, in Oxnard, an hour and a quarter's ride north of the Los Angeles International Airport. Each was preparing for battle, and each was planning his campaign.

Calcutta was behind Count Vaclav Risponyi.

The airplane stewardesses gave him no more attention than they'd pay to any other shaven-headed gnome.

In his pocket was a letter of credit for $175,000, American. The bank manager, Ochterlony, had indicated that if a situation of dire stress arose, Risponyi might receive another $75,000, providing the bank had forty-eight hours' notice to liquidate some of the rare spices in Risponyi's warehouse.

Risponyi leaned all the way back in his seat and closed his eyes.

His mind was awake.

Before leaving the Island of Singapore, K. Y. Smith had

made two telephone calls to Los Angeles. Each was crisp and brief, with very definite instructions, to people who had been on his payroll before.

Shortly after they had seen the last of Paya Lebar Airport, a stewardess had brought the turquoise-eyed Chinaman a pitcher of shaved ice. Talya had taken a chased silver cup from their plane luggage and filled it half-full of the ice. Then she had taken a bottle of crystal clear fermented spirits of high alcohol content and poured it into the cup. It was an Eastern liquor, arrack. It turned milky white when it mixed with the water from the melting ice.

K. Y. Smith reached for the cup without looking at his daughter. He sipped from it slowly and with relish. It seemed to oil the wheels of his thoughts.

Talya ignored the admiring stares of the men on the speeding plane. Her hair hung down her back, fastened with a thick silken cord of glowing green to match her *cheong-sam*. Although the slit of her skirt was more modest, to the knee instead of the thigh, there was no line through the green silk which indicated either a brassiere or briefs.

She was used to attention from men. Attention in return from her was always on her own terms. Now she had no time, for she was her father's handmaiden and an instrument of his will.

Smith drank from the silver cup without taking his empty blue eyes from the totals he was seeing on the abacus of his mind, where he was dividing and multiplying and subtracting, readying for a subtotal.

Killinger had showered after the work-out with Kimo and then they had lunch in the magnificent kitchen of the junk: abalone pancakes, made from a Japanese recipe which Killinger had picked up in Kyoto. Bit by bit, Killinger was teaching Kimo the culture of his grandparents. After all, Kimo was a country boy from Idaho.

Kimo sliced the abalone that he and Killinger had skindived for two days ago on Keith's reef, in the northern part of Malibu. Killinger always left the meat, after it had been taken from the shell and trimmed, in a plastic sack in the refrigerator for a day or two before preparing it. It seemed to be tenderer that way.

They pounded it gently, to keep it from tearing. Next, they chopped the parsley and scallions and combined the whole mixture with flour, using clam juice for the moistener. And for the dip, Killinger mixed cider vinegar, *shoyu,* and hot Japanese pepper sauce.

With chilled white wine, it was delicious.

Katja O'Reilly had no appetite for her ham sandwich.

The two heavy suitcases sat on the floor of the *Katja*'s saloon, not far from a peculiar-looking crate covered with stenciled Chinese ideographs. The crate was bolted to the floor.

The suitcases had airline baggage tags which showed they had originated in São Paulo, Brazil. The man who owned them had just arrived from Brazil, where he had read of the accident to Ejnar Mylius.

After he had eaten his own sandwich, he reached for Katja's, without asking. He gulped it down in large bites, followed by long swallows of warm beer, straight from the can. He picked his teeth with a pinkie, daintily. He belched.

Her eyes hung icicles on him. "João, you always were a pig."

"But, my love, no one else says things like that to me."

"I am not your 'love'."

"Of course you are. I know you haven't stopped your feelings for me."

"You're not only a pig, but you are a very vain pig."

The man across the table from her was a solidly muscled athlete. In his native Brazil, he was a professional soccer player, although only a second-rater. A big, dark, strikingly handsome man, he tended to lose his women when he destroyed the illusion of his appearance by talking. When they listened to his words, they forgot that he was a beautiful animal.

He turned the charm of his white teeth upon her. "I have flown many miles to be at your side in the moment of your deepest need. When I read about your so terrible and unfortunate accident at sea, I knew you would want me. . . ."

His shopworn phrases dropped a curtain of fog between them. And she remembered meeting him, so terribly long ago, perhaps centuries, on the magnificent Copacabana beach that formed a white and sandy line between Rio do Janeiro and the salty sea.

Her father had died and she was a beautiful vessel, full of sadness. She needed someone to lean on. The attentive Brazilian soccer player was very sympathetic, keeping her glass full of champagne and letting her cry on his shoulder. Under the stars that formed the Southern Cross that night, her mood changed under the wild outpouring of his hot words and his hands which touched her, everywhere.

They had torn off each other's clothes and made mad love on the sand. Then they ran into the warm ocean, where they rubbed bodies. When they came out, they made wilder love. The little love bites drew blood. Sharp fingernails ran long red lines across the shoulders. It should have ended there, with hot memories. But he had planned well. He had learned that she was a wealthy woman, and he was tired of playing soccer in the minor cities.

When she learned all this, it was too late. Finally, she did something.

He was now her ex-husband, and he received a small amount of money every month mailed direct from her bank.

His name was João Aranha Mijangos O'Reilly.

He had come to help himself. Not her.

Six centuries before the birth of Christ, the Greeks built a city of white marble in the South of Italy. It was a symbol of Greek gold, Greek culture, and Greek beauty. It was famed throughout the civilized world, in its time. In the year 510 B. C., the city was destroyed.

Sybaris was its name.

The people who had dwelt there were called Sybarites. Today, our dictionaries define a sybarite as a person whose life is devoted to luxury and pleasure.

Killinger left the *Sybaris* to visit the schooner *Katja* and Mrs. O'Reilly. He hoped she was as lovely as van der Helft had indicated. He was as dressed up for the occasion as he would be for anything important. He wore a tight-fitting navy-blue turtleneck with his white Levi's, and thonged zori sandals.

The guard, Cornelius, was on duty in clean dry clothes.

He saw Killinger coming, and his lips turned down into a sneer. This time, he'd be the one to get in the first shot. The man who hits first, wins. It was all a matter of timing. Maybe a punch in the bum's gut. Or, better, just kick him in the balls. Mrs. O'Reilly would back him up.

Killinger reached the schooner's gangplank and stood in front of the guard. A cool smile. "Figuring how to take a shot at me?"

"Uh . . . how'd ya know?"

Long pause. "If it'll make you happy, I'll give you first try."

Cornelius looked at the man in front of him. The snug turtleneck showed a hard body. The bum was standing kinda funny. His feet were spread wider than his hips, toes pointed out. His knees were bent slightly, and his arms hung loosely at his side. Cornelius couldn't figure it.

He didn't know that it was a variation of the Karate *fudodachi* position. Killinger was ready to block any blow. He wouldn't attack unless strongly provoked by physical action.

Cornelius shook his head and exhaled a long sigh. "Okay. What do you want?"

Killinger had brought one single business card with him: elegant parchment, discreetly engraved with only the name, Jedediah Killinger III. He handed it to the guard. "Please tell Mrs. O'Reilly that this is in reference to her Marine Insurance."

Wordlessly, Cornelius went aboard the schooner to the saloon. He handed the card to Mrs. O'Reilly. "It's the bum who threw me in the water."

32

João took the card and listened to the story of what had happened earlier, from Cornelius' point of view. He liked fights and the body contact of soccer. This might be fun. He turned to Katja. "My darling, I shall take care of this." He started for the deck, the guard following, anxious to see the action. Katja was not far behind.

Killinger saw the two men come toward him, down the gangway. His attention shifted when he saw her. The slight breeze outlined her full body against the fabric of her dress. Her red hair hung loose and moved in the air gusts.

Katja looked at this terrible man who had assaulted an employee of Mylius Shipping Lines. She hoped he would receive his deserved punishment. Her eyes brightened at the thought, and she held her breath, as excited as though she were at a bullfight, and the brave bull was about to die.

Their eyes met.

The psychic and sexual magnet was turned on. The fields of force around the magnets attracted. They both felt it.

João confronted Killinger. "You are not wanted here."

Killinger looked him up and down. "I'm here to speak with Mrs. O'Reilly."

"I am *Mister* O'Reilly."

Killinger figured that van der Helft had been mistaken about a so-called divorce. However, his instructions were specific. "Very interesting. However, it's still *Mrs.* O'Reilly I'd like to speak with."

João leaned close to the guard and dropped his voice. "We must hit him together. You go for the knees. I'll get him in the head." They took a step together, moving forward. João snapped out: "Now!!"

Both men threw themselves at Killinger.

Chapter Six

Two ICBMs were in flight over the Pacific, warheads activated and guided with laser beam accuracy to a wooden crate on a schooner in Oxnard harbor.

Count Vaclav Risponyi had twenty hours of flying time. K. Y. Smith had seventeen.

Each thought he was alone on this mission. For they had not yet picked up any blips on their radar screens.

Their intention was clear to Killinger.

When they increased their pace for the attack, Killinger reached to the side and grabbed the iron pole at the foot of the gangplank, to which the handrail was attached. He pulled himself to the side as he jumped to clear his legs from the ground.

Cornelius had launched himself, and his arms were outspread to grab Killinger's legs. He missed and rolled, falling from the gangplank into the water. For the second time.

João's reflexes were faster, from years of soccer. He changed direction and threw a punch at Killinger's head. Killinger rolled under it, untouched.

Katja watched this explosion of male action with a thrill.

João grinned with the pleasure of a fight. He threw a left jab at Killinger's heart. It was stopped and pushed away by a stone wall . . . .

Killinger had brought his right arm up, fist pointing at the sky, elbow bent and as in a ballet movement, his forearm caught João's punch at the wrist, turning it aside. João stood before him, frozen and wide open. It was a beautiful spot for Killinger to use the *hizakinkeri*, or knee to the groin.

Instead, he stepped back a pace and called up to Katja.

"Mynheer Heinrich van der Helft asked me to speak with you."

"The man from Holland?"

Killinger nodded. "The Association for the Improvement of Marine Insurance."

João had stopped his movement and was listening. Cornelius was trying to climb from the salt water to the dock.

Katja looked at Killinger's card. With the thrill of the clash she had just witnessed pumping her blood faster, she smiled at him. "Mr. Killinger, would you please come aboard?"

The three paintings were a Kees van Dongen, a Rouault, and a Matisse. The saloon was designed in a clean Scandinavian fashion, with no expense spared: Killinger appreciated its good taste.

His thoughts were interrupted by João, who wore his greatest man-to-man charm. "I am João Aranha Mijangos O'Reilly, Mr. Killinger." He offered his hand. "Please to accept my apologies."

'llinger shook his hand. O'Reilly's grip was as strong and firm ... his own.

João looked him straight in the eye. "My actions were based on a piece of misinformation." He turned to Katja. "We really must get rid of that uniformed lout."

Katja paid him little attention. She spoke to Killinger. "It would seem that I am getting unusually excellent service from my insurance company." She smiled: "Would it be that Mylius Shipping Lines carries heavy policies?"

Killinger laughed. "That might have something to do with it."

"Then we understand one another. You are really a good-will ambassador." More crisply: "Will you be taking care of this whole situation? Repairs and such?"

Killinger grinned at her imperiousness. He made a very small, slightly mocking bow. "Those were my orders, ma'am."

Exposing all of his teeth once more, João moved to Katja. He kissed her cheek. She gave no response. His smile and charm were unblemished. "Unfortunately, this business talk is away from me. So, if you will pardon me, my love, I shall unpack and change."

She looked at him coolly. "I'll see you later." She couldn't throw him out in front of this man from the insurance company.

Killinger caught the chill of the byplay between them.

Katja sat on the only piece of furniture which had not been knocked apart in the wreck. "Tomorrow, I shall order new chairs and tables. Meanwhile . . ." She indicated the only sittable thing in the salon.

Killinger sat on the crate from Hong Kong. When he tried to move it closer to her, he was unable to: it was bolted to the floor and held by metal straps.

The sand box was square, twelve feet by twelve, four inches deep. The two dogs and the two cats put it to good use, there in the open, on the junk's stern. Kimo kept the sand fresh and raked. Auric was there, doing his duty, when he saw Killinger leave the schooner to come aboard the *Sybaris*. He barked and alerted Copper. When they ran to greet Killinger, Kimo had joined them.

Kimo was curious. "How was the pretty lady?"

"Married."

"Too bad." Grin. "And the pretty lady's husband?"

Killinger let a pause float by. "Can't figure him." He looked around. "Where's Samantha?"

Kimo indicated the office on the bow of the junk, hidden behind the now raised wooden ports, where it seemed a part of the craft. "Doing the report on that big salvage job." He picked up Lollipop who had come by to see what was happening. The cat purred as he stroked it. "Don't be mad if she's a little behind. Going to school keeps her pretty busy."

"Things'll slow down for her. I got a new secretary coming aboard later."

Kimo looked a question at him.

Killinger shrugged. "Never met her. Recommended by my attorney. Supposed to be great at office work."

"What's she look like?"

Killinger grinned: "We'll know in a little while." He leaned down and patted Copper and Auric. "Funny thing, she has teaching credentials in both economics and bookkeeping."

"Sounds like a drop-out."

"Enough of that. Let's work up a shopping list. I'm having company for dinner."

"Wild. How'd you get rid of her husband?"

"Mr. O'Reilly will be coming with Mrs. O'Reilly." Killinger headed for the circular staircase which led to below.

Kimo followed, and the Vizslas trailed them both.

At Los Angeles International Airport, a long, sleek, heavy black Mercedes-Benz limousine had its trunk open. K. Y. Smith and Talya sat comfortably in the rear seat waiting for the chauffeur to pick up their luggage.

Hamid's turban, heavy silk of opalescent dark green, struck an exotic note above the black uniform and black shoes. A big man, he handled the baggage with ease. He slammed the trunk and climbed into the front seat. Soundlessly, the Mercedes-Benz 600 left the curb. It started up the coast, the Pacific Ocean at its left, all the way to Oxnard.

Count Vaclav Risponyi was three hours behind.

Chapter Seven

The Singapore Lobster Curry was hot.

Killinger had added extra crushed and dried red chili peppers to the recipe from India. Aside from the garlic and onions, he had used eight spices, from coriander to ginger. The lobster came from Keith's reef, off the Malibu coast. Killinger had grabbed them, skindiving.

Kimo had made the coconut cream from fresh coconut meat, following Killinger's directions.

Samantha put the side goodies into their separate little dishes: peanuts, ground coconut, raisins, pineapple chutney, peach chutney, and small hot peppers. She was a big, broad-shouldered, full-hipped surfer Kimo had met at Rincon, above Ventura, on the way to Santa Barbara. This wonderful-looking girl in her minimal bikini and short shagged hair rode the waves better than most men. She and Kimo were the only ones who hadn't chickened out on a ten-foot wave. That was enough to build a friendship, which had then blossomed into a love. She went to the University of California, Santa Barbara, where she majored in English literature.

Samantha was striking as she set the table, her micro-mini of cowhide matching her boots, and her wide-open crochet knit sweater pulled tight by the fine, full breasts over pectoral muscles hardened by paddling her surf board.

A Texas girl from the heart of the cattle country, where Chicanos and Blacks were called greasers and niggers, she didn't know how to explain this Japanese boy to her family.

He had gotten her a part-time job aboard the junk, and they were together constantly.

Valhalla, according to Teutonic mythology, is the hall of Odin wherein dwell the spirits of heroes slain in battle. It was also the name of a seventy-five-foot, yawl-rigged sailing yacht across the harbor from Killinger. It had been dark and unused for two months, with a "for sale" sign giving the name of the yacht broker, George Medley.

Now, suddenly, its lights went on. Dark figures moved about in the night. The "for sale" sign was gone.

From its anchorage, the *Valhalla* had a clear and uninterrupted view of the broken schooner, *Katja.*

And, by chance rather than design, had a view of the Chinese junk.

The salad had been made and put in the refrigerator in a plastic bag. Killinger had made the dressing. All was ready for company.

Killinger looked around and was satisfied. "Everybody on deck for a celebration." He started up the spiral staircase and the others followed. He went to the wine cooler in the large living room and took out a bottle of champagne. "Kimo. Three glasses."

Kimo took out three chilled glasses, and Killinger popped the champagne cork. Samantha was entranced. Killinger filled the glasses and they went out on deck to count the stars. Music from the stereo followed them and helped build a lovely mood.

Killinger noticed the lights of the yacht. He turned to Kimo. "Who bought the *Valhalla?*"

Kimo looked. "Beats me." A grin. "Tomorrow, I'll check it out."

Samantha looked across the water at the sailing yacht. "Why bother? Ah bet it won' be anybody interestin'."

K. Y. Smith sat in a comfortable chair on the deck of the *Valhalla.*

The small table at his side held a clay crock of Holland Gin, shaped like a bottle and made by Wynand Fockink of Amsterdam. Next to the crock was his small, solid glass, three-quarters full.

In his hands, held to one eye, was a 40-power telescope which seemed to bring the shattered *Katja* within touching distance. He examined her thoroughly, bow to stern. Normally a telescope of such magnification must be held on a support, for even breathing can cause enough movement to make viewing impossible. However, K. Y. Smith was a cold and immovable rock with physical control that enabled him to hold the telescope unwaveringly. He put it down and reached for his Holland Gin.

"The schooner should have sunk." A rumbling chuckle started in his belly. "I consider it my own personal good fortune that she remained afloat." The chuckle grew into laughter.

Talya stood behind him, a pair of 8 x 30 binoculars in hand, looking carefully at the *Katja*. In the sweep of her examination, she picked up the stern of the Chinese junk and saw its name, *Sybaris*. She smiled, for she knew of that ancient Greek city. She had read about it in English at Wellesley and in French at the Sorbonne.

She wondered who the owner might be and whether he was a sybarite. In the backward sweep of her binoculars, she saw a man and a woman leave the *Katja*. She told K. Y. Smith, and he trained his telescope on them.

The dogs and cats liked the redhaired lady.

Katja wore her hair braided like a crown for a Scandinavian queen, in a coil around her head. The single, large, cabochon cut emerald that hung pendant from an antique gold chain and rested in the warmth between her breasts matched the color of her eyes. Her sheer gown was a blazing crimson, ending between knee and thigh top. A belt of darker, bolder red cinched her in tightly at the waist, its color matching her boots.

João was striking in his black suede bell-bottoms and

ruffled green silk shirt. He had gravitated immediately toward Samantha.

Killinger poured each of them a glass of champagne.

Katja took hers and walked idly, provocatively toward the bow of the junk. As she looked over the rail toward the ocean on the other side of the rock breakwater, her hands traced the designs carved into the teak. She heard Killinger's footsteps behind her. Without turning, she said, "The first time I saw you, I thought you were an animal."

"Thank you."

"The second time, I knew you were an animal."

"Thank you twice."

She turned slowly, facing him, looking up into his face. "A very male and very interesting animal." Her eyes and lips smiled. She moved the half-step that brought her to Killinger with barely enough space for a breeze to drift between them. She waited for him to block out that breeze.

Killinger did not move. He smiled and finished his champagne.

Katja moved forward three-sixteenths of an inch. The breeze was forced to go around them. Her breasts leaned on his chest. She rose on her toes, pressing her pelvis hard against him.

Killinger stepped back. "You've won the first round."

"Only cowards concede."

"Occasionally it's better to sidestep married women."

She laughed and put her glass on the flat top of the rail. "I am not married."

"Is Mister O'Reilly married?"

"Not to me." Her arms started their climb to around his neck. "The gentleman's luggage is no longer aboard the schooner. It's in a hotel." She moved her mouth to his, her lips open. Quickly, she fastened her teeth onto his lower lip and bit. She stepped back. "Did I draw blood?"

The telescope and binoculars missed nothing.

"I want a complete file on that man."

"Yes, father. You shall have it."

41

"It may be necessary for you to establish a personal relationship with him." A dry cackle-laugh. "I know you will not mind."

Talya smiled as she watched the man with Mrs. O'Reilly.

"Does the name K. Y. Smith mean anything to you?"

Killinger shook his head. "It doesn't ring a bell."

Katja explained: "At the hospital, there was a gigantic floral piece for my grandfather. The card with it said, 'To my dear friend, Ejnar. With all good wishes for a speedy recovery and more chess games together.' Signed K. Y. Smith."

The chauffeur was as English as the beige Rolls-Bentley.

His name was Hawkins, and he carried Count Vaclav Risponyi's luggage to the car after it had been cleared through Customs. With gray hair, lined face, and a neat pudginess, his five feet four complemented Risponyi's own five feet two.

During the drive from Los Angeles International Airport to the Beverly Hills Hotel, Risponyi kept the car-telephone busy.

Chapter Eight

The envelope held one hundred $100 bills.

Carelessly, Risponyi placed it in his breast pocket. He had made a point of having the manager, the desk clerk, and the bell captain present when he put his letter of credit for $175,000 into the hotel's safe. This would be advertising and an assurance of fine and prompt service. Also, he had dropped the fact that his motion picture production company was preparing two properties to be shot in the next few months.

While the bell captain and Hawkins took his luggage to his bungalow, he went to the Polo Lounge to learn the results of his phoning. This famous meeting place of filmdom's élite is not named after the polo of mallets and horses, but rather, as an ancient Persian print on the wall attests, after Marco Polo, the famous traveler, dedicated to other travelers.

He identified himself to the maître d' and was shown to the table he had reserved. From the envelope, he took two of the hundred-dollar bills and gave them to the maître d', asking for change The maître d' looked into the envelope, and was impressed.

Count Vaclav Risponyi was aware of the power of money.

He waited, toying with his Scotch and water. After a while, two striking young ladies with long blonde hair entered the Polo Lounge and were shown to his table. They might have been sisters. Both were tall and slim and wondrously full-chested, and were dressed in the absolute minimum of gossamer fabric.

Introductions identified them as Carolyn and Leona. And they were both thrilled to meet the movie producer from Calcutta.

"Beautiful young actresses should not be forced to pay their own taxi fare when they are going on an interview for an acting job." He laid a fifty-dollar bill in front of each of them. "No strings." He smiled. "Only for taxi fare. Please take it. I insist."

The money disappeared into two small purses.

Hawkins and the bell captain entered the lounge and crossed to Risponyi's table. Hawkins had his cap in hand. "Everything is in order, Count Risponyi."

"Thank you, Hawkins." He smiled a thin smile. "We shall leave at nine-thirty. After breakfast."

Hawkins nodded.

The bell captain dropped the bungalow key in front of Risponyi. Risponyi dropped a ten-dollar bill in front of the bell captain. He was not purchasing anonymity. The bellman would not forget him. "Thank you, sir. When you need anything, my name is Heffler."

The chauffeur and bellman dismissed, Risponyi picked up the key, toyed with it, and placed it between the two girls. "Now, regarding the motion picture ... It will be shot on location in a yacht harbor. It will require an actress who looks exceptional in a brief bathing suit."

Carolyn and Leona took simultaneous deep breaths and thrust their breasts forward.

"Of course, there will be several shots requiring complete nudity. . . ."

The first twenty-four-hour period since the *Katja* had struck the barge was marked several hours later that night.

Ejnar Mylius was in the hospital, in a coma.

His granddaughter Katja slept fitfully, and alone, aboard the schooner.

João snored heavily in a hotel room, an empty bottle for company.

Risponyi lay with his arms around Carolyn in his kingsize

bed in the bungalow in Beverly Hills.

K. Y. Smith seemed never to sleep. He sat on the deck of the *Valhalla* planning his campaign.

Talya tossed and turned, wondering about this man on the junk her father wanted to know.

Killinger had gone to bed with a clear mind, thinking how fortunate he was not to have a difficult insurance problem to occupy his time.

The crate from Hong Kong sat securely bolted to the saloon floor of the *Katja*.

the
second
day . . .

Chapter One

Kimo wanted information.

George Medley knew everything that happened in the Peninsula Harbor. Besides, the seventy-five footer that had suddenly lit up was handled by Medley. So Kimo asked questions.

"No, Kimo. I didn't sell the *Valhalla*. It's a rental."

"Two hundred and fifty a day is found money."

Medley grinned. "Three-fifty is better."

They were in the office of Medley Yacht Sales, with a clear view of the harbor. It was early, and Medley was serving coffee. Kimo went heavy on the sugar and powdered nondairy creamer. "No coffeecake?"

Medley sipped his coffee. "I was figuring you might bring it."

"But you weren't expecting me."

"Right." Medley smiled. His eyes were full of hell and fit perfectly with his boyish face and gray hair. His thoughts moved backward. "Paid ten days in advance. Thirty-five hundred bucks."

"Uh . . . what did you say his name was?"

"Kimo, when one gossip is pumping another gossip, he does better if he asks a straight question." Medley looked across the harbor. "Name is Smith. K. Y. Smith." He shook his head. "Never saw a man like that in my life. Six-two, almost three hundred pounds, and built of yellow concrete. Australian accent. Emptiest blue eyes I ever saw."

"Yellow concrete? What are you talking about."

"Yellow's what I mean." Grin. "No offense to Japanese friends, but that's the color of his skin. He signed as Kuan Yang Smith, Singapore."

"Kuan Yang. That's Chinese." Kimo couldn't fit all the pieces together. "What's the bit about the blue eyes?"

Medley's eyes brightened as he looked out the office window. "Here comes his daughter. Ask her."

Kimo turned and saw Talya. He whistled softly. "I don't believe it."

Talya came down the walk to Medley's front door, smiling enchantingly. She wore a crisp sailor-type blue and white denim outfit with full, long pants that swung loose at the ground and held her fanny tight and snug. Her gleaming long black hair was tied with a piece of blue wool that matched her rubber-soled shoes.

Medley hopped up quickly, moving to the door. "Step aside for a dirty old man." Kimo gave him room to open the door.

Talya beamed at Medley. "My father requested that I thank you for your prompt kindness and help."

The sight of her rendered Medley speechless. Kimo's eyes never left Talya.

Talya pointed to the *Sybaris*, moored at its dock. "My father would like to know if, perhaps, that lovely junk is for rent. When may I look at it?"

Medley explained. "She's the *Sybaris*, and she belongs to Jedediah Killinger the third." He indicated Kimo. "If you want to go aboard, perhaps Kimo, here, can arrange it. He works for Mr. Killinger."

She clapped her hands in joy. "How wonderful. Can we go now?"

"I'll have to ask Mr. Killinger." He grinned. "I know he wouldn't refuse."

Her father had put her on a timetable. There was no time to waste. She put her arm through Kimo's, enveloping him with her musky perfume. "Then let's ask him. Together."

It broke Kimo's heart to refuse her. "He's busy aboard the junk right now. "Business."

"What kind of business?" she asked innocently.

Medley answered this one. "Killinger's a marine insurance adjustor."

50

Kimo continued: "After that, he takes his run over on the other side of the harbor, with his dogs." Kimo indicated the direction. "Then back home."

"Thank you. I'll visit Killinger's junk later." She moved to the door. "Good-bye."

As she walked away, Kimo and Medley admired every fluid motion.

K. Y. Smith sat on the fantail of the sailing yacht, binoculars in hand.

He watched Talya across the harbor as she left Medley Yacht Sales. Obviously, the two people in the office were men. Therefore, obviously, she would have gotten information from them. His daughter was most efficient. That was how she had been trained.

A member of the Lascar crew set a silver tray at Smith's side. The large silver pot was filled with thick Turkish coffee. The two smaller pots contained sugar and cream. The sugar had a subtle flavor of vanilla bean, and the cream was extra-heavy. A small exotic bottle contained a liquor made of the fermented sap of the toddy palms.

He mixed the ingredients to match his mood of the moment.

Her eyes were the green of dark jade.

She was black from the top of her wild Afro hairdo to the tips of her dull-leather boots. Five feet one, with full curves and slim legs, she did great things for her open crochet-work black blouse and tiny black skirt. Her skin was lightened with a rich creaminess from some white ancestor.

Samantha took her to Killinger.

She looked Killinger up and down, deliberately. Without a smile, she said: "My name is Marjorie Stafford. Mr. Berkowitz sent me."

Killinger smiled. "Welcome aboard, Marjorie Stafford." He turned to Samantha. "This is the girl I was telling you about. Berkowitz is my attorney." Back to the black girl: "Did you bring your luggage?"

Coolly: "I haven't decided to stay, yet."

"Anyone Jack Berkowitz recommends is welcome." He turned to Samantha. "Show her the office, and explain the problems. But be nice. I think we want her to join the crew."

Samantha smiled to the newcomer. "Mah name's Samantha. Y'all call me Sam."

Almost militantly, Marjorie said, "I don't know why it is . . . but I can't get away from Southern accents." Then she broke up, laughing.

Samantha and Killinger laughed too.

"Call me Marjorie. I hate the name Margie."

The girls started for the office in the bow. Killinger called after them. "Marjorie!" She turned. "You'll be in charge. Samantha's part-time."

The chauffeur wore a green turban.

He sat in the front of a long black Mercedes-Benz 600, parked at the curb of Oxnard beach. Killinger thought that the area was now attracting a new clientele. He put the key under the mat of the little red T-Bird, grabbed a towel, and followed Copper and Auric to his favorite spot on the sand.

It was occupied by a big blue towel and a blue beach bag.

He dropped his towel nearby and started his daily two-mile run. One mile to the turn-around marker, and one mile back. For the dogs it was an eleven-mile romp as they ran in circles, zigzagged, chased birds, and had fun.

There was a figure a quarter of a mile ahead of him, running. It was a female. Her bikini bottom was a strip of cloth. Her long black hair floated in the wind behind her. She was moving fast.

Killinger had a great curiosity about her. He ran faster than usual, working to catch up. He was closing the distance between them when she reached the turn-around. She went around the post and started running directly toward Killinger. The front view fulfilled the promises of the rear. At the moment of their passing, she called to him: "You will never catch me."

He picked up his pace, reached the marker, and started

back. He saw that the dogs had started playing around her and that she had tripped over Copper. Instead of getting to her feet immediately, she waited for Killinger to come close. When they were side by side, their speeds were identical.

Talya moved faster. Killinger stayed exactly with her. She sprinted the last two hundred yards, working hard. Killinger remained level. It had become a dead heat.

Chest heaving and straining the thin bra, she said, "You did not beat me."

"Also, I did not lose."

"It is important never to lose." She spun and raced to the ocean.

Killinger caught up with her. As they ran, close to one another, she grabbed his hand and held it.

"Now, no one loses."

They dove into the first wave . . . as one.

Chapter Two

K. Y. Smith walked down the dock to the schooner *Katja*.

He exuded an atmosphere of power like a heavily armored battleship steaming serenely on a smooth sea. His yachting clothes were impeccable, tailored in London. His mind, independent of the movements of his body, was reviewing and sorting details in his mental filing cabinet.

Cornelius was on guard duty at the foot of the gangplank. He looked up and saw a large Chinese gentleman with odd blue eyes bearing down on him silently on rubber soles. The turquoise eyes bored a hole through him. The voice chuckled in good humor, and the lips smiled. The eyes didn't blink.

"Please announce me to Mrs. O'Reilly." He gave Cornelius his card.

"Sir" was a word he would never use to a Chinaman. However, the respect was automatic. "Yes, sir." Cornelius trotted up the gangplank.

K. Y. Smith waited, moving neither his head, his eyes, his hands, nor any part of his body. Yet, somehow, he was relaxed.

Cornelius returned. "Mrs. O'Reilly will see you, sir." Again the respect.

The big man walked up the gangplank which bent under his weight. Cornelius watched, fascinated, until the Chinaman's bulk disappeared down the companionway.

Katja rose to greet him. She had been sitting at the dining table in the saloon, a pot of steaming Dutch chocolate before her with a shallow silver dish piled high with whipped cream, and plates of croissants, sweet butter, and cherry jam. Her red hair was brushed, shining, and loose. She wore a full mandarin robe of silver-threaded silk with Tang horses embroidered in gold and crimson.

K. Y. Smith descended the steps lightly as though he tiptoed on springs. His eyes divided the room with mathematical precision, mapping it for his records. The empty blue eyes filled very briefly with a sudden light, which disappeared immediately. He had seen the small wooden crate.

He spoke first. "It was with great regret that I learned of your grandfather's misfortune." A sad little smile. "We are old friends."

"Your flowers were very thoughtful, Mr. Smith. I hope he will be able to see them soon, and read your nice note."

"Have the doctors said how long that will be?"

She sighed. "There will be no answers until after surgery."

"A shame." K. Y. Smith moved directly to the crate from Hong Kong. He bent and touched it lightly with his fingertips. Unintentionally sensuous, it was the stroking of a lover who has finally found his missing beloved. "Ejnar Mylius is a fine man." The pull of the crate was so positive that he had to will himself to stand and move back a half-pace.

He had lost control over his eyes. They tried to swallow the wooden container. "Your grandfather has been holding my treasured statue close to him. And safe." A question to test her. First a chuckle. "Of course you have seen it?"

She shook her head. "He never discussed it."

Greatly relieved, the yellow-skinned Australian permitted himself a tiny sigh. He heard a sound behind him. Without visible motion, he faced the noise. He saw a man sipping hot chocolate. He looked a question at Katja.

Katja introduced him to João. In K. Y. Smith's mental closets, João Aranha Mijangos O'Reilly was a tagged and hanging piece of merchandise. At the moment he had no use, so the blue eyes moved back to the crate. His hands followed, stroking the rough wood.

"According to legend, I am a descendent, on my honored mother's side, of the famous beauty, Chin P'ing Mei." His hands rested, palms-down on the box. "For years I have searched the halls of treasure and the bazaars without success." He shrugged. "Ejnar Mylius and I had discussed the bronze statue many times over many games of chess. Finally, an agent located Chin P'ing Mei. It was in Hong Kong."

55

Katja found the story fascinating, but she interrupted. "Would you like a cup of chocolate?"

"It would be my pleasure, Mrs. O'Reilly. And if you are Ejnar Mylius' granddaughter, I know you will serve it with thick cream. Naturally, the chocolate will be Dutch ground." The rich laugh and smile were manufactured. The eyes were remote.

"For reasons which your grandfather will someday explain to you, it became necessary that he act on my behalf in the purchase of Chin P'ing Mei." She handed him a cup of chocolate, high with whipped cream. He sipped it appreciatively. He exhaled. "Hah. It is his same chocolate. By Pieter Djeerte."

She smiled at this friend of her grandfather.

"I shall arrange to have this unwieldy crate removed as quickly as possible. You have been put to enough inconvenience already."

They drank their chocolate. João sat at the table, stuffing himself with croissants and cherry jam.

"For your records, I shall sign any paper you wish." The Australian pronounciation became more evident as his excitement heightened. He took a neat folder of papers from his breast pocket and began sorting through the documents. "First, I shall give you the bill of lading. You will need it for your records."

Killinger's voice was heard as he called before coming down the companionway. "Mrs. O'Reilly!"

K. Y. Smith faced the sound. Katja turned. João put more jam on his croissant. Killinger entered.

Katja introduced him. "K. Y. Smith, this is Jedediah Killinger III."

The Chinaman inclined his head.

Killinger smiled a greeting. "Glad to know you, Mr. Smith." The big man with the turquoise eyes fit the description Kimo had brought him. Killinger went to Katja's side. He laid out a set of triplicate forms interleaved with carbons. He gave her a pen and indicated a line. "You sign here." A smile. "Where the X is."

Without a word, she signed and gave him back the papers. Killinger tore the middle sheet free, handing it to her. "This is yours." She folded it and placed it in her pocket.

K. Y. Smith had gone back to the chest. He was unable to keep his hands from it.

She turned to him and apologized. "Please forgive our rudeness, Mr. Smith, but I'm finishing the details on the insurance."

He stood and programmed himself for a friendly grin. "Don't bother to explain. I understand business necessities." At Killinger, he aimed a hearty bellow of good fellowship. His eyes were tuned in to their own channel. "When I was a child, I heard fabulous stories of the original Jedediah Killinger and his exploits in the China trade." A pause and a smile. "Was he not your grandfather?"

"I wouldn't be surprised." A grin. "From what I hear, he was an unbelievable man."

"True. True." Talya had done her job well. K. Y. Smith had checked his file cards, and where there were blanks, he had been able to fill them in by making long-distance phone calls around the world. "Your father, Killinger the Second, was known to me in Australia, where my own father had struck it lucky in the opal fields of Andamookay." More friendly chuckles. "We must discuss these remarkable people."

"Perhaps you would be my guest on the junk alongside."

"A pleasure, sir. I was admiring the craft." A small bow to Katja. "After I relieve Mrs. O'Reilly of the responsibility of my crate, we shall get together. Indeed we shall." He indicated the crate. "I will have my people take care of the matter." Explanation to Killinger: "My very dear friend, Ejnar Mylius had been kind enough to hold it for me."

Killinger turned to Kuan Yang Smith. "What does the case contain?"

Head bowed in humility. "A bronze statue of one of my honored ancestors. It is called Chin P'ing Mei. In English, the Golden Lotus."

Killinger looked at Katja. "I see that the straps are still secure. That means that the contents haven't been verified."

From the side, the great voice boomed out in reasonable friendship. "Really, Mister Jedediah Killinger the Third, I dislike seeming impolite. But this matter is truly not your concern." Dismissing Killinger, he turned to Katja. "I shall have it out of your way within the hour."

Flatly, Killinger stated his case. "Mrs. O'Reilly may not give you the crate."

The wheels within the Chinaman's head began to speed an answer from his inner computer. *This Killinger the Third seems to be a nuisance. However, he would not make such a statement without knowledge, for he is not a fool.*

Katja was brought up tight. No one, but no one, could give her orders. Haughtily: "Mr. Killinger, I think you have overstepped your bounds."

João sat at the table, happily stuffing himself. He did not like this beach bum from the junk. He said, "Mr. Killinger, you are interfering."

K. Y. Smith made note of the various reactions, for future reference.

Killinger waved the papers which Katja had just signed. He spoke softly, as a good diplomat should. "According to these papers, this schooner, and everything aboard her belongs to The Association for the Improvement of Marine Insurance." He smiled and tried to make them understand. "Let me explain. This is a Danish boat. It was insured in Holland. It was in an accident in the territorial waters of the United States. Claims for damages have been made. Under the terms of the original insurance policies, when claims have been made, the schooner and everything aboard, as I have said, becomes the property of the Insuror. Nothing may be released without specific instructions from Amsterdam." He smiled again at Katja. "Please understand. It is for your protection. Also, it is my job and duty to enforce all provisions."

Katja relaxed and was apologetic. She put her hand on Killinger's arm. "I'm sorry, Jed. Of course, you are acting properly." She smiled graciously at K. Y. Smith. "If the statue has been out of your hands for so long, do you really think another week or so will hurt anything?"

58

The Australian accent was sharp, but the reply was programmed not to be unfriendly. "Of course not, Mrs. O'Reilly." The crate would have been his if Killinger had not shown.

João was against anything that Killinger was for. "Mr. Smith was a friend of your father. I believe you should trust him and end this awkwardness."

K. Y. Smith took greater note of João. A fool. But undoubtedly he could be used.

Katja ignored her ex-husband.

The big Chinaman offered Killinger his hand. "Please forgive my impatience, sir. I was not aware of your responsibilities in this situation." He squeezed Killinger's hand in his powerful paw. The empty eyes swallowed his opponent and examined him for reactions of pain or backing down. Killinger's hand did not give. His expression did not change.

The disappointment within K. Y. Smith was replaced by a greater respect for this Killinger the Third.

The turquoise eyes surveyed the saloon once more, rephotographing everything so there would be no errors. The yellow-skinned hand touched the crate in a gesture of fond farewell before K. Y. Smith departed.

The fond farewell was but temporary.

Chapter Three

Risponyi's binoculars were small but powerful.

He was examining the *Katja* from a table against the glass wall of a restaurant called The Lobster Trap. He had a view of the Peninsula Yacht Harbor from his seat opposite Carolyn. The damages to the boat were obvious.

Earlier, when Hawkins drove the Rolls-Bentley to Oxnard, Carolyn was at his side. She had won the contest at the table in the Polo Lounge, and afterwards, in the bungalow, she had scored very high marks. He had needed a certain type of girl to help him in his plans.

Risponyi had ordered two Bloody Marys, and when the order was given to the bartender, Joaquin, he made three. The third was for a man down the bar who stared morosely through the glass windows at the sailboats in the marina. It was João Aranha Mijangos O'Reilly.

To get him out of her hair, Katja had put him up at the La Sirena Hotel, all expenses paid. João had learned that he could put his bar charges on the hotel bill, so he was permitting his ex-wife to pay for his unhappiness.

As he drank, his eyes drifted to the couple at the table on the other side of the bar. The woman was splendid. The man was almost a gnome, with a shaven head, a thick moustache, and a foppish taste in clothes. João tried to catch her eye. After all, if it was a man she wanted, he'd like to explain the good points of Brazilians to her.

Risponyi paid no attention. He watched the *Katja*.

So, too, did Kuan Yang Smith.

He shifted the telescope to the side and saw Killinger come up on deck, watching him with great interest. After what had happened earlier, the marine insurance adjustor had become an enemy. The more one learns about an enemy, the more successful the war against him.

Killinger left the junk and headed for the schooner.

"Talya."

"Yes, father."

"Mister Killinger is no longer aboard the *Sybaris*. It is the proper time for you to visit and learn what you can, before his return."

"Yes, father."

Count Vaclav Risponyi had left Carolyn alone at the table in The Lobster Trap, saying he would be back shortly. She watched him through the glass as he made his way to the dock where the *Katja* was berthed.

João watched the little man with the long arms as he went toward the schooner. It was an opportunity he took advantage of. He moved to Risponyi's still warm seat with his glass and sat opposite Carolyn.

She turned to him with a frosty look. "That seat is taken."

"I am aware." He indicated to the boats. "The gentleman who was sitting here has gone to a sailboat in which I have an interest." He smiled ingratiatingly. "Perhaps you will be kind enough to try to help me. . . ."

The ice had been broken. Carolyn was curious. João called the waitress over and ordered two more drinks.

Katja could afford them.

The vibrations were wrong.

Both women felt it immediately. Marjorie had been a good and efficient secretary when she told Talya that Mr. Killinger was not aboard. Talya had been insistent that she be permitted to stay until Mr. Killinger's return.

"Frankly, Miss Smith, this is my first day here. Mr. Killinger didn't give me any instructions about visitors."

Coolly: "I'll wait."

"If you insist."

"I do insist."

At that moment, Talya turned toward the dock. She saw Count Vaclav Risponyi walking toward the dismasted schooner. She knew what she was about to ask would build further difficulties. But she had no choice. "May I use the phone?"

Marjorie hesitated.

"I assure you that it is not long distance."

Grudgingly, the black girl took Talya to the living room area, leading the way with a stiff-legged militancy. She pointed out the red telephone. Both women froze. Marjorie wanted to hear whether it really was a long-distance call. Talya wanted absolute privacy. Talya outwaited Marjorie who excused herself, saying she had work to do.

Talya dialed. The phone rang three times.

On the third ring, K. Y. Smith answered. "I am listening."

"Count Vaclav Risponyi went aboard Mrs. O'Reilly's schooner."

"I saw him." The pause was unnoticeable. In that brief time period, a plan was formulated, run through the computer, and declared workable. "Excuse yourself, and wait in the parking lot for Hamid. You will follow the Count and learn where he is staying. And everything else possible." He hung up.

After instructing Hamid, the turquoise-eyed Australian with the yellow skin picked up his telescope and aimed it at the *Katja.*

Killinger had been reviewing the damages and repairs to be made when Cornelius brought the visiting card. Katja was not familiar with the name, so she handed the card to Killinger. "Perhaps he's looking for you."

Killinger looked at the card and handed it back. "Don't know him."

Katja told Cornelius to send the gentleman in.

Risponyi paused at the top of the steps to pop the monocle into his eye. Slowly he descended and approached Katja with an elegant smile. "I am the Count Vaclav Risponyi." A small bow.

62

"How do you do. I am Mrs. O'Reilly, and this is Mr. Jedediah Killinger III."

Risponyi acknowledged each with a formal bow, inclining his head and clicking his heels. In another man, this might have been a laughable performance, but Risponyi had sufficient flair to carry it off.

Katja waited for the odd gnome to explain his presence.

Risponyi's eye was caught by the wooden crate with the Chinese writing on it. He floated to its side, dropped to one knee, and made love to it. His soul was in his eyes. "It is here. It is safe."

Killinger wondered why Risponyi was so deeply affected by a bronze statue of Kuan Yang Smith's ancestor.

The Count forced himself to stand and move from the crate to Katja. "Mrs. O'Reilly, I have come to discuss a personal matter which concerns your grandfather." He turned to look at the crate, as though to reassure himself that it was still there. "How soon may I speak with Ejnar Mylius?"

Katja sighed and shook her head sadly. "I wish I knew. He is in a coma."

"How unfortunate." With a sad smile. "You must know that your grandfather had always considered my own father to be one of his closest friends" Remembrance of things past. "They had shared many adventures together." Making a vague point. "Many."

Risponyi returned to the crate and placed both of his palms on it as though to communicate with what it contained. His eyes were closed in ecstasy. His inner explosion, with the bursting of billions of stars, was greater than ever he had received in climax with a beautiful woman. The noise of a feather-quiet hum in his throat was a low, controlled frog croak.

He opened his eyes. They were glazed. "This is a long lost treasure, belonging to my father. It had been stolen from him, almost thirty years ago."

He stood and faced them. "Your sainted grandfather aided in the long search." A deep sigh. "The physicians would not permit my father to leave his hospital bed." Several deep sighs. "Fortunately, his last moments were made happy when he heard that Ejnar Mylius' search had been successful." A smile found its way through the sadness. "I am now able to relieve you of its responsibility."

The beautiful words and thoughts floated in the schooner's cabin like perfect smoke rings in a still wind.

Risponyi took a folded piece of paper from his pocket. "This is the bill of lading. You will need it for your records." A charming smile. "It's from Hong Kong, you know. And some of the writing is in Chinese."

Killinger asked simply: "Count Risponyi, what does the crate contain?"

Katja knew the answer would be *Chin P'ing Mei.*

Killinger looked hard into Risponyi's black eyes under the thick black eyebrows. They were guileless.

As he spoke, the shaven-headed little man popped his monocle from his eye to his hand and proceeded to polish it with his breast pocket handkerchief. "Two things." He held up two fingers. "First, a series of metal tablets, inscribed with many lines of writing, in Cyrillic."

Katja's eyes widened as she listened close.

Killinger did not miss one word or one inflection.

"Second, the sealskin case in which the tablets are held." A far-off sad smile. "The name of my grandfather is written upon it." He inclined his head slightly. "It says 'Vaclav Risponyi'."

He replaced the monocle in his eye.

Chapter Four

Hamid was at the wheel of the black Mercedes-Benz 600. Talya sat quietly in the rear, watching the schooner so that she would not miss seeing Count Risponyi. She must not lose him.

She changed the angle of her view and looked across the harbor to where the *Valhalla* was berthed.

K. Y. Smith sat under an awning on the fantail. The day was warming rapidly. He called a few words in Chinese back over his shoulder to one of the crisply uniformed and turbanned servants. The man went inside.

With the telescope in hand, he kept everything and everyone in view. He had seen Talya step into the car and knew she was waiting for Risponyi to appear.

The telephone on the table was an instrument he used efficiently. When he had called the hospital to ask after Ejnar Mylius, it had told him that Mr. Mylius' condition was unchanged. Proper pressure on the floor nurse had brought him the knowledge that a Doctor Martin Oberhauser would be coming to Oxnard from Boston for the operation.

The oiled cogs, wheels, and rotor arms that never ceased their motion inside his head had just completed a preliminary read-out. He knew that the Count was attempting to get the crate from Hong Kong. He knew that Killinger would be the protector to foil the attempt.

This time.

The read-out said that Killinger would not tell Risponyi about K. Y. Smith's visit. It said that now suspicions had been aroused aboard the *Katja*. It said that João Aranha Mijangos O'Reilly was a weak man and not overly bright, concluding

65

with the possibility that he might be used as a way to get to his ex-wife.

The servant brought the Chinaman what he had ordered: a frosted silver mug with a curled slice of cucumber-peeling in the drink, Pimm's cup Number 2. Not heavy on alcohol, but cooling and exhilarating.

He began formulating a series of alternate plans for obtaining the crate . . . in case the long-armed little man made a serious error and caused actual alarm.

"Cyrillic is the script in which Russian, Bulgarian, and Serbian are written. Of course, my grandfather's name is written in Cyrillic." The charming little smile. "The sealskin case is hand-tooled and decorated with four small rubies, second grade, and three badly flawed emeralds, with seed pearls in the outline of a map. The map is of the mine near the Ural Mountains from which my grandfather founded his fortune, in the year 1884. On the tablets is the story of the mine."

Risponyi addressed Katja. "I shall have the crate removed and out of your way within the hour."

She indicated Killinger. "Jed, will you please explain to the Count why I may not release the crate."

Killinger did, fully.

Count Risponyi hid his disappointment with all the skill of a master poker player running a bluff for a big pot. He smiled and started up the gangway.

Katja leaned to Killinger while Risponyi's back was turned. In the faintest of whispers. "Which one told the truth?"

Killinger threw a simple question at the foppish nobleman. "Count Risponyi." He looked down from the top of the steps. Killinger continued. "Do the words Chin P'ing Mei mean anything to you?"

Risponyi looked blank. Then he smiled. "I do not speak Chinese." He inclined his head to Katja. "Mrs. O'Reilly, thank you for your hospitality." More coolly to Killinger: "And Mr. Killinger, I shall return soon. Good day."

He stepped out on the deck and disappeared from sight.

The eye of the telescope stayed with Risponyi as he crossed the parking lot and entered The Lobster Trap.

Risponyi stared unpleasantly at the big, handsome man in his seat. He seemed drunk.

"Darling, this is Senor João Aranha Mijangos O'Reilly." To O'Reilly. "Senor O'Reilly, I would like you to meet Count Vaclav Risponyi."

O'Reilly rose, swaying, with a big foolish grin. "A pleasure." He sat with a silent splash.

"Mr. O'Reilly, you are sitting in my chair."

Carolyn put her hand on Risponyi's arm, smiling reassuringly.

The odd little man was in a terrible mood. He had flown twenty hours from the other side of the world for the crate, and he had been rebuffed. Why had he bothered with this girl? Now she was beginning to annoy him.

Carolyn continued: "Please don't be angry. Mr. O'Reilly said he had an interest in the schooner you were visiting."

Risponyi brightened. Could this be good fortune? "You are the O'Reilly of Mrs. Katja O'Reilly?"

João beamed twistedly. "The very same."

Risponyi called for another chair to be brought to the table. Happiness engulfed him. "Mr. O'Reilly, I would be honored if you would join us for lunch."

"Very kind of you. I accept your invitation."

Count Vaclav Risponyi was certain that the key had been placed in his hand. He had but to find the lock.

Chapter Five

Copper and Auric greeted Killinger with love and kisses.

He walked to the office on the bow of the junk to see how Marjorie had been managing in her new job. He looked in, and she was working as confidently and as hard as though she'd been doing it in that same spot for a long time. She heard him behind her and turned, handing him a paper.

"Kimo left a note for you."

He opened and read it. Laughing, he read it aloud. "Don't forget your work-out. Samantha and I went to catch a surfing flick. We may never come home." He put it in his pocket. "He's my voice of conscience."

"Maybe you need one."

"I'll be in the gym, downstairs." Killinger scratched the two cats who'd made themselves comfortable near Marjorie. Lollipop slept with his head on his paws. Coco Chanel was twisted on her side atop a pile of papers. "Looks like the cats trust you."

"Don't wake them." An elfin smile. "A Miss Talya Smith was here."

"Did she stay long?"

"Unh unh. Soon's she arrived, she used the phone." Resentment. "Couldn't wait 'til I left. So she could have privacy."

"What's so different about that?"

"She said she had to make a call, suddenly. Like, right after she saw some funny-looking little guy with his head shaved and carrying a big, thick moustache. He went on the boat behind us. The *Katja*."

Killinger recognized this description of Risponyi. He put the pieces together.

"Till she got on the telephone, she acted like she was going to wait for you. If it took all day." She patted Coco Chanel. "Then, boom, she was gone."

"Thanks."

Marjorie got back to work, and the typewriter sounded like a machine gun, nonstop.

A hard worker. Can't lose her. "Marjorie . . ."

She looked at him.

"What are you doing tonight?"

"Oh, nooo . . ." She faced him directly. "Don't tell me I'm supposed to work all night, too."

"Hardly." A grin. "Do you have any plans?"

"Yes, Mr. Killinger." Evenly and flat. "Shortly, I will start to collapse. When that happens, I will try to get to my little trundle bed before I fall down."

"If you have enough strength when you pass by, speak to me a moment."

"I'll try."

Killinger crossed the deck to the circular stairway. Marjorie started pounding the typewriter. Lollipop talked in his sleep.

João's head was on his crossed arms on the table. He snored.

His presence was immensely cheering to Risponyi, for Risponyi had decided to enlist him in the shock troops. For pay. João had said he was really without money and would like a way to find some.

The Count was grateful to Carolyn. He leaned over, kissed her, placing his hand on her thigh. "Thank you."

"You're welcome." She returned his kiss. "Now, tell me. Thank you for what?"

He avoided an answer by running his fingers up her bare thigh. She shivered. Her skin was smooth velvet. The combination of the good happening with João was added to the excitement of the chase after the crate and brought to a high boil by Carolyn's sighs when he slipped his fingers under her briefs, beneath the tablecloth. She closed her eyes and nibbled his ear. Her hand wandered to his lap and stayed, moving and touching. His fingers caressed her lightly and insistently.

João belched.

The mood was destroyed. Besides, there were more important things.

João sat up, grinning foolishly. "Hi."

Risponyi smiled back. "Hi." He began to slide his hand out from under Carolyn's briefs. She grabbed his wrist and held him there.

João spoke. "Good lunch. Very good lunch." He looked at Carolyn and was aware of her closed eyes and uncontrolled breathing. "Whassa matter, Carolyn?"

Risponyi answered. "Carolyn has a lovely friend in Beverly Hills who would like to meet you." He turned to Carolyn. "Isn't that so?"

Her wild bottom was squirming. She kissed him on the lips hard. Her eyes opened slowly, and she focused on João. "Of course."

Risponyi offered an invitation: "Why don't you come to the Beverly Hills Hotel with us? It will be very interesting."

João's sleepy eyes went from one to the other. He made the big decision. "Why not?"

This time when he belched, he seemed embarrassed.

Hamid followed the Rolls-Bentley at a reasonable distance all the way to Beverly Hills. Talya used the car phone to keep in touch with her father.

Chapter Six

Karate is a martial art.

Daruma Taishi started Karate about 525 A. D. He was the founder of the Zen sect, and Karate was the weapon of the Zen priests of the Shorinji Temple when they overthrew an unpopular local government. Karate moved to China and Korea, where its various styles evolved.

Shorei Ryu originated in Southern China among the men who worked on boats. The upper half of their bodies was well developed, so the Shorei Ryu form of Karate used the upper half's strength and developed into a greater use of hands and arms. Shorei Ryu is also called Nanpa Ken.

Shorinji Ryu, sometimes known as Hoppa Ken, originated in North China, where people were horsemen and had strong legs. Therefore, Shorinji Ryu emphasizes legs and feet.

There are now, through travel, adaptation, and refinement, thirty-six principal forms of Karate. With minor styles, there are over fifty forms.

All are deadly.

Killinger's style was a combination of Shorei Ryu and Shorinji Ryu, called Goju, with more use of upper body.

After the grades of brown belt, there are ten grades of black belt. Karate Masters, or Sen Sai, may go as high as a red belt or a red and white belt. This requires constant work and practise, all day and every day.

Killinger had made black belt six dan, or sixth grade. To maintain it, he worked out every day. To go higher, he would be required to give up everything else. Working alone and going through the movements, he did the exercises called Pinan and Saifa. After that, weights and dumbbells.

As he worked out, his mind and body went their separate

ways. One of the great benefits of constant exercise is the mental relaxation it affords. While the body goes through its regimen, the thinking part of the brain is free. Killinger examined every minute aspect of the meetings and conversations with K. Y. Smith and Count Vaclav Risponyi.

Did the mysterious crate contain a bronze statue?

Or metallic tablets covered with Cyrillic script?

Whether it was one of these, or something else, there was an item of great worth in that simple wooden box. And two men wanted it very badly.

About the bills of lading . . . the turquoise-eyed Aussie had one, and the Count with an English public school accent had one. That added up to two.

Yet there can only be one!

Meaning that one of the two bills of lading proffered must be a forgery. Or were they both forged?

He was now responsible for the safety of that item of great worth. Legally, at this point, he could not open the crate. It must remain closed and guarded.

Here he was—in the middle of a situation. And all because he had listened to the blandishments of a Dutch friend and business associate, who, at this moment, was probably home, asleep and dreaming of the wide world of Insurance.

At least he was in physical condition for the problem. His heart was strong. His pulse was slow, about fifty-nine beats per minute. And since a well conditioned man requires ten to twenty percent less sleep, he had more time to be a sybarite.

The workout was over, and it was time to live the good life. A glass of nice, chilled California rosé wine would hit the spot. So, a cold tulip glass from the refrigerator and the jug of rosé, and he was in business.

While he was sipping appreciatively, Marjorie came down the circular staircase on the way to her cabin. Room and board were part of the job. She stopped before him wearily. "I'm beat." She tried a smile. "I know you wanted to say something. Can it wait 'til after I take a hot bath?"

Wordlessly, Killinger took out a second cold tulip glass. He poured wine into it and handed it to Marjorie.

She held it up to the light, looking through its warm color. "You live too rich for me." Then, defensively: "You sure it's all right? Drinking with the help?"

Killinger laughed. "Everyone aboard the *Sybaris* is either a friend or an enemy. Enemies go."

"And I'm staying?"

"I hope so."

Marjorie held up the glass, toasting him. "Okay, friend. It's a deal."

Killinger drank with her toast. "When can you pick up your things?"

She giggled. "I've already done it. Couple of hours ago, when I decided that living on a wild Chinese junk is absolutely the greatest."

Killinger held up his glass, touching hers. "Good."

They drank together again.

Marjorie looked into her glass admiringly. "That's good wine." An elfin smile. "Living rich is fun."

"You said you needed a hot bath . . . ?"

She put down her glass deliberately and looked at him, stony-faced and defensive. "Is that a hint of some kind?"

Killinger smiled as he refilled their glasses. "My, we *are* tender."

Marjorie rose, ignoring her glass. "I'll take my shower now. The head doesn't have a tub."

"Well, there is a big tub and plenty of hot water." He picked up both their glasses. "May I show it to you?"

Sullenly: "All right."

Killinger handed her the wine glass and turned, leading the way. Marjorie stopped and sipped her drink. She never did feel quite at ease with Whitey. Killinger opened the door at the end of the passage, past the kitchen, and waited. Marjorie glanced at the large room, frowned, and looked angrily at him. "This your bedroom?"

"Right." He turned left and pointed. "There's the tub."

Suspiciously, she moved after him and looked down. Surprised, she said, "It's made of wood."

"Right." He walked away from her. "Carved teak."

"Carved teak? Isn't that a bit much for a gal from the ghetto?"

"The ghetto was yesterday. We hope that tomorrow will bring an end to all ghettos and everything that built them."

"Talk talk talk." She shook her head. "That's all everyone does." She stared at him, hard. "Just jivin', that's all it is." While Killinger watched her, saying nothing, she surveyed the room slowly, hiding her approval with defensive causticity. "What kinda game you playing, anyway?" She swung her arm around in an arc, indicating the whole area. "No walls. And over there, a big, big bed." She faced him directly. "What am I supposed to do? Freaky things? Walk around bare-assed naked? So you can lie over there and get your jollies?"

Killinger looked at her expressionlessly.

"Does it say in small print that I gotta sleep with the boss?"

"Wouldn't it be better not to worry about that?" Killinger smiled. "At least, until you're asked?" Killinger turned and left the room. Before closing the door, he flipped the switch, turning on the stereo music. The door shut silently.

Coco Chanel and Lollipop were left in the bedroom with her. As though they had been trained to do a part of their act, they sat and stared at Marjorie.

She stared back, her anger showing. Then suddenly she laughed. "No reason a cat can't look at a queen."

Standing in front of the mirror, she slowly removed her clothes.

Smith's night glasses swept the *Sybaris*. There was no apparent activity. His mind was picking Killinger apart, adding and subtracting and dividing. The glasses moved a bit and picked up the *Katja*. The guard was sitting in a captain's chair on the deck, at the head of the gangplank, chewing his cigar as he listened to the muted tones of his little radio.

The phone at the Chinaman's elbow rang three times. It was picked up on the third ring. K. Y. Smith listened as Talya reported in about Count Risponyi and João O'Reilly. They were staying at the Beverly Hills Hotel, and O'Reilly was drunk. When Talya finished, her father gave her an explicit blueprint to follow, then hung up.

Without turning his head, he called behind him softly, in Chinese. A dark green turban suddenly appeared, the rest of its owner clad in crisp whites. K. Y. Smith ordered very carefully, in Chinese. The English translation was for corned beef and cabbage with very hot mustard and chilled black German beer, preferably Ritterbrau. Bring the first beer immediately.

The dark green turban faded back into the night to do its master's bidding. . . .

Chapter Seven

In the ghetto, rats running in and out of rooms and biting sleeping children were a way of life. Garbage was thrown from windows. People urinated in the hallways and defecated in the alleys. Couples made love in doorways and under the stairs.

Marjorie's father kept changing names and shapes. Sometimes tall and thin. Sometimes short and fat. Sometimes her father was called uncle. And every nine months, there was another baby in the house.

Marjorie was never picked up and kissed and mothered. No one had time to kiss her and stroke her hair with kindness. No one had time for her. She was bright and questioning, but there was no one who had the answers. She lived inside her imagination.

When she was almost twelve years old, she was raped by a drunk under the brush in an empty lot. He did not kiss her as she lay there still and quiet. In spite of the monstrous pain, she would not cry. Her fine mind remained intact.

It was this mind that brought her into the arena of higher education when her teacher got her the first in a series of scholarships. She was eternally grateful to this fat little Jewish man, Isidore Rosenbloom, whose avocation was being human. Now, these many years later, she held papers which said she was an accredited teacher at high school level.

Marjorie stepped from the wondrous teak bathtub, and from the pile of towels, she chose a super-large one the color of her now-gone wine. She stood before the gold-antiqued mirrors, examining herself critically in their softened reflections and searching her flaws. They were few, and they tended to accentuate the perfections. The one that bothered her most was the scar that ran down the right breast into the valley, almost touching the roundness of the other. It was a memory of a bottle fight at the age of nine. Small dark scars marked her knees and long, beautifully tapered legs. They were from her tomboy days. And she wondered whether her legs showed too much muscle, built up when she spent years of hash-slinging at night to pay for her schooling.

As she rubbed herself with the towel, her nipples hardened and gathered, pointing out at the world. When she laughed happily, the near perfect teeth were a beautiful line of brightness, the incisors a little long and sharply pointed, giving her smile a feline quality. The eyes were wide apart and more golden than brown. Marjorie Stafford made the color of Black beautiful.

Grabbing her clothes in one hand, and wrapped in the towel, Marjorie peeked out the door. Seeing no one, she ran like mad for her cabin. The cats followed. At her door, the towel fell from her, leaving her nude. No one watched except Coco Chanel. But that was permissible. It was woman to woman.

It was woman to woman in Beverly Hills. Carolyn had picked carefully among her friends and had come up with a Peruvian pepperpot named Elena, giving João something in common with the girl. Like, South America. Or something. Elena had done some bits in movies. Carolyn had expected the rapport between João and Elena to be instant and with all the chunky flavor of a hot *salsa verde.*

But João was too drunk to appreciate his passion flower.

Count Vaclav Risponyi kept pouring strong coffee into the Brazilian while he worked out a business transaction. A thousand dollars in cash as a down payment was a greater sobering factor than the coffee. To celebrate, they had dinner in their two-room bungalow at the Beverly Hills Hotel.

The two men in the lobby of the hotel were almost twins. Smooth, swarthy, thick-bodied, in black Italian silk suits with white shirts and black ties and black hats. They had taken up their posts after having spoken with Talya. And now Talya was in the long black Mercedes-Benz 600, with Hamid driving carefully, observing all traffic regulations. They were returning to the Peninsula Harbor Yacht Anchorage.

77

As her father's daughter, she was an extension of K. Y. Smith's will. She was a machine which had been ordered to concentrate on Jedediah Killinger III. As she relaxed in the rear of the limousine, her mind seemed to link with and run in random with the Mercedes' silent motor. The thoughts started from the beginning, running on the beach and romping in the surf.

The waves had pushed them together. Then torn them apart. The ocean's passions had entered their blood. They had touched. They had kissed underwater. They had put their hands under each other's bathing suit.

It was a good game.

Talya wondered whether she would have to destroy Killinger.

K. Y. Smith watched the new guard on the deck of the *Katja*. The guard who replaced Cornelius was named Johnson. He emptied his bottle of beer and carefully placed it in the beer cooler at his side as he took out another fresh, cold bottle. He adjusted the radio's dial, unscrewed the bottle's cap, and dropped it into the cooler. The yellow-skinned Australian's computer took note of the guard, his beer-drinking, and his habits, putting all the details on tape. Added to this was Smith's estimate of the guard's size. About six feet two inches, 247 pounds, and ill-conditioned.

The computer worked independently, noiselessly singing and making soundless clicks with each operation.

K. Y. Smith's telescope moved to the *Sybaris*. The unblinking turquoise eyes examined carefully. No movement. A button was pressed, and the computer read-out began. Facts and figures and mathematical probabilities ran through quickly. Count Risponyi in Beverly Hills. Talya returning shortly. Smith's crew, efficient and completely obedient. Killinger quiescent.

The computer printed a basic plan of action. The computer calculated every microsecond of the plan's operation. The computer said the time to begin was *now*.

Chapter Eight

K. Y. Smith was the complete gourmet. His chef was superb. The reason Talya barely touched her trout amandine was lack of appetite, as she listened closely to her father's instructions. They concerned Jedediah Killinger III and were specific in detail and in timing. When he had completed the run-through, she rose and said, "If you will pardon me, I had better get ready."

"Sit," he snapped at her, "and eat your dinner."

"I'm not hungry."

"You will not do your work on an empty stomach. Further, it would be an insult to Armand." A small sigh. "And you know how difficult it is to hold a chef of his ability."

Talya sat, and, like an unhappy but obedient child, she started to eat.

Meanwhile, Smith had dialed St. John's Hospital and asked for Ejnar Mylius' nurse. "This is Mr. Mylius' friend, Mr. Smith, asking after his condition."

"Mr. Mylius' condition remains unchanged."

"Is the operation scheduled for tomorrow?"

"Perhaps we shall know in several hours. Mrs. O'Reilly arrived a short while ago with the surgeon who had flown in from Boston. There will be a consultation shortly."

Now, the real reason for the phone call. "Uh . . . is Mrs. O'Reilly there?"

"She has taken a room here for the night. She's asleep right now."

The chill blue eyes showed nothing. The lips did not smile. But the Chinaman was gratified to know that Katja O'Reilly would not be aboard her schooner. The computer grabbed this morsel and put it in its proper place.

K. Y. Smith tapped a small gong on the table three times with his fork. Silently, four of his men in green turbans entered. Their group commander was a slim and cold-looking man with pockmarked skin and a face with all of the charm of a rusty broken knife. His name was Teffki.

The phone rang. On the third ring, a big yellow hand picked it up. "I'm listening."

"This is Vincenzo, sir." A brief pause. "Count Risponyi and Mr. O'Reilly remained in their bungalow with the two women. Also, they had dinner served there."

"If there is any change, phone immediately."

"It shall be done, sir."

K. Y. Smith replaced the phone and turned to Teffki. "Is Aldera at the motorboat?"

Teffki nodded. "Those were your instructions, sir."

K. Y. Smith trusted no one. He picked up the two-way radio and pressed the switch. "Aldera, where are you?"

Through the small speaker. "In the motorboat, sir."

"Did you bring the bundle of work clothes?"

"It is by my side. I swear it."

"Stay there. Teffki will arrive shortly." The radio was turned off. To Teffki: "Are there questions?"

"No questions." Teffki was a cruel and efficient man whose soul had been bought by K. Y. Smith. He made a small bow of respect to his master, then turned and left silently, followed by the other three green turbans.

Smith's huge bulk floated to its feet and walked to the *Valhalla's* fantail carrying the telescope. A servant followed, a step behind, with the two-way radio and the telephone on its long extension cord.

Killinger had taken a well-aged side of beef from the meat cooler and sliced two magnificent New York steaks from it. He'd invited Marjorie to join him for dinner. When she arrived in the kitchen, full of suspicions, he was making the salad dressing. She had watched silently. Finally, "Do I get lucky and wash the dishes?"

Killinger laughed as he pushed lettuce and tomatoes and

greens toward her. "Electric dishwasher behind you." He indicated them. "There's a knife and salad bowl. Chop 'em up."

Marjorie got to work, and Killinger poured them Cabernet Sauvignon, handing her a glass. "Try this."

"Wine?" She sipped. "Good." A smile. She held it up to the light. "The color of blood. Beautiful."

After eating, Killinger put the dishes in the machine and turned to Marjorie. "How about some ice cream?"

"Why not?" Big smile. "You're a good cook."

"Thanks. What's your favorite ice cream?"

"What ya got?"

He pointed. "Look in the freezer. Bowls and spoons are right behind you. See you upstairs." Copper and Auric followed him up the circular staircase. Lollipop and Coco Chanel stayed with Marjorie.

Danger sat in the dark, nearby in a quiet part of the yacht harbor.

The motorboat was wide beamed, all wood, no ornamentation. A man on shore held the line. He was dressed in nondescript khaki. Another man near him carefully folded the white crisp uniforms and put them with great care into a big gray canvas sack. He placed the five green turbans within the same sack, which he tied tight and put under the brush near the boulders which rimmed the landing. No lights were used. No sound was heard.

There were four men in the motorboat. Waiting. . . .

The silence was broken by K. Y. Smith's voice, distorted by the small speaker of the two-way radio at Teffki's ear. It snapped at him: "Teffki!!"

Softly: "This is Teffki, sir."

K. Y. Smith trusted no one. Everything and everyone were subject to check. "How many men are with you?"

"Four others, beside me."

"Their names. Tell me their names."

"Aldera. Parvetin, Khaloush, Chiang-Tsi."

"I wish to hear them. Individually."

Teffki held the radio to the closest man. "My name, Excellency, is Khaloush." The next one identified himself simply: "Parvetin." The third, "Chiang-Tsi." Finally, "Aldera, sir."

The necessary precaution. "Aldera. Start the motor."

Teffki held the radio close to the motor, nodding to Aldera. Aldera turned the key. The motor hummed smoothly. Teffki nodded again. The motor stopped.

"Check your weapons." The transmitter clicked off.

Teffki was aware that the blue-eyed Chinaman listened at his receiver, virtually at his shoulder. So Teffki acted accordingly, with care. This was to be an operation of surprise and silence. Teffki made the others show their long, sharp, curved knives. Each had wires for strangling an opponent from behind. These were displayed briefly.

Now, the rehearsal.

In the center of the motorboat, mounted on thick rubber feet, was a portable tripod crane. The lines for the pulleys were nylon cord with a test strength of four thousand pounds. Under Teffki's direction, they rehearsed taking the crane and pulleys apart and reassembling them. They did this four times.

Teffki carried the only handgun. It was equipped with a silencer.

Talya was a weapon which the big Australian aimed at Killinger.

She had just gotten out of her bath and dried herself. Now, dressed only in heavy musk perfume, she examined her ammunition. It was dark, glowing, jade-green *cheong-sam* of the finest silk. The glow was heightened by the golden threads running through the fabric. The high neck of the *cheong-sam* was more gold then green, a perfect frame for her exquisite face. Her shoes, too, were golden, with four-inch heels, sandallike soles, and the thinnest of golden straps to wrap the insteps of her bare feet.

The four-inch heels were cunningly fashioned of spring steel, with sharp points covered by thin leather. Each one, a deadly weapon.

That was all Talya would wear for Killinger. Body-clinging *cheong-sam* and shoes. The gleaming long black hair would fall loosely, wherever wind or circumstance blew it. The same winds or circumstances would blow wide the long slits on either side of the *cheong-sam*. These were outlined in golden thread and they ran all the way up to where the thigh became the hip.

Talya picked up her shoes, examined the spring-steel of the four-inch heels wrapped in their golden silk and put them on. Next, the *cheong-sam*. It became her skin, hiding nothing.

Her father's instructions had been explicit. She hoped it would not become necessary to cause Jedediah Killinger III to die.

The two cats insisted on walking on Marjorie's bare feet as she climbed the circular stairway to the deck of the *Sybaris*. She carried an ice cream bowl in each hand. Meanwhile, Killinger had adjusted the stereo, and taken out two brandy snifters and a bottle of Remy Martin. He was pouring when Marjorie entered. "What kind did you pick?"

"Rocky Road." Small laugh. "You must have a dozen different flavors there."

"Thirteen. It's my lucky number." He pushed a snifter toward her. "Try a sip."

She put a bowl in front of him. "I hope it's enough." She picked up the snifter glass. "What's this?"

"Brandy."

Marjorie took a gulp, and tears came to her eyes as she coughed.

"Better if you sip it slowly."

Marjorie picked up the bottle and read aloud, "Fine Champagne Cognac." She looked at him and said flatly, "Whatever that means."

Killinger explained, as they ate their ice cream, that brandy, and fine cognacs like Remy Martin, were distilled from wine and that if it consists of grapes from the Champagne districts of France, then it may say "Fine Champagne Cognac." Marjorie sipped her brandy slowly and with relish as she ate her ice cream. Her feelings of hostility went to sleep. She put their empty bowls on the floor for Copper and Auric to lick.

While the dogs enjoyed the last of the Rocky Road, she thought she'd never had a finer day. And she ran her fingers over the bar, in and out of the irregularities. Her eyes moved to her fingertips and opened, at first disbelieving. Then she put her hand to her mouth as she leaned closer. It was the group of intertwined males and females, in positions of joy.

Killinger watched her reaction. He smiled. "Philippine mahogany."

"It's more than that. It's wild."

"An old Siamese friend's memories of the love-making of his youth." Killinger poured a drop more brandy into the snifters. "He believed that making love was the full reason for life."

Marjorie put her glass on the bar counter next to Killinger's. Then she got up from the barstool and moved to him, standing on tiptoe, putting her arms around his neck. Her micro-mini rose, showing her wine-red bikini briefs and lovely round bottom. "I want to thank you for the best day of my life." She kissed him. Suddenly, she pulled her arms back as though Killinger was white hot. She took a deep agonized breath, spun and ran to the circular stairway, disappearing down the steps, sobbing.

Killinger followed, to see her slam her door. He knocked.

The voice inside choked out, "Go away." The painful crying could be heard in the corridor.

Killinger knocked once more. Her footsteps came to the door. She opened it. Her cheeks were wet. She was crying, unable to catch her breath, like a child badly hurt. She finally got control. She looked at him, accusing the whole world.

"I know how to fuck. But I never learned how to make love." The tears and sobbing would not stop. She slammed the door in his face.

With heavy sadness, Killinger went up to the deck. There, he picked up both Lollipop and Coco Chanel and went back down the stairs to Marjorie's cabin. Without knocking, he opened the door and entered. Marjorie was sobbing into her pillow. Gently, Killinger put Coco Chanel on the bed next to her. Lollipop he placed on her back. Lollipop put his ears back and moved to her rump where he began to knead one buttock, his paws rhythmically pumping. Coco Chanel moved to Marjorie's head where she started to lick the lovely, full Afro hairdo.

Marjorie rolled over and picked Coco Chanel up into her arms, burying her face in the cat's fur. The sobbing stopped. She looked up at Killinger. The black elf with the feline smile said, "Thank you. So much."

"Say 'prunes'."

Uncertainly, "Prunes."

"Once more. And don't rush it."

Marjorie lingered over the word. "Prunes." Her lips puckered into a pink flower . . . which Killinger kissed softly.

"Remember. The cats have a love for you. The dogs, too." He started for the door, opening it. ". . . And so do I. . . ." He closed the door quietly behind him.

Marjorie held both cats close.

In this small war, the green turbans were K. Y. Smith's big guns.

Talya was his stiletto.

The telescope moved from the watchman aboard the *Katja* to the Chinese junk where his unknown menace, Killinger, lived. All was quiet aboard the *Sybaris*.

A movement on the dock caught his eye, and the telescope shifted. It was Talya. She stopped briefly at the gangplank, then she started to walk aboard. K. Y. Smith approved of her walking on her toes, to protect her heels.

If they caught between planks and stuck, she would be without a weapon.

Chapter Nine

The sardonic smile revealed over-large and sharp teeth in a huge mouth. The smooth cheeks were full of black dents and pocks. The nose was bulbous and beaten, perfectly centered in the round, fat, ugly face. Large eyes stared into space from under almost nonexistent eyebrows, thin scratches. It was one of the devils of Borneo, Pangkalanbuun, etched into the bronze gong.

Killinger had picked it up in Bandjermasin, on the island of Borneo. Now it stood at the head of the gangplank for visitors to announce themselves. A heavy violet-colored silken cord held the hammer.

He was sipping his brandy when the loud clear voice of Pangkalanbuun called through the night, the vibrations continuing with a deep rumble. The strong muscial note brought Copper and Auric running and barking. Killinger followed.

The dogs were making a fuss over the beautiful Eurasian girl with whom he had run on the beach and frolicked in the ocean. Kimo had told him that she was K. Y. Smith's daughter. Killinger had decided that their meeting had been no coincidence. If she wished to play a mysterious game of intrigue, he would be a very willing partner.

Now she was purposely posing for Killinger as she bent to pet and nuzzle the two Vizslas. The breeze had enjoyed opening the slash of her skirt, revealing the magnificent ballet dancer's legs all the way up to her firm buttocks. Her long black hair covered her face and hung to her breasts.

Killinger whispered to himself, "A girl with a body like

that can't be all bad." He walked to the shiny lady spider in her glowing *cheong-sam*, hoping to be entrapped.

Talya was aware of Killinger. She held out her exciting semi-nudity as a lure. Suddenly, she stood. As a ballet dancer would, she began a spin with her arms out. Her hair went straight out behind her, and with increased speed the panels of her *cheong-sam* acted like the rotor blades of a helicopter, rising from the ground and revealing her as the silken fabric swung away.

Abruptly, she stopped. The skirts bounced and fell back to the ground demurely. Her hair had fallen wildly over her shoulders. The deep V-slit at her bosom was unbuttoned to below her breasts. She ran to Killinger and threw her arms around him. Accusingly, to put him on the defensive, she cried: "Jed! Why were you not here earlier? I waited." As part of her act she pouted her full lower lip at him.

Killinger did not waste words. He put his arms around her, returning her kisses, passion for passion. She laughed and nibbled at his ear. His hands ran down her back until he held a firmly moulded roundness in each hand. She moved into him, sensuously rubbing against his excitement.

He kept his mind clear and apart. He knew she was fulfilling some kind of planned scheme. She hadn't waited for him. She had used his phone to make a report on Count Risponyi. Then she had disappeared. Well, it was her show. If she wanted an audience, he would be the audience. If she wanted a partner, he would be that partner. His fingertips told him that there was nothing under the *cheong-sam* with Talya. And she was more than enough. Too much?

Pelvis to pelvis, she had felt him rise to her, quick and strong. She whispered, close, "We are wasting time." A tongue tip into his ear. "Have you champagne?"

He was more than willing to aid her in seducing him. Killinger took her by the hand and led her to the lush cabin-living-room on the rear deck.

Words were unnecessary. He went to the wine cooler and took out two champagne glasses and a chilled bottle. She looked at the label. "Taittinger!! How wonderful. My favorite."

While Killinger untwisted the wire around the cork, prior to opening the bubbly, Talya looked down at the bar before her. He watched her expression.

She laughed; looked up at him; looked back down. She bent to examine the carvings with professional appreciation. She leaned a bit lower than necessary so that Killinger could see the erect pink nipples and the twin fullnesses. Talya had seen as well as rubbed against Killinger, and she knew he had stayed risen. The knowledge excited her. Twisting and turning her body for his eyes, she felt his appreciation. Her eyes shared the pleasure of their thoughts as she turned to him briefly. Then she ran her lips softly over the entwined figures in the Philippine mahogany, created by the lecherous old Siamese. Occasionally she would pause at one of the frozen-in-motion figures of love and touch it with her tongue.

Killinger put a glass before her, popped the champagne cork, and poured for them both, properly putting the first drop in his glass and tasting. They toasted silently, touching glasses. They sipped as she made a point of smouldering into his eyes. She felt she had him entrapped in her web. Now, to be certain, she indicated the many positions of fornication she had just kissed. "Do you have a favorite?"

"I have several. Must I choose one?"

She moved from the bar. "Yes. And while you make up your mind, I shall turn off that bright lamp near the window." Quickly she moved to the lamp; turned it off.

Killinger could not help but wonder why she had wanted darkness. Certainly, Talya was proud of her body. And the lamp was across the room.

K. Y. Smith had chosen the light on the port side as a signal. Immediately it went out, he clicked on the two-way radio. "Teffki!"

The small distorted voice: "This is Teffki, sir."

"Start the motor."

Teffki's voice said, "Aldera! Start the motor." The low roar of the motor came over.

"Proceed."

"Yes, sir."

The sound of the motor as it engaged the propellor came over the small speaker.

Count Vaclav Risponyi was in Beverly Hills, making plans to acquire the crate which was aboard the *Katja*. He had been trying to explain certain details to João Aranha Mijangos O'Reilly. As they talked, João drank himself back into near-insensibility. Risponyi would have gladly left João . . . if he could have. But he needed the Brazilian as his key to the lock.

Risponyi sent the Peruvian pepper, Elena, to João's room. She stayed twenty-seven seconds, and then came out into the living room. "He is drunk, and he snores like one hundred pigs. Have you got a good book?"

Risponyi laughed and turned on the television set for her. Then, he took Carolyn with him to his room for some active relaxation.

He wouldn't have relaxed if he'd known that the box with the Chinese lettering was in grave danger.

At that very moment.

To Smith, exercises in strategy and planning were far more exciting than any woman. Adrenalin had been dripping into his blood. He was ready. The computer and abacus of his mind were waiting, clicking rhythmically and heard by no one. His cold blue eyes did not change. Nor did they blink. Nor did he smile in anticipation.

He sat at command-post on the deck of the *Valhalla*, a table on either side of his chair. The one at his right hand held the implements of his battle, two-way radio, binoculars and telescope with night lenses, two telephones with muted bells, and closest to him a large timing clock with a sweep second hand. Black button to start. Red button to stop.

The table at his right held the small pleasures which heightened his enjoyment. A bottle of Grand Marnier, a small brandy glass, and a plate of petits fours with thick sugar-icing.

He turned the receiver loud, to hear everything happening aboard the motorboat. The brandy glass was enveloped in one great hand. The other hand fed his mouth a petit four which he ate with a careful daintiness which did not seem to fit his bulk.

He focused the binoculars on the *Katja*. Johnson was alone, drinking from a new bottle of beer and listening to his radio.

The light was still off aboard Killinger's *Sybaris*. Talya was in control there.

The binoculars picked up a squat motorboat moving at a slow pace with controlled power, innocently circling the open harbor area. It held five men, dressed in khaki-colored work clothes.

The binoculars swept back to the *Katja*—and froze.

A blond man with a moustache stood on the dock at the foot of the gangplank leading to the *Katja*. He leaped into the eye on that dark night, dressed in a white suit and wearing a white Panama hat. A businesslike dispatch case was gripped firmly under his arm. He started up the gangplank.

Johnson saw him and stood, putting his beer down next to the radio and loosening his snub-nosed .38 in its holster. He approached the man in white. His tone was flat. "Can I help you, sir?"

The man in white dipped his head with a smile as he came closer, holding up the dispatch case as though to indicate that he was there on business.

Johnson was doing what he was paid to do. "Mrs. O'Reilly isn't aboard. Better try tomorrow."

The man with the white dispatch case came closer, smiling apologetically. He opened his mouth as though going to speak. Instead, he took a deep breath and held it. He aimed the dispatch case at Johnson's face and pressed a button. A cloud of mist surrounded Johnson's head.

Johnson fell, his hand on his gun. With surprising ease, Johnson was lifted from the deck and placed in his chair and arranged sitting naturally. His breathing was shallow and irregular.

The man in white removed his hat and blond wig and moustache. Before taking off his white suit, which he wore over khaki work clothes, he aimed a small pen-flash at the *Valhalla* and flicked it on and off four times.

Simultaneously, K. Y. Smith spoke one word into the two-way radio and pressed the black button of his split-second timer-clock. The word was, "Now."

Chapter Ten

Teffki's two-way radio was secured by a chest harness so that K. Y. Smith could hear every word, every breath. And Smith's every thought would come across clearly.

For the big yellow man with the turquoise eyes was right there. The six men were his hands. His mind directed each motion and action meticulously. The victory was his. His alone! He refilled the small brandy snifter with Grand Marnier, and, with great control, he ate another petit four in little nibbles, though it was tiny enough to be popped into his mouth and be gone in one bite and one swallow.

His eyes were the binoculars.

The businesslike dispatch case held more than the device which sprayed a mist when a button was pushed. It held a small tank of oxyacetylene gas, under high pressure, and a miniaturized welding torch as well as a neat welder's mask.

The dispatch case was now open on the floor alongside the crate from Hong Kong. Now out of his white suit, the man was lighting the stream of gas coming from the welder's torch and adjusting its flame. With his eyes protected by the mask, he began cutting the crate free from its four bolts.

Meanwhile the powerful launch had pulled up alongside the *Katja,* holding to the schooner's deck with sharp three-pronged hooks, so there would be no time lost in tying up or untying when the operation had been completed.

The five green turbans had been well rehearsed.

Khaloush moved to the open door of the hatch which led to the steps to below. He carried the collapsible tripod crane which was made of titanium because it was lighter and stronger than steel. He erected the crane so that it could lift the heavy chest from the stateroom to the deck of the schooner.

While Khaloush locked the legs of the crane with titanium pins dropped into paired holes, Chiang-Tsi snapped the pulleys and nylon lines to the hook at the apex of the crane. He had carried these aboard.

Parvetin had climbed onto the deck carrying a strong dolly whose wheels had been carefully oiled. This was for rolling the crate to the edge of the schooner, after it had been brought up from where it was now being cut free by the hot flame of the torch. In seconds, Khaloush would move the crane to the edge of the decking, lift the crate once more, and lower it tenderly into the stern of the powerboat. Aldera stayed aboard, the motor throttled down and the power to the propellor disengaged.

Parvetin placed the dolly at Chiang-Tsi's feet and ran below, taking the nylon line from the crane with him. He had the hook end. Khaloush would operate the pulleys by hand while Chiang-Tsi would guide the precious crated cargo to the dolly.

Parvetin moved quickly to the side of the man with the welding outfit. He was now finishing the second floor bolt. Two more to go, and all six men would disappear, together with whatever was really in the wooden box.

Teffki was everywhere at once with the two-way radio in the middle of the action. He had helped with the crane, the pulleys, the dolly, and the welding. Now, he was putting the nylon line around the crate so that as soon as the last bolt was cut through, the heavy box would begin to move.

The large sweep-second hand crawled, never hurrying.

K. Y. Smith's computer knew exactly where each man was supposed to be, at every millisecond. Teffki's muffled commands came over the speaker. The grunting and heaving and curses were constant background to the work going on.

The petits fours were eaten daintily, and the Grand Marnier was sipped appreciatively.

According to the timer, the read-out said that the third

belt was now being worked on. The voices over the speaker confirmed that the plans were being carried out smoothly. Perfectly.

The binoculars took an area sweep before coming to the Chinese junk. The *Sybaris* was quiet and dark. Never had his daughter given herself in a better cause. In case of emergency, she was more than adept with her twin four-inch stilettos.

A movement in the dark. The binoculars searched into the area where motion seemed to live. Two dark figures. Like two men on their hands and knees. Why were they keeping low? They moved forward on Killinger's upper deck. If they stood, or reached the stern railings, they would be in position to look down at the activity on the *Katja*.

Discovery would endanger the group. Teffki might be forced to use his gun. Silent killing would be permissible. Gunshots could not be permitted. His computer read-out said that forty-seven percent of the marina's boat owners had firearms aboard, for their own protection and the protection of their neighbors. In a minor war, the computer said, his position was untenable, and he would lose. He could not afford to lose. However, he could afford to withdraw, regroup, and plan another attack under more favorable conditions.

He spoke into his transmitter. "Teffki!"

"This is Teffki, sir."

"Stand ready to abort."

"But, sir, we are in a position to—"

The cold, hard voice cut him off. "Abort immediately. No shooting." The binoculars watched the two figures on the junk above his men as they moved forward, bent low.

"Immediately, sir." Teffki's voice giving instructions on a well-rehearsed abort operation came clearly to the Australian's ears.

Not many minutes before, Talya and Killinger had been sipping their chilled Taittinger champagne. She had stood at the bar counter, close to the frieze which illustrated an old Siamese gentleman's conception of heaven. Her fingers had caressed the carved mahogany bodies paired and frozen into permanent ecstasy. Her smile had been a challenge. "You have not yet stated your favorite."

"That is like asking me which is my favorite brand of champagne." He paused, toasting her and sipping. "Many bubbling wines are called champagne. Too few are fine champagne. Those which are *great* champagnes are all my favorite."

"Of these great champagnes, you must have a choice."

He laughed as they played the game. "It is a choice of the moment." He tilted his glass at her. "What is in the glass that is offered to me."

Talya placed her glass on the bar, stepped carefully from her shoes, and spread her bare feet wide apart so that her legs were no longer concealed by the loose panels of the *cheong-sam*, her satin skin gleaming.

The green and gold garment of silk was fastened along the right side, starting under the arm and continuing to the top of the slit. Talya stood before Killinger, her bare legs wide, her pelvis thrust forward, and her eyes fastened to his while her fingers went their own way, busy.

Silk-topped button by silk-topped button, Talya was freeing herself from her second skin as the buttons were pushed through their heavy silk loops. The top of the *cheong-sam* came open, from the right shoulder, down, exposing a wondrously soft but firm breast . . .

. . . and, without warning, it happened.

The binoculars were fastened to the two figures on the junk's rear deck. They had stopped moving at the same time. A quick flash of light from some boat's searchlight hit them briefly.

They were the two dogs, Copper and Auric, doing their duty in the big sandbox above Killinger's living room.

K. Y. Smith put these facts into the computer, and while it was deciding whether to call off the abort, all decisions were taken from the big man and his mental machinery.

Copper and Auric suddenly heard the noises aboard the schooner below them. The cursing of the men. The movement of the crane. They began to bark, running to the rear rail.

Teffki and his green turbans speeded up their disengagement of the operation. They ran across the *Katja*'s deck to their boat, taking their equipment with them. The dogs laughed and cheered, their barks making the men move faster and with carelessness.

Killinger moved automatically, jet propelled. Talya tried to stop him, but he shook her hand free. She picked up one of her golden shoes and ran after him.

Her father's instructions had been explicit. Keep Killinger from interfering. No matter how. As she ran, she unscrewed the leather heel which capped the stiletto's point.

Killinger had gone up the steps in three jumps. In three more, he was with Copper and Auric, watching the man scramble into the motorboat. The dogs' barking became more frenzied.

Talya came up behind him, the golden slipper now a weapon in her hand. She stopped in shock as Killinger flicked the switch that snapped on three 150-watt floodlights. His back was to her. Talya looked over his shoulder as the last two men jumped into the motorboat which immediately became lost to sight amidst the forest of masts and yachts and docks.

The dogs turned to Talya. Killinger spun with them.

To keep him from moving, she threw her arms around him and kissed him, trying girlish laughter. "Darling, what is this excitement?" She had no way of knowing whether her father's mission after the crate had been successful. Nor did she know whether Killinger had seen enough of the boat and men to identify them.

Killinger tried moving, to get from his junk to the schooner. But Talya was a strong woman, and for a moment he was held still.

The point of the stiletto grazed his shirt.

Chapter Eleven

K. Y. Smith accepted the blame as his own. A leader can do no less. In dispassionate analysis, he would review each action and piece of information that his tapes held. A man always learns, his whole life long. Better, though, to learn from success than from failure.

His binoculars crept over the *Katja*'s deck. It seemed normal. The guard would not sleep for long. And his memory of what had happened would be vague, as though it had been a bad dream. He would have a small headache. That was how the drug worked.

He looked at the rear deck of the *Sybaris*. There, outlined in a reflection of the floodlights, he saw Killinger in Talya's arms. And he saw clearly the golden slipper in her hand, heelpoint aimed at a spot behind his heart. With the operation's having been a failure, Killinger's demise might very well make any further actions on his part an impossibility. He realized that Talya was trying to make a decision based on his instructions. She did not know that a fatal stabbing might lead to insurmountable complications. He put his fingers to his lips and gave his distinctive whistle which started low in tone, climbing to a shrill peak and then chittering into a group of separate notes. The sound was loud and clear and strong.

The shoe dropped from Talya's hand, falling to the water over the rail, sinking with the barest of splashes.

She released him, unlocking her arms. "What is happening?"

"C'mon and see." He ran fast, and she followed.

Killinger's mind was working as he ran to Katja O'Reilly's wounded schooner. As representative for the Dutch Insurance

Company, he had a large area of responsibility if anything had been stolen. Especially since he had taken possession on behalf of Mynheer van der Helft.

His primary concern was possible theft. A little bell in his mind was ringing and trying to tell him something. Something about Talya. He'd worry about it later. And that funny loud whistling. It sounded like some kind of a signal. To the thieves? To whom?

In his speed, he had left Talya way behind. Aboard the *Katja,* before jumping down the companionway to the saloon, he saw Johnson relaxed in his chair, seemingly asleep. He took a fraction of a second to ascertain that the guard was breathing, then a quick examination below, before Talya's arrival. First look at the chest showed that it was still there. Second look told him that the bolts which had held it had been burned through. A fast look on one knee confirmed this by showing a scorch on the floor.

He had wondered about Talya's chasing him, coming to the junk earlier, and then tonight. Keeping him busy. Turning off the light. He heard her running aboard, almost silently, for her feet were bare.

When Talya came into the saloon, Killinger's back was to the companionway and to her. He was checking the paintings hung on the walls. Covered by glass, they acted as partial mirrors. He used the glass of the Matisse as a mirror to watch Talya behind him. She had gone straight to the crate. Then, after looking at Killinger's back, she dropped to a knee to check it. Killinger was certain that she had seen the burned-through bolts for she had pulled the small rug close, throwing up its edges to cover them. Quickly she moved to his side.

Obviously, what had just hapened must have been instigated, masterminded by her father. Again, the little bell was ringing some sort of a signal to him. Something that had happened that was not quite right. About Talya. But he had to make certain that she would feel he had no suspicions. He smiled and indicated the pictures. "Looks like nothing was stolen."

She felt a relief. "Is that what it was? Robbery?"

"Maybe that was what it was *supposed* to be." He grinned. "Fortunately, Copper and Auric scared the people away."

Talya had to test him. "Is there enough of value here to tempt thieves?"

"Oh, yes."

She wondered whether he knew of the crate.

Killinger continued. "These pictures must have great value." Pointing to them as he spoke. "This is a Rouault. I do not know its worth. Nor do I know what this seascape by Kees van Dongen might bring on the market. The others are in a similar price range. And they're still here."

"Do you think money or jewelry might have been taken?"

"There will be nothing positive until Mrs. O'Reilly returns."

Talya looked around the saloon with a pretended offhandedness. She indicated the heavy box with the Chinese lettering. "That wooden case. Is there anything valuable in it?"

Killinger shook his head, playing his scene so that she would tell K. Y. Smith that the insurance man believed what he had heard. "Not really. A heavy bronze statue with a certain sentimental value."

Talya was glad that she hadn't put the stiletto into his heart.

They walked up onto the deck. Johnson was in the same position in his chair. Killinger walked over to him and shook his shoulder. Johnson gave no reply. His breathing grew deeper, verging on the sound of snoring. Killinger leaned down and smelled his breath. The odor was sweet and cloying, with an undertone of a medicinal aroma. Killinger's brows moved together in a sign of puzzlement. Definitely not alcohol.

Talya saw the reaction. "Is something wrong?"

Killinger covered by reaching down to the small cooler at the guard's side and lifting out an empty beer bottle. As though angry, disgusted. "The man's drunk. Passed out." A headshake. "He'll be replaced in the morning."

"And tonight?"

"Tonight, the floodlights stay on. And the dogs will keep a watch for me." Killinger slid Johnson's gun from its holster and stuck it into the waistband of his trousers. "He'll get this back in the morning."

Talya walked down the gangplank, and Killinger followed to the dock. She stretched and yawned. The movements were feline. Like a tigress exercising its claws. "I'm so tired." On her tiptoes to kiss him good night. "Till tomorrow." She let her lips linger, and her tongue moved into his mouth, touching his. Abruptly, she disengaged and laughed, repeating herself. "Tomorrow." A promise.

Killinger looked at her bare feet. "What about your shoes?"

She ran a finger lazily down his chest as a hundred thoughts raced through her mind. All of them about the twin stilettos. "Put them at the side of your bed." A sensuous smile as she licked her lips provocatively. "I'll be by to pick them up." She walked from him, her lovely bottom undulating. Then, a few paces away, she remembered that she must cover the fact that one of the shoes was not aboard the *Sybaris*. It was under water, at the bottom of the harbor. "Keep my lovely golden slippers away from your dogs. They might lose one." Satisfied that she had explained in advance about only one shoe aboard, she drifted away into the night.

He knew that Copper and Auric never touched any articles of clothing. They had been broken of that long ago.

Why had she made such a point of her "lovely golden slippers"?

The warning bell started again in the back of Killinger's skull. He barely heard it.

Chapter Twelve

Tonight, a forty-eight-minute sleep was enough for Count Vaclav Risponyi. He had important planning before him, and he could not afford more time. Like a large chimpanzee in a cage, he could not stay still. He paced back and forth, sat in a deep chair, bounced up, and now he was waking the drunken Brazilian.

He was laying out his basic blueprint of operation. When it was complete, he would be ready to make his move for the crate from Hong Kong. Slow and careful thought was the answer. He had enough time to work so long as Ejnar Mylius was compelled to stay in the hospital.

João drank cup after cup of coffee, at Risponyi's insistence. João was needed for answers. About the guard. About the schooner. And especially about what-is-his-name . . . Killinger. What power did this insurance person have over Mrs. O'Reilly?

João told what he knew.

Then the Count started explicit questions about the case from Hong Kong.

João laughed. "You're as bad as the Chinaman."

All expression was wiped from Risponyi's face during a very long pause. If possible, his black eyes seemed to grow harder.

João tightened, as though the Count had been pulling on his nerves. "What is wrong?"

The silence continued. Then, in a faint whisper, "The Chinaman. Tell me about him."

"He wanted the wooden box that's bolted to the floor."

"His name!! What was his name?"

"Smith."

"His eyes. They were turquoise?"

João nodded. The little man's reaction had been incredible.

Risponyi pressed his eyelids together and tore up his blueprint. He no longer could proceed at his leisure. Time had become his enemy. He laid out a new sheet of blue paper, opened a new bottle of white ink, and straightened his T-square and compass and his broad-nibbed drawing pen.

"Did I say something wrong?"

Risponyi started at him. "Unfortunately, you said something right. But you should have said it sooner."

An excuse, for protection. "You never asked me about anything."

The Count began moving about the room rapidly and erratically. A chimpanzee jumping from branch to branch.

Jedediah Killinger III sat with his hand on the phone.

He knew the sheriff's telephone number. And a crime had been committed. Or had it?

If he called, he was certain the conversation would go like this:

"Ventura Sheriff's office. Sergeant Walters here."

"My name is Killinger. Jedediah Killinger III."

Politely. "Yes, Mister Killinger."

"I want to report a robbery."

"Yes, sir." The sergeant would tiredly start writing on the top sheet of the pad before him. "Where did this alleged robbery take place?"

"At the Peninsula Yacht Anchorage."

"Could you please list the missing items."

Embarrassed: "Nothing is missing."

"But you said a robbery, Mister Killinger." Pause while this new non-information was being recorded. More carefully, now. "Can you identify the alleged robber, sir?"

"It's night, and there was no moon. Besides, I was about twenty feet away, about fifteen feet above the men."

Picking up the word. "Men?"

"Yes. Five or six of them."

"Yes, sir." Talking more slowly, as though to a drunk or a child. "Can you describe these five or six men?"

"They were wearing work clothes."

"Work clothes." The sergeant would be wondering what kind of a kook was at the other end of the line. "How did they get away?"

"In a motorboat."

The sergeant had expected to hear that it had been a helicopter.

End of imagined phone conversation with Ventura County Sheriff's office.

Killinger realized that bringing in the law would help nothing. In fact, it would certainly embarrass Mynheer van der Helft if it got into the newspapers. And now, Killinger had received warning of K. Y. Smith's intentions.

Question: all this for a bronze statue?

The door to the deck behind Killinger opened, and Marjorie came in. Her wine-red outfit had been straightened. The micro-mini was cute as ever. The sheer blouse showing the lace bra was still interesting. And a long matching colored chiffon kerchief was twined around her hair. She held two bowls of ice cream, with spoons. She put one in front of Killinger.

He inclined his head toward her, gravely. "Thank you."

She giggled. "It's burgundy-cherry."

"And it matches everything you're wearing."

With ice cream in her mouth: "Glad you noticed." She climbed up on the stool next to him, her excitingly slim legs hanging down. "Know what I think I like better than burgundy-cherry?"

Killinger shook his head in a negative.

She laughed. "Prunes."

He ate his ice cream.

"Do you think I should say it again. But slowly?" Her eyes traveled around the living room. They had been attracted by a golden glow not far from where she was sitting. Instead of pursing her lips softly, she pressed them into a straight line as she hopped off her stool and bent to pick up a high-heeled slipper of golden silk.

She slammed it onto the bar, angrily. "You're got company. And I'm interfering." She sniffed the air. "The perfume is familiar."

Killinger stared at the golden shoe next to his bowl of ice cream.

A bell started to ring. More insistently.

"It's that . . . that Talya woman!"

He didn't bother to explain. He was staring at the four-inch heel.

"Good night, Mister Killinger. I've had enough ice cream." She marched out, erect. Anger did not destroy the rhythm of her hip movements.

Killinger picked up Talya's shoe.

The big Australian with the yellow skin sat on the fantail of the *Valhalla* as he listened to Talya's debriefing. She told the story cleanly and logically. It was never necessary to ask her to repeat or clarify.

He did not anger and curse the dogs. Nor did he feel that misfortune had tapped him on the shoulder.

It was all a matter of mathematical probability. He had not fully programmed his computer.

Killinger was opposed to him, therefore an enemy. If it should become necessary to wipe him from the slate, Killinger would cease to exist.

K. Y. Smith punched the buttons for preparing alternate plans. And alternate plans for the alternate plans.

The phone at his elbow rang. On the third ring, he picked it up. "I'm listening."

"This is Vincenzo, sir. Count Risponyi and Mr. O'Reilly have left their bungalow with the two women. He has put in a call for his chauffeur and his Rolls-Bentley."

"Is there not a telephone in your car?"

"There is, sir."

"Follow them. And call me in fifteen minutes."

"It shall be done, sir."

K. Y. Smith hung up.

His computer said that the Count had learned from João that K. Y. Smith had been aboard the *Katja*. Also, that João had told the tale of the statue called Chin P'ing Mei.

There would be a head-on clash between Count Vaclav Risponyi and K. Y. Smith. The computer was positive.

The warning bell no longer rang for Killinger.

He had remembered the dull gleam of gold in Talya's hand when she had followed him to the poop-deck of the *Sybaris* after the dogs had barked. First, though, she had attempted to grab his arm and keep him from running to see what had caused the trouble.

Evidently she had known that the motorboat and men were to be busy in their attempt to take the heavy crate from the *Katja*. Therefore, she had been sent to meet him on the beach. And to seduce him—after turning out the lamp—as a signal to Smith.

The dull gleam of gold which Talya had held as a weapon had been at his back when she had thrown her arms around him to immobilize him. It had been the other golden slipper. And she had probably dropped it into the water when the odd shrill whistle had been sounded.

Saving his life?

He toyed with the leather heel at the end of the four-inch spike. It moved. He twisted it, and it came off.

He held four inches of Swedish spring steel that had been carefully honed to a needle point.

He laughed as he remembered his earlier thoughts about the shining spider lady in her glowing *cheong-sam.* "A girl with a body like that can't be all bad."

As long as he remembered not to turn his back on her.

Forty-eight hours ago, a barge had brushed against a schooner.

the
third
day . . .

Chapter One

By the clock, it was morning, even though it was dark. Sunrise was several hours away. A heavy low fog had blown in from the sea, hanging over the marina. There was less than twenty-five feet of visibility. All of the lights, from cars, from ships, from lamp posts, had beautiful halos which were lost and isolated, one from another, in the heavy and wet very early hours.

K. Y. Smith's telescope and binoculars were useless. He was without eyes.

However, his ears were tuned perfectly to his telephones and two-way radio. Vincenzo, from his car's telephone, had kept the turquoise-eyed Chinaman informed of the progress of Count Risponyi's trip. Kuan Yang Smith knew that the two couples would come to the marina after leaving the Beverly Hills Hotel bungalow.

It was a matter of learning Risponyi's plans of attack on the heavy wooden case. For attack he must.

There was no sleep for the man on the fantail of the *Valhalla* drinking his Turkish coffee and sipping arrack.

The Rolls-Bentley floated on the California freeways all the way to Oxnard. Vincenzo and the man he was paired with were able to drop a mile behind and follow easily. There was barely any intervening traffic that time of morning. When they came closer to the ocean and patches of fog drifted by, they moved closer.

The Rolls-Bentley also contained a car-radio. Risponyi used it to make reservations at the La Sirena Hotel. João had recommended it.

The little man with the shaven head and the moustache

put Carolyn and Elena in a room together to be out of the way and sleep. Now he had not a moment to waste. He had told the two of them a far-out story about rival movie producers and had told them they would have odd tasks to perform. Their performances would illustrate whether or not they were good enough actresses for his upcoming motion picture.

He gave them each two hundred-dollar bills for their trouble and told them that if they did a good job, they would get another two hundred. This was enough to stop the girls from analyzing his rival-producer story. Besides, they thought it was all fun.

They had no idea that they were now part of a dangerous game.

João, on the other hand, had walked into this situation with his eyes wide open. He had become a mercenary. A soldier of fortune. He believed the crate held a bronze statue.

Risponyi's need for constant motion and physical movement almost put him in the category of hyperkinetic. His days started with rigorous exercise. Now, he did his morning work-out as he talked to João. First, it was a hundred push-ups broken into four sets of twenty-five. On his fingertips. Making his hands strong and dangerous weapons. As he went up and down easily, he asked João: "Have you ever killed a man?"

João answered matter-of-factly, not shocked. "Never."

It was Risponyi's last set of push-ups. "I shall give you an additional four thousand dollars."

"How nice." Figuring. "That will make five thousand dollars."

"You may have to kill a man."

Thoughtfully. "Oh. That is different." A small frown. "Then I think I should have more money."

Risponyi knew that he had found his man. Someone not too smart. Someone greedy. Someone without conscience. "Of course. If you do, you will receive an additional ten thousand. Making fifteen thousand, total."

"Will you aid in booking me a flight to Brazil so I can leave immediately?" A thought. "I mean immediately after I do—uh—what I must do."

The Count had completed his push-ups. Now he took off his shirt. He looked more simian than ever. Monkey hair everywhere except where he was shaved, from the Adam's apple up. He started his next exercise by getting into a handstand and keeping it. While remaining balanced, with his toes pointed at the ceiling, he did handstand dips. That is, he lowered himself until his chest touched the floor. Then straightened his arms, legs still aimed up. Then down again. Ten times. A pause, and then ten. And a final ten, making thirty.

João watched fascinated. Although an athlete himself, he'd never seen anyone able to do this as many times. He'd been thinking about the money, too. Tentatively. "Am I supposed to kill the big Chinaman?"

"K. Y. Smith." A chuckle that was a sound of hate. "He is an old and valued enemy. We have fought in the business jungle many times. Sometimes he won. Sometimes I." The grin was a grimace. "Last time, he almost put me out of business. Order us both a large breakfast, and I shall shower. After, I will tell to you how I was ambushed and left bleeding. Left for dead."

He walked to the bathroom, drawing new white lines on the blueprint of his mind.

João wondered what it would be like to kill a human being.

Outside, the fog stifled all sound.

The waiter had delivered the food and gone. Now Risponyi was hungry. He and João attacked their ham steak, home-fried potatoes, and eggs. João poured the coffee, and they began to butter their rolls as Risponyi spoke.

"The international market for black pepper jumps up and down. It is very volatile. The trick is to be there with the dried and cured peppercorns when the price is at its peak." Risponyi, holding his knife and fork in European style, cut around his fried eggs carefully, neatly cutting away the white. One yolk went on top of the ham steak, the other atop his fried potatoes.

João listened intently.

The Count spoke around the forkload of potatoes he was chewing. "My warehouse on the Island of Celebes was full of black pepper."

"In Indonesia?"

The little man nodded. "Almost twenty tons. The result of two years work and cash investment on my part. Overnight, pepper prices hit a violent high. The first man to deliver would carry away sacks of gold."

João squashed his fried eggs, stirring them around. Then, also holding his utensils in European style, he dipped the ham and potatoes into the gooey mess before stuffing them into his open mouth.

"I had an agreement with a cargo company to fly in a DC-8 airplane. It could carry the twenty tons in one trip. I paid them in advance and gave them a pick-up date, to be at the Celebes. A DC-8 arrived a day early. Most fortuitous. A great stroke of good fate. I helped to load the plane, myself. Anything for speed. It was destined for Singapore." His eyes were hard at the memory as he drank his coffee.

Eagerly: "What happened?"

"Never again did I see the pepper."

"Did the DC-8 crash at sea?"

A quick and thin-lipped cold smile. "Next day, the airplane which I had ordered and paid for . . . arrived."

João's coffee cup stopped on the way to his lips. Eyebrows together.

Risponyi's chuckle was the laughter of a child pulling wings from a fly. "In Singapore, K. Y. Smith was the seller of twenty tons of pepper . . . which had supposedly come from Java by ship."

"Are you saying he stole your pepper?"

The Count's hands gripped the table's edge with fury. For a moment no words came. A deep breath. "He received $446,000! *American* dollars."

"I do not blame you for wanting him dead."

Risponyi looked into his private mental hellfire. "I decided on a revenge that would leave a mark on him forever." His fingers caressed his coffee cup. His coal black eyes shone at

João. "I must have that crate from Hong Kong. It is aboard your ex-wife's schooner."

"Of course. And you shall have it." His puzzled look. "The statue of Chin P'ing Mei . . . Is it worth that much?"

"Of course not." His voice fell to a bullfrog croak of a whisper. "It is pride. As Orientals say, 'face'." Cunning lit the solid black eyes. "Face means more than gold." Sharp, frightening laughter. "Kuan Yang Smith will lose his honor." The laughter came back and made itself heard.

"Will you sell it back to him?"

Risponyi's monocle appeared in his hand from nowhere. He popped it into his eye, highlighting his evil simian grin and his shining and shaven skull. His soft and dreamy answer was an oblique reply. "There is a price for everything."

Chapter Two

Aboard the *Sybaris,* the sybarites were preparing a bountiful breakfast.

Samantha had started early, wearing a skintight pair of gaily patched hot pants and a loose, scoop-necked blouse which hid nothing. Marjorie had thought that since they were working together, they should dress as a team. So she dug out her hot-hot pants and her loose blouse which decorated her hills of promise. They were a bright and fresh and cheery team as they cut the grapefruit, set the table, and served up toast and butter and three kinds of preserves.

Kimo was at the oven, in charge of the bacon. Four extra thick slices per person, broiled slowly under a medium-low flame, letting the fat drip away from the crispening bacon. The plates were on a bottom oven wire shelf, warming.

Killinger was the egg king. A dozen eggs, scrambled in a tin-lined antique copper pan over high heat, with plenty of butter. Constant stirring made them fluffy and moist.

The coffee was ready, made from Killinger's special blend.

To the nose, the aroma of the coffee, blended with the bacon's odor and the buttery smells of the eggs, made a perfect combination.

The gal of all cleanup work, Olga Martinez, had phoned to say she would be late. Last night had been much fun. She had been laughing when she had hung up.

Copper and Auric ate their breakfast, at the side. Lollipop and Coco Chanel waited for stray bacon bits.

The Chinese junk had started its day on a sea of calm.

The typhoon was over the horizon.

Thunderheads are as full of destructive energy as an atom bomb.

114

Electricity builds within them until there is enough to shoot bolts of lightning miles long, reaching down to the earth. The winds they contain have been measured at hundreds of miles an hour in their wild spinning. They contain their own storms in which rain and hail are thrown high, to fall back and be shot upwards again.

The thunderhead on Killinger's horizon sat on the fantail of the *Valhalla*, enjoying a table full of food. The hand-chased silver pitcher at his right hand was covered with droplets of condensation caused by the cold of the freshly squeezed orange juice it contained. Another hand-chased article of silver was the bowl within easy reach. It was filled past the top with fresh strawberries, pieces of pineapple, and slices of mango, sprinkled with lightly crushed mint leaves and powdered sugar. He ate of the fruit with his fingers, daintily. He drank the chilled orange juice in large draughts.

A green turban placed a hot dish before him, containing a high pile of kippers with six fried eggs and sliced onions. The basket of hot buttered crumpets and the jar of gooseberry preserves were to fill any odd corners which might be empty within him.

Talya sat across the table, eating lightly of her fruit. Much of last night was on her mind. She had not uttered one word. When with her father, she reacted strongly to what she felt were his desires. That was how she had been trained. Now she knew he was running his computer, asking it questions and reading its answers. For example: "What has Jedediah Killinger III told the police?"

K. Y. Smith had never learned to lose.

The first battle had been a defeat.

He would win the war.

He put a read-out into words. "Yesterday, my enemy was Jedediah Killinger III. Today, there is not only Killinger—but Count Vaclav Risponyi."

Talya began spooning her small bowl of yoghurt.

"This small man has heard of my visit to Mrs. O'Reilly from this João Aranha Mijangos O'Reilly." A pause, for the read-out from the machine of his mind was not clear.

"O'Reilly has told him that I made mention of a certain statue called Chin P'ing Mei. However, I am certain that he has not corrected O'Reilly about a bronze statue." The laugh was loud and hearty, starting at the boat's deck and billowing to the sky.

He put a gob of gooseberry preserves on a crumpet and nibbled at it.

Talya had given him her absolute attention.

"Count Risponyi will make an effort to get the crate. He will move very fast, for he is aware that I am here." The frozen blue eyes almost smoked from their intense cold. They did not blink, nor did they move when the powerful laughter was thrown forth from deep in his belly.

The laughter was sliced by a Saracen thin blade and died as it floated in the morning air, leaving not a trace. "I have two choices." One finger held up. "The first is to take the crate away before he gets his opportunity." Two fingers held up. "The second is to permit him to obtain the wooden box and then take it from him."

K. Y. Smith picked up the binoculars and aimed them at the deck of the *Sybaris*. The view was clear, for the morning sunshine had pressed the fog down into the sea.

"Mister Killinger is about to take his run on the beach."

Without comment, Talya rose and left the fantail. Her violently red shortie coat covered the impossibly narrow strips of her bikini top and bikini bottom.

Killinger and the two Vizslas trotted down the gangplank to the dock and bumped into Katja O'Reilly. Copper and Auric ran to her, tails wagging and with small barks of greeting. Katja leaned down and kissed them both. Tired as she was from her night at the hospital, she still held herself as magnificently as though she were the Danish Goddess called Nerthus. Her red hair in a gold clip, falling way below her shoulders, and without make-up, the green eyes lit up her face which brightened at the sight of Killinger. She stood. "Good morning, Jed."

"Katja," he acknowledged. "How is your grandfather?"

116

Proud of the grand old Viking, she smiled. "He's tough, and his heart is holding up wonderfully."

"And the operation?"

"Tests will have been completed by noon. Surgery is scheduled for early afternoon."

"Please let me know if there's anything I can do."

She smiled and moved to him. "Of course. And thanks for your offer." She got to her toes to give him a friendly kiss. Immediately, the electricity ran through her. She pressed against him. He helped her. Both hands on his shoulders to push them apart. A smile. "To be continued."

Killinger watched her walk to the schooner. A sad and beautiful lady with great inner strength.

He trotted to his little old red '57 T-Bird, behind the dogs. They were in the front seat waiting when he got to the car.

Pulling in to the parking place, at the beach, he found himself behind the chauffeured Mercedes Benz 600, with a green turban behind the wheel. Copper and Auric had picked up Talya's scent and had run ahead, looking for her. When Killinger saw her, she was petting the two dogs, and they were jumping up and down, anxiously waiting for the morning run to begin.

Talya stood when she saw Killinger, letting her shortie coat fall to the sand. Today's red bikini was as much a part of her as was yesterday's blue one. Perhaps a sixteenth of an inch had been trimmed here and a thirty-second there. The well-conditioned flesh was interestingly held and presented.

Killinger had to make it a point to remember that she was the daughter of the Chinaman with the blue eyes and the Australian accent. The lovely animal with the concealed stiletto.

She pouted enchantingly. "You have found my golden slippers?"

He smiled at her and spoke with great sincerity. "I'm sorry. They had disappeared." He shrugged and indicated the dogs. "You can never tell about Hungarians." Mentally, he crossed his fingers as he lied. He hoped Copper and Auric would forgive him.

She looked down at the Vizslas, shaking a finger at them. "That was a bad thing to do." Inside, she was relieved. Now, Killinger would remain an innocent about possible danger from her. She continued talking to the dogs, her words aimed at Killinger. "Those shoes were supposed to be placed at the side of your master's bed. So I could come back for them."

"There'll be something else in their place."

"A surprise, I hope?"

"Right."

She threw her arms around his neck. "I love surprises."

"Now, let's run."

"All right. But you'd better give me a big head-start."

Talya spun quickly and began running, her hair streaming behind her. He waited until she'd gone a quarter-mile before he started the two-mile course. He caught her in the last two hundred yards, and they ran together into the ocean. Copper and Auric had had their own romp, running circles and games around everyone.

When Killinger came up for a breath, Talya jumped onto him from behind, her legs around his waist and her arms around his neck. He moved to where he was able to stand as the shore-break waves went past them. Holding her arms, he turned so that they were facing each other. She still had him locked in her legs. She brought her head close, as though to kiss him. Instead, she squirted salt water into his eyes. They laughed, and he undid her bikini top. Her breasts were beautiful and pink-nippled, pointing in different directions as they were held tenderly by the ocean. Killinger ducked beneath the surface and took her right breast into his mouth, biting gently and flicking the erect nipple with his tongue. She slipped her hand inside his trunks and held and squeezed him with a loving firmness. His hands moved down the velvet of her back and slid under the bikini, holding her buttocks and pulling her to him. His fingers crawled and explored the edges and inside of the silken band. Talya breathed hard and put her teeth into his shoulder.

The dogs barked.

Talya and Killinger came from out of their private misty

place and looked about. Copper and Auric were swimming next to them, enjoying life noisily. Killinger gave Talya her bra top, and she put it on.

"May I come by for my surprise this afternoon?" Her father wanted Killinger under surveillance and accounted for.

"I'll be there. But I don't know for how long." He answered the question in her eyes. "Ejnar Mylius will be operated on some time after lunch."

She put a finger to her lips, in thought. A smile. "I have decided to consider that an invitation." A farewell kiss, with but a touch of her tongue inside his lips. "So, wait for me."

Talya walked away, without looking back. Each movement flowed into another with consummate ease and in wondrous rhythm. Her body was exquisite.

Why, he wondered, was she making a point of being with him . . . knowing where he was . . . keeping him in sight . . . ?

After several steps, Talya stopped and turned to face Killinger. She had something to ask. It was the reason K. Y. Smith had sent her. She had not forgotten the purpose of her mission. It was supposed to be an afterthought. She raised her voice. "Jed! I almost forgot. What did you tell the police?" She took two steps toward him, to hear his answer.

"Nothing."

Surprise brought her back to him. "Nothing?" She ran a finger down his chest in a lazy and wavy line. "Why not?"

"What could I say? There was nothing missing, and I couldn't possibly identify the thieves." He was more and more certain that they belonged to the big Chinaman, but he knew that proof was impossible and that making big noises would only embarrass the Dutch insurance company.

Talya's smile was inside, where it couldn't be seen. Her father would be elated with this important morsel. She threw him a kiss. "Don't forget. Later." Once again she turned her back and started for her Mercedes Benz 600.

Jedediah Killinger III appreciated the view and the thoughts of 'later.'

Except for one thing.

Next time, where would she hide the stiletto?

Chapter Three

Count Vaclav Risponyi's notations were indecipherable.

Not only were his words in his own form of shorthand, they were written in Cyrillic script. Now, with gold pencil in hand, he was writing on a lined pocket pad which was kept in a slim gold case, in his breast pocket.

His notes were a list dictated by his newest blueprint.

As he picked up the telephone, he checked off the first Cyrillic line. He spoke to the hotel's desk clerk. "Count Risponyi here." A pause for the clerk to be impressed. "Is there a party registered under the name of Smith?"

The overtones of the clerk's voice aggravated the Count's ear. "Smith, sir?"

"Precisely. Smith."

"A Mr. and Mrs. Smith, perhaps? It's a very common name on hotel registers."

Risponyi permitted this piece of Americana to drift by. "This Mr. Smith is Chinese. He weighs almost three hundred pounds, and he is over six feet tall." As though he hadn't given sufficient identification, he added, "His hair is clipped close to the scalp and his eyes are blue."

"Blue, did you say? Amazing." The overtones peaked, and Risponyi held the phone away from his ear with a grimace of pain. "The gentleman you described is quite distinctive. He has not been here."

"Thank you." The little man put a check on the next line. "Would you ring my chauffeur, Hawkins, and tell him to come to my room?"

"Of course, sir." The phone was disconnected.

When Hawkins arrived, Risponyi consulted his handwriting.

"I want a complete list of the companies and places in this marina which specialize in boat repairs."

Hawkins nodded respectfully. "Yes, Count Risponyi."

"This is of great importance." The strong monkey hand reached for an open envelope on the table alongside. "Ask everywhere—I repeat *everywhere*—for a man named K. Y. Smith." He gave the Australian's description to Hawkins. After Hawkins repeated it, Risponyi gave the English chauffeur the envelope. "It may be necessary to buy answers. Do not hesitate."

Hawkins looked into the envelope. It was full of crisp green banknotes, in five- and ten- and twenty-dollar denominations. "Pardon, sir, but how much shall I . . . ?"

The Count cut in on him. "Do not be niggardly. If you locate this K. Y. Smith, do so unobtrusively. Discretion is most important."

"Yes, sir."

"When you find this gigantic Chinaman, I shall reward you with a bonus of a hundred dollars." Hawkins departed quietly.

Again he picked up the phone. This time, he asked for Mr. João Aranha Mijangos O'Reilly's room. When João answered, Risponyi snapped at him: "Be here as quickly as possible." He hung up.

The Count checked the third Cyrillic set of words.

He reached into an inside pocket and brought out his hand. It appeared to be empty until he opened his fingers. What he was holding was a hand-tooled weapon made in Kobe, Japan. An over-and-under hand gun holding only two 7 mm bullets. . . .

The derringer disappeared into his closed fist.

The two-way radio spoke. "Paolo here." Paolo was the second of the two men in black Italian silk suits who wore white shirts and white ties. "Count Risponyi's chauffeur has gone to the Rolls-Bentley. He is starting the motor. There are no passengers."

K. Y. Smith's computer was on standby, the motor and relays clicking silently. "Follow him. Learn what he does . . . to whom he speaks . . . and the words he utters."

"Yes, sir." Paolo clicked off.

The computer's answer to the Chinaman's question was quick and simple. The Count had learned from João that Kuan Yang was close by. The chauffeur would be asking if anyone had seen the big man with the turquoise eyes.

Talya's nugget of information, about Killinger's not calling in the police, was most welcome. However, since it seemed far too good, K. Y. Smith had run it through the machine twice to find a flaw. None showed.

However, the read-out stated that Killinger must not be underestimated.

Talya would look after Jedediah Killinger III.

K. Y. Smith rechecked his totals on the abacus.

Olga Martinez was cleaning the living room. She was a woman of absolute cleanliness. Literally, one could eat from the floor of a room on which she had worked. She shone from her minimum of two baths a day; one at morning, one at night, and possibly another after making love, which could be anytime. She was a woman of moods who, in her middle thirties, lived a complete life of which any female fifteen years younger would have been jealous.

Her glossy hair hung long and loose. Her blouse hung low and loose. Her skirt hung below her knees, full and loose. She liked the feeling of unfettered freedom. No mini's for this boiling hot female. She wore absolutely nothing under her dress, and she didn't want to be concerned with unintended exposure when she bent over to clean. Her face was classic Aztec Indian. Her legs were good, full and strong rather than slim. Her body was full, but hard work kept her waist slim and her breasts from sagging.

When she found Talya's beautiful golden slipper, she tried it on. Then she laughed at its tininess and its not fitting her. Since Killinger had screwed the leather heel-cap back on, Olga was not aware that the silk-covered shoe was a deadly weapon. She had placed it carefully in the middle of the bar, admiring the sculpted nudes in their mad patterns of love.

The dogs barked, announcing Killinger.

Olga greeted him by pointing to Talya's single pump.

"When you start going around with one-legged girls?"

"Don't worry about it. She had exactly the right number of everything."

"Everything?"

He nodded solemnly, repeating, "Everything."

Olga pretended there was a speck near her feet. In bending to pick it up, her blouse fell forward, showing her hard breasts. She remained in that position, aware of her display, and looked up at Killinger. She laughed. "Why waste your time on children? When you want a *woman,* you tell me."

This had become a game between them. Killinger teased in return. "You would only break my heart and then leave me."

"Aaaah, but what a wonderful week we could have. . . ."

"I do not doubt the pleasure." He smiled at her. "But I fear the thought of the pain, afterwards."

"You fear nothing." With a laugh and a pirouette and a spin which almost brought her skirt all the way up, she made her exit.

Killinger held the shoe and looked at it thoughtfully, tapping the long steel heel. He remembered that he'd told Talya that he couldn't find her slippers anywhere. Therefore, he'd hide it.

Beautiful women can be so dangerous.

Elena had picked dusty pink as her color.

Risponyi had instructed her as though it was a scene in the never-to-be-shot motion picture. She was to wear her sexiest clothes to meet a man named Jedediah Killinger III.

So she had started with flat leather sandals of dusty pink, with leather thongs that she wrapped around her calves, almost to her knee. Naturally, no stockings. Her skirt was a mini with a slight flare and a wide leather belt of interlocking enamel designs. Her sweater was of open-knit, showing the skin and absence of brassiere which her free-floating breasts did not need. Her tiny brief was of dusty pink, appearing as though she wore nothing on her lovely bottom.

Risponyi was deadly serious in his questions. "Who is your father, and what does he do?"

Elena was a fast study. "My father is Don Manuel Ruiz

Gontron Varga. He is president of the Varga Tanker and Shipping Company. He has met Senor Jedediah Killinger III three years ago, in the city of Madrid, Spain." Anxiously. "Is all right?"

"Perfect."

The long distance phone had helped the Count get a factual background on an area of Killinger's life.

"This Jedediah? He is attractive?"

"Very."

Elena put her arms around herself, happily. This was going to be very much fun. "How will I keep this attractive man from going anyplace? I mean, in one place?"

Chapter Four

The golden slipper-stiletto stood on the bar.

Marjorie gave it a look which somehow ignored it completely as she saw each little detail. She walked over to Killinger who sat in front of the brass fireplace on one of the facing twin couches. The yellow phone on its long extension cord was before him on the heavy inlaid coffee table made of Coromandel ebony from Bengal.

She placed a slip of paper before Killinger. A comment. "Funniest looking phone number I ever saw." She threw a quick and hostile look over her shoulder at the offending shoe of silken gold.

"The man I'm about to call is in Amsterdam, Holland."

Testily: "Well, it didn't say that in the files."

Killinger called the operator and placed a call person-to-person to Mynheer van der Helft. While he was waiting, he kept his eyes on Marjorie. She had picked up Talya's slipper, examined it judiciously, hefted it for weight, and looked at Killinger. Then she put it on the floor, next to her feet, comparing size. Her next look at Killinger was defiant. Deliberately, she removed a shoe of her own and tried Talya's on for size.

It fit perfectly.

The golden color was complementary to her skin tones. The high heel accentuated her own perfect ankles, swelling into the calf muscles.

She took it off, put it on the bar, and walked to the door, carrying her own shoe.

"Call me Cinderella."

A few seconds after Marjorie limped out, van der Helft came on the line. "Since I expect you to bill me for this conversation we shall have, let us please make it brief."

"All right. Good-bye."

"Wait. Wait. I am aware that you would not be calling unless it was important." A pause for a puff on his green cheroot. "Please to proceed."

"There was an attempted robbery on Ejnar Mylius's schooner. . . ."

Cutting in: "When? When?"

"Last night."

"I trust I heard you properly. You used the word 'attempted', did you not?"

"Affirmative. Nothing was taken. The robbers escaped without leaving any sort of identification."

Fast nervous puffing on the green cheroot. "The publicity. It will be for making terrible explanations. Especially since we now hold title to the schooner and its contents." Van der Helft was distraught.

"There will be no publicity."

Relief. "Killinger, you are a genius. An absolute genius." A slow puff and an exhalation of thick white smoke, aimed at the wood-paneled ceiling.

The accolade was accepted with great modesty, in silence.

"Katja Mylius O'Reilly. Her reactions. What were they?"

"I managed to keep her from knowing."

"You are a double genius. Absolute."

Before van der Helft could ask questions, Killinger laid out the main reason for his call. "I want you to use your international network of business connections to dig up facts on two people."

"You make me sound like a spymaster. Why do you need this information?"

"To save your company money and embarrassment."

"Two excellent reasons. Tell me their names. . . ."

Killinger gave complete run-downs on K. Y. Smith and Vaclav Risponyi. Van der Helft made notes.

Killinger made a suggestion. "Better start looking for them around Hong Kong."

"Hong Kong?"

"Right. They both showed me papers from there." Killinger meant the duplicate bills of lading, but he didn't say it because he didn't want to upset van der Helft more than necessary. "And I have a feeling that something might show on them in Singapore."

"Interesting. Interesting." Thoughtful cigar puff. "Would you like to tell me what this truly concerns?"

Killinger wanted to avoid the detail. "At twelve dollars a minute?"

"Glad you remembered. Write me. Airmail."

Killinger grinned. "Of course." He was a lousy mail correspondent. "Phone me when you get the information."

"Wouldn't a letter be good enough?" Pause. "Airmail?"

"Only if it arrives here from Holland in a matter of hours." Killinger hung up.

Risponyi counted the money in the envelope.

There was nothing missing.

"I'm sorry, your Lordship, but I didn't find the Chinaman." Hawkins was quietly apologetic. "Nobody even seen 'im." With a headshake: "People thought I was jokin'." Disbelieving: "A blue-eyed Chinaman."

The Count gave Hawkins two twenty-dollar bills. Loyalty came with a price tag. "It's a pleasure to do business with an honest man."

Hawkins' joy would bind him to the little monkey man for at least another twelve hours. "Thank you, sir." The money sped into his pocket. "You din' have to do it. Really."

Risponyi held out his hand, snapped his fingers. "The list, if you please."

Hawkins put a sheet of paper into the powerful hand. "All the boat repair people, sir."

"Find Mr. O'Reilly. Tell him we shall meet in the car in five minutes."

Hawkins left. Risponyi picked up the phone and called Elena.

Her instructions had been to sit by the phone. She picked it up on the first ring, breathlessly. "Hello."

"We are leaving. Remember, if you see Carolyn, João, or me . . . we do not know each other."

"I understand."

"See this man, Killinger, in a half-hour. Make him take you to lunch."

She sat on the big and soft bed in the hotel room. "That sounds like fun." Elena smiled at the almost nude girl in the nearby mirror.

"This is not fun. It is business."

Killinger had taken Marjorie to lunch.

She hadn't wanted to go. Instead, she had suggested they eat aboard the *Sybaris*. Killinger had guessed correctly, without saying it aloud, that Marjorie was uncertain in public places full of white people. Especially accompanied by a white man. He had dragged her off before she tried to change from her wild and skintight hot pants and revealing scoop blouse.

The Whale's Tail was a nice, lively restaurant at the marina with an all-glass front for looking at the boats. All eyes seemed to turn on them when they entered. Marjorie was a delicious dish for staring at, but she got uptight. She grabbed his hand and whispered: "All the tables are taken. Let's get out of here."

He wouldn't let her go. "Not while I'm with the wildest chick in the house."

She failed to smile. Panic had her all wrapped up.

"Jed, I don't know how you do it. Each one is prettier than the last!" exclaimed a voice behind them.

Killinger turned to the voice. "Howard, obviously, you're a man of excellent taste." Introducing: "Marjorie Stafford, our host, Howard Conant." Explaining: "Marjorie's my new secretary." Indicating: "He owns the joint."

"I got a great spot for you at the window, where you can keep an eye on the *Sybaris*." He showed them to the table, then he took a set of binoculars and put them in front of Marjorie. "For the interesting sights."

Howard dropped a pair of his famous wooden menus on the table and left.

Marjorie smiled. "He's a nice man."

"All of my friends are nice people." He leaned toward her. "Friend."

Marjorie picked up the binoculars. "Let's see how the *Sybaris* is getting along without us." She smiled expectantly as she aimed and focused the glasses. The smile dissolved into lips pressed together, grimly. She stiffened.

"Something wrong?"

The words came out like small pebbles. "Looks like I'm keeping you from some important . . . 'friend'." The small pebbles were covered with ice. "We can go any time you like."

Killinger took the glasses and aimed them at the *Sybaris*.

The two-way radio spoke.

"This is Vincenzo. One of Count Risponyi's people is going aboard the Chinese junk. A lady dressed in pink."

The big yellow hand held the telescope without a tremor. It moved like a battleship's gun mount, changing direction.

Elena climbed the *Sybaris* gangway.

A turquoise eye watched.

Chapter Five

Talya moved noiselessly.

K. Y. Smith felt her presence. His free hand gave her the binoculars, while he used the telescope. "She belongs to Risponyi."

Talya examined Elena thoroughly. Obviously, if the Count had sent her to Killinger, it would be for the same reasons her father had sent Talya. To entice and entrap the owner of the *Sybaris*. Talya dissected the girl in dusty pink, from her painted toenails peeking through the open flat leather sandals to her full breasts whose nipples were visible at this distance, through the open-knit sweater. Dispassionately, Talya gave the distant girl a very high score in the area of animal beauty. Also dispassionately, Talya graded herself quite a bit higher.

And Talya was right.

Kuan Yang had put this new information into his computer. The female lure which Count Risponyi was throwing before Jedediah Killinger III indicated that the monkey man with the monocle was drawing a blueprint. The read-out said that the beautiful girl who reeked of sex was a preliminary ploy because Risponyi was in the process of building his machine of conquest and theft.

The results were re-run on the abacus.

A distorted voice came from the radio.

"Paolo here. Count Risponyi's car is parked in front of a place on the water's edge. It says 'Lemoyne Brothers, Boat

Repairs'. O'Reilly left the car and is entering the shop. Count Risponyi and the woman remained in the car with the chauffeur."

The computer grabbed and swallowed the words "Boat Repairs," digesting them completely. The silent whirring and clicking picked up speed.

Risponyi's blueprint was taking shape.

In the mind of K. Y. Smith.

Carolyn's hand was on Risponyi's thigh, moving in warm little circles. His fingers were under her almost nonexistent skirt, dancing to a tune of small fires. Her eyes were closed.

Hawkins hopped out from behind the wheel and opened the door for João who sat in the jump seat. He had papers firmly in his hand. When Risponyi looked a question at him, João shook his head in a firm negative.

Risponyi popped his monocle into his eye; took out his list which was written in Cyrillac. With his gold pencil, he made mysterious notations.

Pangkalanbuun roared and rumbled, as a devil from Borneo should.

Copper and Auric came running from the poop deck.

Olga Martinez climbed up the circular staircase from the kitchen.

They found Elena standing before the gong, the hammer on its heavy violet silk cord still in her hand.

When Elena asked for Killinger, Olga's keen ear picked up the accent, and she replied in Spanish. Elena would only speak English.

They measured each other.

And became instant enemies.

The radio spoke once more.

"Paolo here. Mr. O'Reilly entered a place of business called 'Julie's Boat Repair'. It is at the edge of the marina, touching the water. He stayed less than one minute. Count

Risponyi and the lady remained in the car. When he joined them, they drove off."

The voice was flat. The twang, Australian. "I shall be here."

The computer had reached out and taken the words "Boat Repair," then stuffed them into its maw. The transistors glowed. The read-out tube printed its message. It said that Count Risponyi had not yet completed his blueprint. He was searching for a difficult-to-find integral part. Further, that the little man with the shaven head and thick moustache would travel by water.

Kuan Yang Smith pushed the button for another read-out.

The blueprint grew clearer.

But the white lines were incomplete and hazy.

Marjorie sat with the binoculars at her side.

The meal and service had been good. She was really enjoying herself.

She had eaten extra slowly because every time she put the *Sybaris* in focus, she saw the girl in dusty pink waiting for Killinger.

Marjorie had decided that the longer she kept her boss at the table, the longer this girl, whoever she was, would have to wait and stew.

Marjorie's bitchy streak was a yard wide:

Again, the transceiver talked.

"Paolo here. Mr. O'Reilly is inside the shop of a boat yard. The sign outside says 'Carl F. Cooper Fixes Your Boats'. Mr. O'Reilly is coming out."

The big Chinaman sitting on the fantail of the luxury yacht sipped slowly from a tulip glass, drinking his Chardonnay wine as he listened.

"Mr. O'Reilly did not get into the automobile. Instead, he spoke with Count Risponyi. The Count joined him and they re-entered the shop."

Smith's great interest was not visible in the icy blue eyes.

A flicker of a smile raced across his mouth as he spoke.

"You have a Polaroid camera. Take as many pictures as you can. Show any boats tied up to this Carl F. Cooper dock. Show also all pieces of equipment and machinery in the yard."

"Yes, sir."

Carl F. Cooper was a real swinging cat, laughing at the world, always with a cigar butt that he kept relighting between his teeth. Wavy brown hair, blue eyes hidden behind dark and wild squared-off glasses. Over six feet tall, with a little tummy, he was a workman who knew his business. The coolest.

Count Risponyi and João Aranha Mijangos O'Reilly stood in the middle of Cooper's shop, surrounded by pieces of oily motors and broken hunks of metal on the floor. The roof above their heads was on heavy girders which did double duty as supports for the sets of pulleys and wheels and racks.

The little man spoke with a very British accent, from his public school days. O'Reilly's accent was Brazilian. The tailoring of both was impeccable.

This meeting was one of the things for which Risponyi had hired João. The Count had to get aboard the *Katja* with the people and tools needed to carry off the crate. This handsome ex-soccer player was his key to the problem. João had his packet of papers in his hand.

João's task was to identify himself and then connect that identification with the *Katja* strongly enough so there would be no questions. He started by giving his passport to Cooper. "My name is João Aranha Mijangos O'Reilly."

Cooper looked from the passport's picture back to João. "I dig, baby. It's you." He grinned around the cigar. "Someday, explain to me how O'Reilly is a Brazilian name." He handed the passport back.

The two potential customers couldn't quite keep pace with Cooper's use of the American argot. Now João had established himself. Next step was the tie-in to the boat.

João handed Cooper a group of newspaper clippings. "Please to read this."

"I don't know what you dudes are peddling. But I'm probably not buying."

João explained carefully. "These are newspaper stories and pictures of my wife's schooner. It was brought into this harbor after an accident at sea." He pointed to a picture. "That is my wife, Mrs. O'Reilly."

"Like, wow." Cooper's smile was all across his face. "You sure pick 'em."

Courtly: "Thank you."

Cooper relit his frowzy cigar butt.

Risponyi's monocle seemed to jump from his breast pocket into his hand. Like a feat of legerdemain, it next appeared in his eye.

Cooper was fascinated. "Hey. Do that again."

Risponyi's British accent became heavier as he spoke to Cooper in his bullfrog croak. "I am the Count Risponyi." Elegantly cold. "I am a member of the firm of solicitors who handle Mrs. O'Reilly's interests."

Cooper laughed his grin. "That's wild. Absolutely. A solicitor is English for lawyer. Right?"

Meanwhile, João had walked through the front of the shop, facing the dock. He stopped before a wide-beamed converted old tug. The superstructure had been built high and elongated so that it ran from bow to stern. The bow held welding equipment, a miniature forge, and tools to do almost anything.

João jumped from the dock to the tug's deck. He walked straight to the stern and stopped in front of the item he had been looking for in all the other boatyards—and hadn't found. It was a twenty-five-foot-high crane that could swing in any direction. He squatted and examined its workings.

Risponyi had followed, staying on the dock. Cooper had come along to see what the people wanted.

He was proud of the set-up. "Beautiful, ain't it? Put it together myself. No kinda job it can't do."

The English croak was pleased. "Mr. Cooper, you must be prepared to start work almost immediately." A wad of crisp money appeared in Risponyi's hand.

Cooper's eyes couldn't leave the green U. S. Treasury notes. "Beautiful." He laughed. "I impress pretty easy." Back to business tones: "Mr. O'Reilly told me three o'clock sharp."

"Exactly." The Count pulled up his sleeve, exposing his wristwatch. "Not one minute early. Not one minute late."

"Right, baby. Will do."

"Let us coordinate our watches."

Risponyi removed his wristwatch so that he could observe the sweep-second hand more easily. João held out his watch, ready for the Count's signal.

Cooper's timepiece was a big round gold antique from the days of coal-burning railroads. Still accurate. Slowly, he brought it from his pocket, putting it close to Risponyi's and João's.

Cooper spoke softly. "Just like a military operation."

Chapter Six

The green turban placed the envelope and magnifying glass on the table. Then, like the djinn of the Arabian Nights, he disappeared quietly as a puff of smoke in a light breeze.

K. Y. Smith took the four polaroid pictures from the envelope and spread them before him. He had spoken with Paolo over the transceiver and had arranged for the pictures to be left at a drop-off so that the green turban could pick them up.

The first picture was a frontal shot of Carl F. Cooper's boat-repair facility. The second showed the left side, with the equipment in clear detail. The third was not in perfect focus, but since it was of the right side and uninteresting boats and motors were piled carelessly, the Chinaman brushed it away.

Number four was his lucky number. He picked up the magnifying glass to see the detail. Paolo had shot this in perfect focus. It was of the dock in front of Cooper's place. The centerpiece of the grouping was the converted tug, and on the stern of the vessel was a crane with a twenty-five-foot-high movable arm. Squatting at the base of the crane examining it, João stood out as though a strong ray from the sun had acted as a spotlight. To the side, on the dock, Count Risponyi was head-to-head with a man who was obviously the owner or manager of the yard.

The computer behind the frozen turquoise eyes recorded the pictures more completely than a film negative. The transistors activated the calculations. Additions, subtractions, division. A total. A read-out. This converted tug with its long arm would be used to lift the heavy crate from the saloon of the *Katja*. The computer had clashed with Count Risponyi many times, and it had recorded an absolute method of operation for this adversary within its memory files.

A yellow finger flicked on his talk switch. "Vincenzo."

"This is Vincenzo." The loudspeaker distorted the low tones.

"You may now cease observing the girl. On the south side of the marina, at the far end, there is a boat-repair yard. The sign which identifies it says Carl F. Cooper Fixes Your Boats."

"Yes, sir."

"You will go there immediately. Tell the man in charge that you want him to work on a boat this afternoon."

"I am making notes, sir."

"The object of the questioning is to ascertain whether or not he has a prior commitment. Also, whether this prior commitment is of such importance that he will not cancel it."

"I understand, sir."

The same yellow finger flicked the talk switch to the off position.

Stopping abruptly in midsweep, the telescope froze on two men.

The two suitcases were quite heavy.

João carried them both. They contained equipment that would make it possible to cut the metal bolts which held the crate to its deck. Johnson was alert. He rose from his chair, walking to João and Count Risponyi. It was a crucial moment in the ball game he was listening to, so he carried the little radio with him, tuned rather loud.

João used his most charming man-to-man smile when Johnson stood in his way. "Is my wife aboard?"

Johnson turned down the volume. "Beg your pardon—?"

The smile was turned to full volume. "Is my wife aboard?"

"Sorry, sir. The only lady on this boat is a Mrs. O'Reilly." He looked closely at the two of them and saw two men in very expensive clothing who seemed to be "gentlemen." "Mrs. O'Reilly isn't here."

João started walking forward. "That's all right. . . ."

Johnson planted his feet wide. "You must be on the wrong boat."

João put the suitcases down with ease, so they seemed of ordinary weight. He reached into his pocket, taking out his passport and handing it to the guard. Patiently: "This is better than a long explanation."

137

Johnson looked from the passport to João and back. His attitude changed. "I'm sorry, Mr. O'Reilly. I didn't know. . . . It's my second day."

João nodded sympathetically. "Of course. That's why we hadn't met. My plane recently arrived."

Johnson reached for the bags, to be of help and make amends. "You don't have to worry about these, Mr. O'Reilly. I'll take them."

Graciously: "Thank you very much. But you weren't hired to carry people's luggage." With a friendly wink, he reached to Johnson's portable radio and turned up the volume. "Relax. And if anything goes wrong, call me."

"Right, sir."

João carried the bags into the saloon of the schooner, Count Risponyi following close behind, his monocle shining like a misplaced mirror. The little man thought that João had handled the situation perfectly. He felt reassured that he had picked wisely, for the Brazilian had indeed proven to be the key he had needed.

Both men disappeared from sight.

Elena had seen João and Risponyi go aboard the *Katja*.

She had known that they would be on the dock and that they would be going aboard the schooner. Her instructions had been to keep Killinger from seeing the two men. Also, she had been given a strict time schedule. She was to get Killinger off the *Sybaris*. And to keep him away.

No matter how.

As she sat there, alone, there was nothing to do but think. What was on her mind was this mysterious owner of the junk, the one she had become responsible for. Her greatest worry was that he might be unattractive. Looking out the window at the dock, Elena saw a man. A real man. Striding forcefully. Tall. Magnificently built. Longish hair. And she enjoyed making love with a man with long hair. Somehow it added to her kicks. But he had a beautiful woman with him. A black woman, very well-shaped.

They came aboard the *Sybaris*. Too bad this man was occupied. He appealed to her.

Copper and Auric greeted Killinger and Marjorie at the head of the gangplank. Marjorie's stiffness when she cut away from him was due to the fact that she knew some female dressed in dusty pink was waiting. She went into her office in the bow of the junk and slammed the door behind her.

Killinger's curiosity had been warmed by the sight of Elena through the binoculars at the Whale's Tail. He started for the living room on the stern when Olga Martinez rushed up the circular stairway and hurried to him.

"There is a very sexy girl waiting for you." Time out for a haughty sniff. "Only a girl. Not a *woman*."

"I know. I saw her from the Whale's Tail."

"You be careful of her." Olga leaned close to give a confidence. "She have told me she is from Madrid, Spain." Lips pressed together and a confirming nod. "But she speaks with an accent of Peru." Making her point. "Peru! You hear?"

"Thanks for watching out for me."

Insincerely: "You are welcome."

Killinger started away. Olga grabbed his arm briefly. A whisper.

"I think she wants your body."

Count Vaclav Risponyi was close to orgasm.

His hands petted and touched. His fingertips examined every crevice and opening. With his eyes closed, he breathed deeply and hard. His passion was greater than he had ever felt for a woman's body.

João watched disbelievingly.

Risponyi tore himself away from the crate from Hong Kong and stood. His now opened eyes were beyond his control, held by what was inside the wooden box. He spoke over his shoulder. "Assemble your equipment."

João opened the two suitcases, placing the tanks and hoses in proper position, then attaching the acetylene torch. He laid the welder's mask alongside.

"This must be freed from the floor before Cooper brings his boat here."

João nodded. Preparing for the task ahead of him, he pulled the rug away that Talya had placed there to cover the burned-through bolts. Surprise struck him. He called: "Count Risponyi! Look at this!"

Risponyi's reaction was of utter shock.

The first possibility to hit him was K. Y. Smith. But he knew that if the big Chinaman had gotten that far, he would have finished the job. Nothing, Risponyi thought, could have stopped him. There were many ways the burning of the floor bolts might have occurred. The Count couldn't ask the guard. That might lead to insurmountable difficulties.

Could it have been Mrs. O'Reilly or Jedediah Killinger III?

Thoughts of Killinger brought the little man with the shaven head to one of João's open suitcases. Within it, wrapped in chamois, lay a Colt Cobra hand gun, .45 caliber and with a small four-power scope screwed on between the sights. It carried a magnum load. The bullet's trajectory would be absolutely flat for the first two hundred yards of its flight.

For the killing of a man, it was the equivalent of an elephant gun on a game hunt.

Holding the Colt Cobra lightly and checking its ammunition, although he had loaded it himself, he walked to the bottom of the open gangway to make certain that the view of the stern of the *Sybaris* was clear. It was. The rear windows of the deck's living room showed cleanly.

He picked up the nearby telephone and walked it on its long cord to where he could watch the rear of the Chinese junk. He put the Colt Cobra down in order to take his pad of Cyrillic writings from his breast pocket. He translated the numbers and began to dial.

While the number was ringing, the apelike bemonocled Count aimed the gun at the right rear window of the junk. A man figure stood there. With his finger on the trigger, standing in classic target-shooting pose, Risponyi looked through the four-power scope.

Elena's face stared back at him.

Chapter Seven

"Hey, friend. Got a little job for you."

Carl F. Cooper turned around to look at the voice. He saw a wide and swarthy type who looked like a barrel, dressed in a black Italian silk suit with white shirt and white tie and a black fedora. And wearing a smile he'd carefully copied from a shark.

"Always interested in an honest buck." Cooper wondered whether this cat in black silk had ever had an honest buck. "What's gotta be fixed?"

Cooper was operating his welder's torch. His cigar had gone out, and he adjusted the torch's flame to relight the ragged butt.

The shark's smile spoke again. "Smoking's bad for you. It could kill you."

Cooper laughed as he flicked the torch off and stood. "You die your way. I'll die mine."

The shark shrugged. "Whatever." He moved closer. "Got any spare time to come look at my boat, I'll pay you double rates."

"Sounds like a great offer. But my afternoon's booked. And paid for in advance."

Vincenzo continued the probe K. Y. Smith had sent him to complete. "More'n double money for your time?"

Cooper nodded. "You better believe it."

"Maybe you could squeeze me in ahead. Just a few minutes is all I need." Vincenzo flashed a roll of greenery.

Cooper hated to lose a good cash customer, shark smile or not. "Maybe if you can hold off 'til about four-thirty? It's only two hours."

"Maybe." Vincenzo's friendly eyes came from the same shark as the original smile. "When's this job start?"

"Three o'clock. On the button."

"Three o'clock." The voice was flat. The Aussie twang crept through.

The impersonal blue gaze brushed over the large electric timer, with its sweep-second hand waiting for a signal to start, to the clock, which it absorbed.

"You spoke of a crane on the stern of the tugboat. How high is its arm?"

The speaker distorted Vincenzo's speech. "Approximately twenty-five feet, sir."

"The girl is still aboard the junk. Return and keep her under surveillance." The yellow finger flipped the speak switch to off.

Kuan Yang's computer delivered a newer blueprint of Count Vaclav Risponyi's operation on its next read-out.

The big Chinaman poured his Pernod slowly over the crushed ice in his glass. The clear Pernod became a thick milky white. K. Y. Smith enjoyed the strong licorice taste of the anise. He found its chill refreshing. And, though Pernod is a substitute for the outlawed absinthe, he missed the drugging wormwood effect of the original.

Electric crackling preceded the voice. A different voice.

"Paolo here. Count Risponyi and Mr. O'Reilly are still out of sight aboard the *Katja*. However, they will have a visitor shortly. A man from a truck asked directions to the schooner *Katja*."

"Describe the truck."

"Yes, sir. A sign on the side says 'Marve Googe, Contract Hauling'. It is a one-and-a-half-ton pickup. Color, dark red. Extra heavy tires with new tread. On the flatbed are three heavy-duty roller dollies. Also, a series of four-by-four interconnected and grooved wooden sections, as well as several steel alloy runner tracks. Also grooved."

"How many men in the truck?"

"One man, sir. Very big."

"Stay there."

The Chinaman might have been a giant ventriloquist's dummy. His eyes were wide. His mouth was slightly open. And from somewhere, the sound of laughter crept in and held him. The rumble seemed to start rolling in his belly, rising to his mouth and pouring out.

His face was not betrayed by a sign of expression.

The computer did its calculations in micromilliseconds.

The newest blueprint, as drawn up by Count Risponyi, showed on the big tube for K. Y. Smith's pleasure in examining the read-out.

The big yellow man with the turquoise eyes did a rare thing. He spoke aloud, with himself as the sole audience.

His glass of Pernod was raised in a toast, honoring Count Risponyi.

"To my cat's-paw."

The rumbling laughter gushed out, poured across the deck, and fell into the waters of the marina.

Elena did not know that she was in Count Risponyi's gunsights.

She knew even less that it had been a dry run on the little man's part. Practising for Killinger. If it should become necessary.

Elena had been told that if for any reason Killinger should refuse to leave the *Sybaris* with her, she should arrange it so that he stood in that same window from which she had been seen. She had no idea of Risponyi's plans.

She saw Killinger finish his short talk with that awful Mexican, Olga Martinez, and enter the living room area. She approached him quickly, and putting her best features forward, she aimed her breasts at him.

He smiled at the juicy wench before him. "You wanted to see me?"

"If you are Jedediah Killinger III." She licked her lips to make them shine.

"I am."

"Then I bring you greetings from my father, Don Manuel Ruiz Gontron Varga."

"Thank you." He looked puzzled.

She pouted at him. "My father is president of the Varga Tanker and Shipping Company. He met you three years ago, in the city of Madrid. That is where we have our home."

Killinger remembered the general occasion. There had been a large series of meetings in Madrid at that time between insurance people and the Continent's big shipowners. He had met many men at once, and he couldn't remember their names, although he'd probably know them on sight. He answered vaguely: "Ah, yes. Don Manuel." He walked to the bar. "How is he?"

Count Vaclav Risponyi's use of the long-distance phone had paid off. He had learned of an occasion when Killinger had been part of such a large group that he would not be able to remember all of those who might have attended. Elena had been instructed well, and she was proving herself to be a good actress.

"His health is splendid." She climbed up on a bar stool, aiming both knees at him. Her legs were a little bit apart. "Wouldn't *my* health be of more interest to you?" She laughed. "You shall call me Elena."

"All right. Elena, would you like a Margarita?"

She sneaked a quick peek at her wristwatch as she answered brightly: "It is my most favorite afternoon drink." She wiggled her cute bottom into the bar stool's cushion. Her almost nonexistent micro-mini virtually disappeared, showing a small glimpse of her wispy dusty-pink brief and an interesting darkness behind the fabric.

He laid out the limes, tequila, orange curaçao, ice, and a dish of salt. As he did so, he looked at her. The sweater hid nothing, and its effect was to make her more desirable. Her perfume was provocative, her face was lovely, and she was a delectable package. Her animal excitement reached out and touched him, and touched him again. He found himself responding. So much so that he barely heard the tinkling of the little bell in his mind.

144

The second beautiful girl in two days to throw herself at him. Not that he minded. But why? The little pieces came back. Olga had said, "She have told me she is from Madrid, Spain. But she speaks with an accent from Peru."

Whatever this Elena wanted to do, Killinger would go along with it, trying to find out what she wanted. He took a quick look at her shoes. Sandals with flat soles. No stiletto hidden there.

She saw his glance at her feet. She pointed them at him, legs straight. "You like my legs?" She did seated ballet movements, showing all.

"Indeed." He put the drinks before them. "Ankles, knees, and thighs."

Satisfied, she picked up the drink, making a "toast" motion, and sipped. "You are a fine bartender." Another sip. "Very, very good. And I am an expert."

"Thank you." A little thought sneaked into the mood. He wondered about Katja at the hospital. If she wanted him by her side during the operation, he would go, for he had promised. Besides, he was concerned about Ejnar Mylius.

Elena crossed her legs comfortably.

Her animal excitement touched him again and played with him.

Killinger never carried a watch, nor any kind of personal jewelry. Remembering the hospital, he asked Elena for the time.

She looked at her watch. "The time is half past two o'clock." At least, that's what her watch had said. Risponyi had had her put it fifteen minutes *behind*, purposely making it slow. He had said it was part of the whole joke.

He hadn't told her what the joke was.

Elena realized suddenly that she was running behind schedule. She had to get Killinger out of there because it was really two forty-five.

And Carl F. Cooper was due at the *Katja* in fifteen minutes.

With the crane.

Chapter Eight

Marve Googe had a gray soul.

The rest of him matched. Silver growing in his black hair. A salt and pepper two-day beard. A gray uniform that had never met an ironing board. Matching gray shirt with a grimy leather bow tie, readymade and probably once black. His leather cap matched his bow tie, and it was strategically worn over his bald spot. Six feet four inches, with a pot belly.

He was a startling contrast to Count Risponyi and João, standing in the center of the *Katja's* luxurious saloon. Sullen and gloomy, he waited for someone else to open the conversation.

"You are from the Googe Trucking Company?" João had started things.

A surprisingly small, high voice made itself heard. "I am Googe."

"I prefer to deal with the man who bears the responsibility."

"Me too." His eyes wandered as he spoke. "You the lawyer who called me?"

"It was I who spoke with you." Count Risponyi took over. His low bullfrog croak had a stranger than normal sound after Googe's voice.

"You said you'd put up cash in advance. That's why I came." His eyes had covered the saloon several times, and he hadn't really seen anything. It was a constant nervous habit. "Can't trust employees with money. So I came myself." The constant motion of his eyes had picked up nothing more than the feeling of wealth. "My price is thirty-five dollars an hour."

"On the phone, you said twenty-five."

"Maybe we had a bad connection. Anyway, instead of a

one-ton, I came in a ton-and-a-half pickup truck." His mouth changed shape slightly. It was his personality smile. "Thirty-five bucks includes labor."

Risponyi recognized greed, and he knew how to use it. He took his roll of money from his pocket. Googe's gaze pressed against it. The Count carefully removed a hundred-dollar bill from the other assorted greenery.

To Googe, it was beauty incarnate.

Risponyi held the bill to Googe's face. "This will belong to you when you finish the job I have for you." He folded the currency and placed it in his own breastpocket. That was the incentive to make certain Googe would do as he was told.

"How much work I gotta put in?"

Risponyi indicated the crate. "This is the box I spoke to you about."

"Why all the business with dollies and tracks, and that stuff?" Googe moved to the crate as though to pick it up. "Looks kinda small to me."

Risponyi grabbed Googe's arm to stop him. Googe, knowing himself to be a big and powerful man, pretended that the Count hadn't touched him. He continued the arm movement. Then, suddenly, he stopped. A grimace of pain leaped to his face and clung there. "Hey. Whatcha doin'?"

Risponyi had squeezed hard. Without answering Googe's question, he removed his hand. Googe massaged the sore place on his arm.

The Count continued, ignoring the interruption. "At precisely three o'clock, a boat with a crane will arrive. The crate will be lifted from here in the hold and moved to the dock. You will be ready with your dolly." A pause. "This 'small' box weighs over one thousand pounds."

Googe was impressed.

Risponyi impressed him further by taking a fifty-dollar bill from his thick green wad. He handed it to Googe. "This fifty dollars is an advance."

Awed. "Over and above the hundred?"

Risponyi nodded. "You will wait in your truck until the

boat arrives. When it will have gotten into position to lift the crate, you will return with your dolly."

"Got ya." He turned to leave, but stopped and asked his question. "Where do I gotta take it?"

"Oxnard Airport. There is an airplane waiting."

Time is unstoppable.

K. Y. Smith had double proof of this in the form of the two timepieces on the table. One was a large clock, with the exact time. Its minute hand moved slowly to three o'clock. Its second hand jumped forward in half-second measures, moving in silence. The other was his large sweep-second timer, waiting for the go switch to be pressed. The oversized dial had lines radiating along its outer circle. Some were minutes. Some, seconds. And the finest lines measured tenths of seconds.

The binoculars followed Googe from the *Katja* to the truck. The unmoving eyes took note of the fact that Googe had left the schooner with empty hands. A message to this effect was sent to the computer. A memory cell held on to the fact.

Over his shoulder. "Talya. Write a note."

She picked up a pad and pencil. "I am ready."

He dictated. "Print what I tell you in block letters." He swung the binoculars to the far end of the marina. " 'You will not move from where you now stand until the clock says three-thirty.' "

Talya wrote the words in clear and easy to read block letters. She placed the pad of paper, with what she had just written, in front of Smith.

The computer had been spinning and whirring, reacting to the Chinaman's commands. The picture on the read-out tube was nearing completion.

Kuan Yang snapped out: "Teffki!"

Seemingly without prior movement, Teffki appeared alongside the big Chinaman. He waited to be spoken to.

"Take the top sheet from the pad, and fold it into four parts."

Teffki took what Talya had written and followed instructions.

The turquoise eyes took note of what the computer stated as fact. Jedediah Killinger III was aboard the *Sybaris*. Killinger's presence spoiled the Master Plan. Unless Risponyi succeeded, up to a point, then K. Y. Smith's plans would be unable to move forward. Killinger was in the way. Only minutes were left.

"Talya, bring the phone close."

It was fourteen minutes before three.

Elena's wristwatch said twenty-nine minutes before three. It had purposely been set incorrectly. Elena remembered what she was to say to Killinger to make him leave the junk. "My father has given me a sealed envelope for you. It is important that you read it. He said that it is imperative for you to speak with him." She looked again at her watch. "He will be phoning me at three o'clock, our time. You must be there."

A highly improbable story, but Killinger would play along. Perhaps he'd learn what she was trying to accomplish. About her weapons, he thought her shoes looked safe. Obviously nothing was hidden under her clothes. Even she wasn't hidden. Two things to be careful of. Her purse. And wherever she wanted to take him.

Killinger appeared to accept her story, and they were about to leave the living room on the stern of the *Sybaris*. The phone rang loudly. Killinger caught it on the second ring. "Hello."

The female voice with the French accent lilted: "Mr. Killinger, please."

"Speaking."

"This is Madame Boulanger, of the St. John's Hospital."

"About Mr. Ejnar Mylius?"

"Perhaps. I am phoning for Mrs. Katja O'Reilly. She have said that you must be here as quickly as possible."

"Madame Boulanger, what's wrong?"

No answer. She had hung up.

It was eight minutes before three.

Risponyi was becoming restive. Not even the close proximity of the crate calmed him. Elena had been unable to get Killinger to leave the junk. He took a silencer from João's open suitcase and began to screw it onto the Colt Cobra .45.

Although it was a sudden relief to see Killinger and Elena leave the *Sybaris,* he kept the weapon of death in his hand.

K. Y. Smith's chuckle caused the table to vibrate.

He, too, watched Killinger and Elena run down the gangplank.

It was seven minutes before three.

Chapter Nine

"Explodes" is the description of an antelope's instantaneous movement which takes him from grazing to running. Muscle response is electricity-fast and powerful. This is caused by a high amount of adrenalin pushed into the blood by a pair of ductless glands located above the kidneys. Hunters have learned that adrenalin in the muscles causes the meat to have a bitter taste; therefore, if you want to eat good-tasting antelope meat, you must shoot the poor animal while it is grazing, from a distance.

A rifle was designed for this particular kind of immediate kill: the .257 Weatherby Magnum. Each part of this excellent shooting piece is carefully crafted by hand. Including the bullets.

K. Y. Smith's .257 Weatherby had a hand-chased stock, inlaid simply with gold and ivory. Mounted on its barrel was an Italian Unerti scope, with controlled magnification giving, in five steps, from ten to twenty-four times vision. The Unerti was set for twenty-four times. Its thirty-four ounces added to the weight of the rifle, so that for long waits between shots, it was best supported on a bipod, that is, two rods which joined and held the rifle by the barrel, slightly behind the muzzle.

Two green turbans had just finished setting up a three-sided canvas shelter on the fantail of the *Valhalla*. A third green turban stood inside the blind, ready to make a long-distance shot.

On a signal from K. Y. Smith.

The transceiver spoke. "This is Vincenzo. Killinger and the girl have gone to the La Sirena Hotel. He took her key to open the door to her room."

While driving to the nearby hotel, Elena had convinced

Killinger that he should take the envelope of papers with him to the hospital, to read. She had kept her hand in his lap, manipulating her fingers, while they drove.

Now that they were in her suite, she had him wait in the living room while she went into the bedroom "for the papers."

He heard much rapid motion through the open door, and he was intrigued by the girl. Also warmed by her hand. He thought it was a shame that he had to run off to the hospital. Finding out who she really was and what she was attempting would have been more than just fun. Oh well, duty always comes first. He heard Elena's voice calling.

"I cannot move this big trunk. You must come to help me."

The least a gentleman could do is accommodate a lady. Especially in her bedroom. So Killinger entered. She was nowhere in sight. He stepped in to look for her, when suddenly he was pushed hard from behind. He rolled forward to the bed, twisting his body so that he was ready for any physical assault. His hands and feet were hard weapons. And lethal.

K. Y. Smith's clock said that it was Zero Hour.

He pushed the black button on the oversized timing clock. The hand moved to its first tenth-second measurement as Carl F. Cooper's tug touched the *Katja*.

Count Vaclav Risponyi and João were ready to help Cooper.

A green turban, Teffki, stood at the side of the parking lot above the *Katja* and the *Sybaris*. He carried binoculars and an envelope.

Marve Googe leaned against his truck, waiting for a signal.

Jedediah Killinger III was prepared to fight an unknown assailant.

A green turban, named Khaloush, had his eye at the Italian Unerti scope atop the .257 Weatherby Magnum rifle. His finger was on the trigger.

Two of the classic movements in a war are the Pincers Movement and the Encircling Movement.

152

Basically, Pincers Movement reaches in and takes, with sharp and decisive action.

On the other hand, the Encircling Movement is a maneuver in which one force surrounds and envelops the opposing force.

Count Vaclav Risponyi had worked rapidly and brilliantly. He had blueprinted a speedy Pincers designed to pick up the heavy box from Hong Kong and spirit it away before any one of his enemies was aware.

Kuan Yang Smith's computer had designed an Encircling Movement. His forces were ready to surprise and entrap Risponyi and his people, taking the crate from under the Count's big brush moustache.

The battle was now joined. But one side was not yet aware.

Another small war was in progress.

The eternal battle between men and women.

Killinger was ready for an enemy. But it was Elena who jumped on him, laughing, as he lay on the bed. While she had been alone in the bedroom, she had removed her clothes. After all, she had had her instructions to keep Killinger in her room. "No matter how." She liked him; found him exciting; and used the earthy approach. Elena unzipped his trousers.

Chapter Ten

Carl F. Cooper secured his tug to the schooner *Katja*.

He found himself face to face with Risponyi. The Count's speech was crisp. "Follow me."

Cooper hopped aboard the schooner, ragged cigar stub held tightly in his teeth. "Got a match, baby?"

The little man glared at him.

"My cigar ain't makin' it."

"Smoking is bad for you." Risponyi headed for the companionway.

"Everybody's worried about my health." Cooper shrugged and followed the bald-headed gnome. The cigar butt was still in his mouth. When he caught up with Risponyi, the Count was standing alongside the crate, stroking it as though the rough wood with the stenciled Chinese lettering were really the perfumed and oiled skin of the most beautiful woman in the Orient. João was a step behind the foppish little man.

"Mr. Cooper, this is the box about which I had spoken with you."

"Don't look heavy." Cooper's sight examination was practised. A grin. "But I'll take your word." He squatted next to the crate and gave it an experimental push. Nodded to himself. "Where do I put it?"

"On the dock. How long will it take you?"

A laugh around the dead cigar. "If everything goes wrong, maybe ten minutes."

"Do not permit anything to go wrong."

"Nothing to worry about, baby. Just a figure of speech." He tried one more heft at the corner of the crate. "I'm gonna need a hand with the ropes and hooks."

Risponyi's eyes embraced the crate. "Mr. O'Reilly will assist."

154

Cooper ran up the steps to the deck, João following. In a matter of seconds they had both returned, carrying rope and hooks and a strong metal crowbar. Risponyi had not moved.

Cooper ran the crowbar under a corner of the crate to lift it so that João could slide the rope beneath it. When Cooper strained and lifted, the wooden slats of the box wailed, like a baby at the moment of birth.

The Count closed his eyes and prayed to all of his gods.

Marve Googe had been watching the operation on the *Katja* intently. The grooved tracks were piled together and bound so that he would be able to move immediately on Risponyi's signal. In his left hand, he held the two metal dollies easily.

Googe paid absolutely no attention to the green turban who moved unhurriedly to the Count's Rolls-Bentley and the chauffeur, Hawkins. It was Teffki carrying the two simple items which soon would assume great importance. They were a pair of binoculars and a white envelope.

K. Y. Smith's sweep-second electric timer said that it had been six minutes and fifty-two point three seconds since Cooper's tug had first bumped the schooner. He was satisfied with what he saw through his telescope. His computer had neither additions nor subtractions to make to the last read-out.

Killinger had been conquered.

However, he enjoyed the kind of small battle in which, even if he lost, he would end up on top.

Elena had rolled on him, mashing her exquisite breasts into his chest, nibbling his lips, exploring his tongue with hers. All the while, she was trying to remove his trousers. Her fingers held him and stroked him and squeezed him while she moaned in a hard and fierce whisper: "So big. Oh, so big . . ."

The mood was destroyed by that damned Madame Boulanger from the hospital who had hung up. Grudgingly, he rolled free and picked up the telephone. He would make an excuse, and then when he arrived later, he would bring flowers. He asked for the number, trying to control his heavy breathing and unsuccessfully attempting to get Elena to calm down, even if briefly.

"St. John's Hospital."

"Madame Boulanger, please."

Teffki had finished a short conversation with the chauffeur, Hawkins. Hawkins was now walking quickly to the schooner and Count Risponyi. He was carrying a pair of binoculars and a white envelope.

The sweep-second hand said that seven minutes and forty-eight point three seconds had been used up.

The crate from Hong Kong had been securely wrapped in heavy nylon line. The hooks had been attached. Cooper was ready to have the crane lift the heavy box. Risponyi had insisted on holding the guide rope.

Hawkins rushed down the companionway breathing heavily. "Count Risponyi . . ."

The little shaven-headed man spun and swung at the same time. Hawkins was thrown back against the bulkhead. "Get back to the car."

Hawkins had slipped to the floor, his mouth bleeding. In his hands he held the binoculars and the white envelope. He wanted to cry. Instead, he whimpered: "The Chinaman . . . with the blue eyes . . ."

Risponyi stood over the quivering chauffeur. Rage was in his black eyes. "The Chinaman! What about him?"

Hawkins could only point to the steps down which he had come.

Roughly, the Count grabbed the chauffeur's shoulder with one hand and lifted him to his feet. "Show me."

"These are for you." The chauffeur trembled in fear as he held the binoculars and white envelope to the enraged little man. Risponyi seized them with the speed of a hawk piercing a pigeon in midflight with its talons.

"Show me where this Chinaman is."

Hawkins preceded the Count to the deck, blood running down his chin.

He was crying.

The voice at the hospital was puzzled. "I am sorry, sir. But there is no one on the staff by the name of Boulanger."

"But she just called me, fifteen minutes ago."

The operator was firm. "Sir, I have worked at this switchboard for almost five years. For the past hour and a half, I have been alone here, and I have handled all of the calls." More firmly. "There is no one at St. John's Hospital named Boulanger."

Killinger slammed down the phone and rolled to his feet.

Hawkins wiped his mouth before he pointed. The blood on his hand was his own.

Count Vaclav Risponyi aimed the binoculars at the fantail of a luxury yacht named *Valhalla*.

He saw a telescope aimed at him. It was held by one huge yellow paw.

Risponyi's blood stopped moving. Its flow had been halted by hunks of red ice in his veins. His stomach began to hurt, fiercely . . . .

With his free hand, K. Y. Smith made a sweeping motion to the canvas behind him. The Count's binoculars peered at the indicated place. He saw a canvas blind with the open side facing him. Pulled back, inside, a man in a green turban stood with his eye at a telescopic sight and his finger on the trigger of a rifle which had its barrel supported on a bipod. He recognized the gun as a .257 Weatherby Magnum.

K. Y. Smith made more motions. They were those of a man tearing open an envelope.

The Count looked at the envelope in his hand. Dazedly he ripped it open and read its message. In Talya's handwriting. "You will not move from that spot until the clock says three-thirty."

The little man felt the cross hairs of the 24X 'scope as they pressed against his heart.

Chapter Eleven

Knife in hand, Vincenzo waited for Killinger.

And Killinger ran straight at the blade.

Moments ago, when Killinger had learned that there was no Madame Boulanger, his mind had leaped to the crate aboard the *Katja*. The first phone call, from the woman with the French accent, had been designed to get him off of the *Sybaris* immediately. He had left with another woman, one with a Peruvian accent. Elena, too, had done her best to make him leave the junk. The two of them had a common goal. He had pulled his clothes together and had started racing on foot to his boat in the marina. For some reason or other, a man in an Italian black silk suit who wore a white shirt and tie and a black hat stood in front of him holding an open switchblade knife.

Vincenzo had been told that this Killinger must be kept away from the dock that held both the *Sybaris* and the *Katja*. He hadn't been told how this order should be enforced. He would inquire of K. Y. Smith, using the transceiver which he held in his left hand. Vincenzo pointed the knife at Killinger's belly as he made a polite request: "Please do not move, Mr. Killinger."

Killinger did not slow his pace, and as he moved, years of practise made him respond to the threat automatically, with Karate. As he dodged to the left, he used his left hand to chop Vincenzo's elbow joint. With great speed, almost making it a simultaneous action, Killinger's right hand, in *uraken*, hit Vincenzo in the right side, breaking two of his ribs. Still in motion, Killinger flowed into putting all of his weight onto his two hands, on the ground. He used a *maegeri*, kicking Vincenzo in the abdomen with the ball of his right foot.

Flipping into an upright position, Killinger started a two-hundred-yard sprint to the *Sybaris*.

Vincenzo lay still, a pile of human rubble.

Cooper worked the crane.

João handled the guide rope as the wooden box moved lightly from the saloon of the *Katja* and floated above the deck.

For some reason unknown to João and Cooper, Count Risponyi stood rooted to the deck looking through binoculars. He neither spoke to them nor did he answer their questions.

A shout reached them. "Cooper!! Carl Cooper!!"

Cooper looked toward the sound and saw Killinger running toward him, across the dock. He waved a cheery greeting and grinned.

"Hold it, goddammit! Wait for me!" Killinger was rapidly moving closer.

Cooper stopped all motion of the crane. The crate swung back and forth, wrapped safely in its rope cradle.

The sound of Killinger's voice had ripped K. Y. Smith's timetable into little shreds and blown them away.

The large yellow hand closed into a fist, crushing the telescope.

A yellow finger pressed the broadcast button of the transceiver.

While the turquoise eyes turned inward to examine the ruined computer program, K. Y. Smith spoke into the microphone. His voice was devoid of expression. "Abort. All procedures are cancelled. Repeat. Abort. All procedures are cancelled. Return immediately."

The three-hundred-pound Australian rose gracefully from his seat at the table on the fantail of the *Valhalla*, turned, and walked into the interior of his yacht with a steady and measured tread.

Count Vaclav Risponyi used the binoculars to watch his enemy disappear. When he saw the green turbans break down the canvas blind and roll it up, he took his first deep and relaxed breath in eleven minutes and seventeen point six seconds. When the .257 Weatherby Magnum was disassembled, he took his second deep breath.

Carefully, not quite believing he was still alive, the little man did an about-face.

And looked directly at Killinger's chest.

Chapter Twelve

Cooper's crane moved alongside the junk, still holding the crate.

João and Risponyi followed Killinger aboard the *Sybaris*. The Count had no choice. He would go wherever the wooden box went. And João Aranha Mijangos O'Reilly followed the Count, because that's where his money came from. To insure a diplomatic silence from João, the Count had given him an additional thousand dollars behind Killinger's back.

Count Vaclav Risponyi believed that the best defense was attack. He drew himself up to his five feet two inches of dignity and took his monocle from his breast pocket. He polished it deliberately as he tried to stare Killinger down. Then, seemingly without movement, the monocle appeared in Risponyi's eye.

The shaven head seemed to shine with honest indignation. The bullfrog croak became its most proper and its most British. "Mr. Killinger, I expect an apology from you."

Killinger almost laughed. "If you deserve an apology, you will receive an apology."

Risponyi pointed above them where the crate swayed back and forth, held by the crane. "That is my box. What is inside it belongs to me." He whipped out a folded piece of paper and presented it with stiff formality. "This bill of lading says that it is so."

João's interest was magnified. The last bill of lading he had seen for the crate from Hong Kong was held by K. Y. Smith when that Chinaman had attempted to claim the bronze statue called Chin P'ing Mei.

Risponyi gestured with a grand sweep at the box which moved over their heads, back and forth like a metronome beating the time for a funeral march. "I give you permission to open that wooden box for a limited examination." He waved one finger under Killinger's nose. "With this one limitation. You may not look inside the leather case which I described to you . . . ." Pause, for emphasis. " . . . so long as the description matches what I say."

Killing said not a word.

"I shall repeat that general description." He ticked off the points on his fingers. "Hand-tooled sealskin."

João listened to every syllable. What the Count was saying differed greatly from what the big yellow man had said.

Ticking off another finger. "The date, 1893." And another finger. "A brass lock with my grandfather's name over it." The clincher. "And that name is the same as mine." A small bow with his head. "Vaclav Risponyi."

João looked to Killinger for a reaction.

Killinger spoke softly. "I cannot release anything aboard the schooner without permission in writing from the company for which I am now working."

Risponyi seemed relieved as he smiled. He reached into his inside breast pocket and brought out a sheet of paper folded in three parts. He opened and handed it to Killinger with an attitude that said "This settles all of our problems. As you can see from this document, the insurance company and you, Mr. Killinger, are completely protected."

Killinger unfolded the paper. It was imprinted with the name of a large Beverly Hills Bank. The signature was identified as that of the Executive Vice President. The letter was addressed to Jedediah Killinger III as agent for an insurance company based in Amsterdam, Holland and called The Association for the Improvement of Marine Insurance. It stated that there was $50,000 on deposit, being held as a bond to guarantee the actions of Count Vaclav Risponyi in the matter of a certain wooden crate. Further details covered the bill of lading and its number.

Again the Count made a small bow. But with irony in its feeling. "Now, sir, may I take my property?"

Killinger looked above him. The writing in Chinese calligraphy was there for him to read. But he could not decipher it. He exhaled a long sigh. Then he refolded the letter and gave it back to Risponyi.

It was all past João's comprehension.

The monocle flashed in the sun. "I repeat, sir. May I take my property?" As though it was settled his way, Count Risponyi tacked on another question. "Will I now receive my apology?"

Killinger's answer was short. "Negative."

"Negative? I beg your pardon. . . ."

Killinger looked down into the black eyes that seemed to have no pupil. "Negative. Like in 'no'."

Talya had been sitting in her father's chair, binoculars aimed at the *Sybaris*.

When K. Y. Smith returned, she gave him a quick run-down on what she had seen. In essence, it was that Killinger had held conversation with Risponyi, with João very much in the background. That the Count had offered some papers to Killinger which had been returned. Then the Count had left, walking very stiffly and followed by João who acted like a dog waiting for somebody to throw him a bone.

The big man with the turquoise eyes figured that João Aranha Mijangos O'Reilly was a hungry piranha from his native Brazil. That João would as soon bite the hand that fed him as the food it held. K. Y. Smith would offer food to this O'Reilly. But he would exact a price.

Information was put into the computer, to store away against later questions.

"Talya."

She moved close.

"Does Mr. Killinger find you exciting?"

Talya thought first before answering dispassionately, "He does."

"Your weapon is your femininity." A pause—sip a little twenty-year-old Scotch whiskey. "Make yourself ready."

Dutifully, Talya left.

The binoculars stayed with the crate above the deck of the junk.

Kimo had come to help Killinger move the hatch covers.

There were three of them. The first was in the ceiling of the living room on the top deck. The second was immediately beneath the first, on the floor of the same living room, which also was the ceiling of Killinger's bedroom. The third was also in a straight line down, on the floor of the bedroom.

When removed, there was a clear shaft from the topmost deck to the hold of the *Sybaris*.

Carl F. Cooper, his cigar still dead and smelly, followed Killinger's directions in the lowering of the small heavy crate. Killinger had taken over. He gave signals and instructions to Cooper on the water below until, finally, the crate was over the long shaft that led to the hold. Killinger called down to the tug: "Okay. Drop it slowly."

"You ain't payin' the bread," Cooper laughed. "But you're sure sayin' the words." He followed Killinger's instructions exactly.

K. Y. Smith watched the crate being lowered to the top deck.

He thought it would stay there.

But it disappeared from sight.

He watched the large spool which held the cable as it continuously unwound. He tried to gauge how much cable was running. When enough had been released to permit the crate to reach the floor of Killinger's topside living room, K. Y. Smith was sure it would stop.

But it kept running.

The spool released cable at a controlled, slow, steady pace. Ten more feet went by. Then ten more. Finally motion stopped. Killinger left his position of signalling to Cooper. He looked down at what K. Y. Smith now assumed was a shaft and signaled a complete stop.

Seconds later, the rope and hook came back up into the sunlight, as the spool reversed its motion.

There was no crate.

Down in the bottom hold, Kimo had released the hooks and rope. The crate rested on the concrete ballast which ran the length of the hull, like a pathway. Killinger ran down the circular stairway to join Kimo.

When Killinger had ordered the concrete for the hull, in Hong Kong, he had also bought a huge old safe. This had been imbedded in the concrete so that it was immovable.

Kimo had put one of the junk's dollies beneath the wooden box when it was lowered. Now Killinger opened the safe and rolled the crate into the safe. He slammed the door and spun the dial.

Kimo's curiosity was killing him. "What's in that box that's so important?"

"I wish I knew."

"What keeps you from opening it and looking? Ethics?"

Killinger grinned. "There must be a short cut on the sharp and rocky road of ethics. And I'm going to use it."

Talya shone as she drifted to her father's side.

He sat in his chair on the *Valhalla*'s fantail, watching the Chinese junk.

Talya's silk sheath was of a cerulean blue, heavily interwoven with silver metallic thread. It was more exciting than a mere skin over her own skin. Somehow, it had become the skin *under* her skin. Her full body leaped out, demanding to be noticed and appreciated and used.

"I am ready to visit Mr. Killinger, Father."

K. Y. Smith sighed as his binoculars followed a moving figure. He sent his hand to search the table for sweets.

"Mr. Killinger has left the *Sybaris*."

Chapter Thirteen

The two green turbans carried Vincenzo between them.

Killinger had seen the two men step from the black Mercedes-Benz limousine and walk to where Vincenzo sat, crumpled in a chair. He had recognized the car as being the same one which had brought Talya to the beach that morning and yesterday, when they had run and played with each other in the surf.

As the limousine drove away carrying Vincenzo, Killinger climbed the steps to the balcony of the hotel. From that height, he watched the car's slow progress around the marina. When the car stopped in the parking area behind the *Valhalla*, Killinger knew these had been Smith's people.

Now he was on his way to find out what Elena's involvement had been.

The mouthwatering Peruvian pepper had been utterly confounded.

Never in her life had a man run from her bed. And with such speed. And such an attractive man. And so much of him. A shame. A pity.

She had taken a shower to cool herself. It had helped, a little.

Drying herself, she stood before the hotel room's full-length mirror and examined herself critically. Dropping the towel, she lifted her arms high. Her breasts were good. She dropped her arms, and the breasts stood proud and firm. Very unusual for chichis that large. Her hips were full, showing that if she weren't careful, they would become too much. But that was in the future, after she got married and had children. The roundness of her thighs was not yet fat, and they met nicely, highlighting a soft and dark triangle. In profile, she patted her tummy which was saved from flatness by a small hill below her navel.

How could a man who was truly a man fly from that body?

As she was rubbing a scented body lotion into her skin, there was a knocking. She picked up the towel, wrapped herself, and moved to the door. "Who it is, please?"

"Me. Jed Killinger."

Elena flung the door open. She grabbed Killinger's arm and dragged him in. Then she slammed and locked the door. With her back against it, she crossed her arms in great seriousness. "This time you will not get away."

"I don't *want* to get away."

"Then please to tell me what you do want." She turned the radio on and adjusted the dial until she found music with a Latin beat. "Perhaps I can help you." Her smile was full of mischief as she swayed and moved her bare feet in time with the Spanish love song in the background.

Killinger's voice was flat. "Who sent you to visit me on my boat?"

Elena's mouth fell open. She hadn't been expecting this kind of a reply. She forced an expression of minor outrage onto her face. "My father. I have already told you this."

"Your father? In Spain?"

Elena nodded.

"Where did you get your Peruvian accent?"

Elena was silent.

"And who gave you instructions to have me off my boat at three o'clock?"

Ten thousand lies and evasions spun round and round in Elena's mind. She was certain that none would work. She decided to tell the truth. Piece by piece. She smiled. She laughed. And she grew warm all over. "I have been told a story. I have been given instructions. I have been paid money."

"I'm listening."

Elena laughed again. "But I will say no more." A wider smile and a licking of the lips. "Not until later."

"What is your price?"

"That is the question I wanted to hear." Elena undid the tuck-in knot that held the towel. It drifted to the floor. Only Elena stood there, legs apart. "My price is . . ." She stepped to Killinger and put her arms around his neck. Her next words were a husky whisper. " . . . that you will make love with me." She kissed him, her lips wide open.

Killinger accepted by putting his arms around her. He felt it was one of the best business deals he had ever been offered.

Elena's tongue strolled slowly around his lips and then crept into his mouth, moving languidly. Her breasts pressed into him. Her soft dark triangle moved in continuous circles against him. When she felt him rise to meet her, she reached down and opened his zipper, putting her hand inside.

Killinger's hands moved down the velvet smoothness of her back until he held a firm, exciting cheek in each hand.

She started at the bottom of his shirt, unbuttoning it and working her way up. When she had it undone the whole way, she slid it from his shoulders. She was growing more excited with each moment. Finally, with explosive laughter: "If you do not remove those terrible trousers, I will rip them from you."

He stepped out of them. "I may need them another day."

"There is no other day but today. There is no other time but right now."

Nothing separated their nakedness.

Killinger swept her up into his arms and took her to the bed.

Elena put her teeth into his shoulder, deep enough to mark without breaking the skin. He lowered the two of them onto the turned-back sheets. She moaned as they rolled exquisitely close.

Her eyes opened and glowed hot. "If, when you are inside of me, you hurry, I shall kill you."

Killinger nibbled her ear. While one hand held the magnificence of a breast, toying with the erect nipple, the other hand was under her undulating bottom, exploring and caressing. "If I do hurry, I deserve to be killed."

Elena's fingers examined Killinger, millimeter by millimeter. What her fingers liked, her lips kissed, and her tongue tasted.

Touching her was wondrous sensual pleasure. Her belly was a delight, and the moist insides of her thighs were delicious walls leading to a special heaven.

Elena purred into his ear, "Lover, turn the radio very loud."

His wonder was evident.

She laughed. "I scream when I love."

He turned up the radio.

They loved. She screamed into his shoulder for a very, very long time.

In joy.

A small black car followed the Rolls-Bentley to the airport.

Paolo was at the wheel, and he was expert in trailing without being seen. When the Rolls-Bentley slowed, he slowed. When it stopped, he pulled in behind some low scrub trees and watched. Count Risponyi stepped from the car and entered a small building with a sign that said, "Airplane Charters—Griff McLellan." He spoke into his transceiver. "Paolo here . . ."

The big Chinaman listened to the electrically distorted voice. " . . . I am at the Oxnard Airport. Count Risponyi just entered a small building that says 'Airplane Charters—Griff McLellan'. The chauffeur is in the car in the front seat with Mr. O'Reilly. The blonde lady is alone in the back." A pause. "Mr. O'Reilly is getting out of the car. He is walking in a different direction from the one Count Risponyi took."

The empty blue eyes looked at nothing—and saw everything. Australian twang filled the two-way radio. "Listen carefully. There are specific instructions which you will follow. . . ."

João opened the door of the coffee shop and took a seat at the nearly empty counter. He told the bored waitress that he would like a cup of coffee and a dish of strawberry ice cream. She put the coffee in front of him first. The saucer held almost as much of the coffee as the cup. While João was mopping it up so it wouldn't drip on him, a man sat in the seat next to him. His annoyance compounded, João turned a supercilious stare on the newcomer. He saw a swarthy man in a black Italian silk suit, wearing a white shirt and white tie, with a black fedora square on his head.

The man didn't look at João. His eyes were on the menu tacked to the wall. He spoke out of the side of his mouth. "Mr. O'Reilly, pretend like I'm not here."

João tried to pretend, but the shock of a stranger knowing his name, especially after the fiasco on Killinger's boat, was almost too much.

Paolo's whispered growl reached João's ear. "Mr. K. Y. Smith told me to tell you that he is a much richer man than Count Risponyi."

João heard each word with great clarity.

"If you are interested, phone this number." Paolo pushed a folded piece of paper at João's elbow, rose from the stool, and glided through the door, closing it silently behind him.

João Aranha Mijangos O'Reilly picked up the paper and opened it. A telephone number was written very legibly. He smiled to himself and glanced around. No sign of the Count.

He refolded the paper into a smaller square and placed it in his shirt pocket, on the left side.

Over his heart.

Chapter Fourteen

Elena had told Killinger every detail she knew about Risponyi.

The price, indeed, had been right.

He lay there on her bed sorting the information, when she came in from the shower, toweling herself. "I am the cleanest girl in town. First a bath. Now a shower." She leaned down and kissed Killinger gently. "You are a man, and you make me feel like a woman." She sat next to him, fingers idly tracing invisible lines on his skin in the nice touching which comes with liking another person. "You are a good man, Jed Killinger. Someday, if I am a lucky woman, I will find someone a little like you."

He sat up and put his arm around her hip. He kissed her lightly on the neck. "Elena, I'm going to ask you a favor."

She put her hand on top of his. "A favor is a thing you ask of a friend." Her eyes found his eyes. "I am a friend." A deep sigh as she leaned her head against his shoulder.

"Thank you, Elena."

"What is this favor?"

"I want you to phone me, from time to time, and tell me what the Count is planning and doing."

Elena's smile grew into a small portion of laughter. "There will be a price."

Killinger looked at her, waiting for the surprise.

"It is . . . that I will be a guest on your Chinese junk." Sad afterthought: "For a little while." After having given all, she was suddenly afraid of her boldness and a possible rejection. She closed her eyes, afraid of his answer.

He kissed her eyelids softly. "Of course. That would be wonderful."

Her eyes popped open and sparkled. "I will be your personal spy." Her tongue tiptoed over her even teeth as she wrinkled her nose in thought. "And, like they do in the movies, I picked myself a code name."

"What is it?"

"Mata Hari."

"Okay, fellow sybarites, it's time for a drink."

Samantha and Marjorie turned to look at Kimo who was at the door to their office on the bow of the deck. Samantha glanced at the wall clock. "Quitting time."

Marjorie stretched. "Sounds groovy. Where should we go?"

Kimo played it straight. "To the world's sexiest bar. The Club Sybaris, of course."

Marjorie giggled. "It sure is. What'll the boss man say?"

"He's gonna give me all kinds of hell if you chicks don't. I got orders to stay aboard 'til he returns and keep the pretty ladies happy."

The girls had closed up the office and followed Kimo to the big room on the stern of the junk. They were on their second drink when Copper and Auric ran out to the deck to greet Killinger.

He walked in to them, where they were relaxed and listening to the music. "Kimo, I'll have one of whatever you people are drinking."

Kimo made him a screwdriver with tangerine juice instead of orange juice. They toasted and drank.

Samantha stood and pulled Kimo up with her. "We're going to help Marjorie move some things in Kimo's van. But we've got things to prepare, first." To Marjorie: "Be ready in about seven minutes." Kimo left with her.

Marjorie sipped her drink. "I'm one ahead of you."

"I'm in no hurry. Where's your stuff?"

"Santa Barbara. Mostly books." She emptied her glass. "My ex-roommate said she's having a big party, so maybe we'll stay over."

"Be careful when they pass the prunes."

With extra dignity: "I'm certain that they won't carry my favorite brand." She broke herself up and giggled. She got serious again and leaned close. "There won't be any of that love-making stuff." Her soft laugh was earthy and low. The two drinks had gotten to her. "Don't you think I should practise lesson number one? Like, if there's some interesting dude?"

Gravely: "Practise is always suggested."

Marjorie held his shirt front lightly between thumb and forefinger. She raised on tiptoes and whispered. "Prunes."

To Killinger, her lips were a soft and sweet-tasting flower. The petals opened. Killinger kissed it, barely lingering. Quick as a hummingbird, her tongue darted out and then was gone.

Killinger pretended shock. "When did you start on lesson number two?"

Marjorie got her delightful fit of giggles.

K. Y. Smith had been on the fantail with a new telescope in his right hand. His left fed him macadamia nuts from a priceless Ming bowl. Before him, a Singapore Gin Sling, long and cool.

He had seen Killinger return and had put the information into his computer. His chill blue eyes gazed inward at the newest read-out on the tube. It said that there were three important blank spaces. They concerned Killinger. The speed with which Killinger had returned to the *Sybaris* at eleven minutes and fifty-four point eight seconds past three o'clock indicated that he had not gone to the hospital, as he should have. After all, Talya, pretending to be Madame Boulanger, had done her job perfectly.

Also, Killinger had just appeared and boarded the *Sybaris* moments ago. Where had he been? With whom had he spoken?

Finally, and of primary concern, where was the precious crate? What had happened to it after the crane's drum had continued to turn, letting out more and more rope?

Once again, Talya was at his shoulder. She would obtain for him the necessary answers to the questions.

Over his shoulder: "It is time you saw Mr. Jedediah Killinger IH. He has returned."

Like a weapon aimed by her father, she moved to the target.

Chapter Fifteen

Killinger had saved his life.

But he didn't understand how and why. If Killinger had not shown exactly when he did, K. Y. Smith would now have the wooden box from Hong Kong, and he, Count Risponyi, might have been shot by the man in the green turban.

Since gratitude would be pointless and an obvious waste of time, he had sent for Elena to learn what had happened, the reason Killinger had come to the dock in the marina.

Elena was happy in her new relationship with Killinger, and she wanted to be careful not to excite the little man with the shiny head and the bullfrog croak of a voice, so she wore her simplest clothes with the longest skirt and the loosest, highest blouse. And no make-up.

In questioning her, Risponyi used the carrot-stick technique. That is, first the promise of something good; then the threat of something bad.

The carrot. "Elena, you look lovely." He indicated a deep chair. She sat. He smiled. "Would you care for a drink?" She shook her head. He patted her hand solicitously. "Later, then."

The stick. He sighed an unhappy sigh. "Elena, I am afraid I won't be able to use you in my picture." He shook his head in sadness. "I asked you to do a small acting part with Mr. Killinger, and you failed."

She had been prepared by Killinger for this type of

approach, and she was ready. She gave the best dramatic performance of her life. "But acting is everything to me. I must have the role in your movie." Her tears were convincing. "I did not fail."

Still the stick. His hand crept around her forearm. "Ah, but you did." The fingers closed gradually. He increased the pressure until she opened her mouth for the beginning of an acting sob. The sob became real. His hand remained, but the pressure faded. "You are a disappointment."

She looked unbelievingly at the red marks his fingers had left on her white skin. "I did as you instructed. Even more." A touch of triumph through the wetness of her cheeks. "He was even removing his clothes."

"But this Killinger did not stay." The fingers began to close once more.

She yanked her arm away. "He made a phone call to the hospital." She looked into his solid black eyes. "He asked for a woman named Madame Boulanger."

"Madame Boulanger?"

"Yes. She had called him earlier, when we were on his boat, and told him that Mrs. O'Reilly would need him at the hospital at three o'clock."

The Count thought that the timing, exactly three o'clock, was more than mere coincidence. "Why didn't he go to the hospital?"

"I convinced him to come with me to the hotel room. From there, he could phone Madame Boulanger with an excuse."

Risponyi nodded. "I presume he did phone this woman."

"Absolutely." Dramatic pause. "That's when he left me."

The little man fondled his brush moustache, his curiosity showing.

"There was no Madame Boulanger!" Another perfectly timed pause. "Before he ran out, he said, 'Someone wants me off the junk at three o'clock'." She put her hands out in an expressive gesture. "And that's what happened."

Risponyi rose and paced rapidly, his long apelike arms

swinging. Unexpectedly, in painful and rumbling bullfrog croaks, he began to laugh and laugh.

Elena stared at him uncomprehendingly. Somehow, she felt that she had been a good spy for Killinger and had said the right thing. He would appreciate this information when she called him.

Count Vaclav Risponyi stopped pacing, clenched his fists, and looked up at his gods. He spoke in ecstasy, as though part of a prayer.

"Kuan Yang Smith, you have defeated yourself."

The devil god from Borneo, Pangkalanbuun, growled when he was struck.

His low tones swam across the waters of the marina to where the *Valhalla* was moored. K. Y. Smith heard as he watched Talya strike the bronze gong to announce her arrival aboard Killinger's junk.

Magnified by the telescope, Talya knelt to pet the two dogs who came out to greet her.

At his side, the telephone rang. On the third bell, he picked it up. "Yes."

Muffled, as though it was close to the mouthpiece, the voice whispered. "I am João Aranha Mijangos O'Reilly. I was told that you wanted me to call. That is, if you are Mr. Smith."

The little fish was in his net. "I am Mr. Smith." The good-humored laugh was reborn low in his stomach. "I gather you find it interesting that I have more money than Count Vaclav Risponyi."

"I do. But I, as yet, do not understand how that affects me."

"Where are you calling from, Mr. O'Reilly?"

"A pay telephone, here at the hotel."

"I am prepared to pay you good money, Mr. O'Reilly. And to do so in large amounts."

João's pause and heavy breathing betrayed his avarice.

"However, Mr. O'Reilly, there are conditions. The first of

which is that the good Count must not be aware of our friendship." The laughter in his stomach grew until it poured from his open mouth.

The sound hurt João's ear. He held the phone away. from him. "It is agreed."

"Shortly, we shall meet and talk. At that time I shall make a substantial deposit in advance for your time." The laughter erupted like lava from the volcano of his belly.

"I am to meet with Count Risponyi in a matter of minutes. When I am through, I shall call you."

The laughter swelled and swelled. K. Y. Smith chopped it off when he hung up his telephone.

The heels of Talya's shoes were four-inch slim spikes. . . .

While Killinger appreciated how they accentuated Talya's legs, he reminded himself never to forget that each was a stiletto. The shoes were a cerulean blue, matching her sleek silken sheath.

She was a beautiful picture as she bent to Copper and Auric, scratching their ears and cooing love sounds at them. Her long hair was worn in a coronet braid, and the polish on her long nails was an iridescent blue, the same color as the fabric that was part of her.

When she rose to greet Killinger, she flowed to her feet with the grace and potential danger of a female leopard. She was conscious of her challenge. She stood, daring him, as the breezes from the nearby Pacific Ocean played with the cerulean silk, moulding her body.

She pretended a haughty stare. "I am trying to find a certain Mr. Jedediah Killinger III."

"Perhaps I can be of assistance."

"I doubt it." She posed voluptuously. "My name is Cinderella, and I have come about a pair of golden slippers."

"There's a shoe store down the street."

She pouted. "But I was told that whatever girl was able to fit into the golden slippers . . ." She lifted her skirts higher than necessary to display her long slim legs. ". . . would become the Prince's lady."

"Old wives' tales." He looked at her feet. "Besides, your feet are too big."

She stepped from her shoes, holding her skirt high and pointing a lifted foot at him. "I think my feet would be exactly the right size."

Killinger laughed and swept up her shoes. He turned and went inside the living room.

Her haughtiness gone, she trotted after him, barefoot. "You are a peasant."

Killinger put the twin stiletto-type shoes on a high shelf behind the bar. Now they would be easier to keep track of. As part of the newly-invented routine, he stepped out of his thonged zoris, picked them up, and gave them to her. "This puts us on an equal footing."

She laughed, took them, and threw them across the room. "Fortunately, I prefer peasants to princes." She put both hands around his neck and anchored them in his longish hair, pulling his head down. She kissed him with little biting nibbles.

He bit and chewed and kissed her ear until she began breathing more heavily. "And the reason you prefer us peasants is because we are more basic and much earthier."

She bit his tongue. "Animal."

He made a mock bow and touched his forehead. "You are too kind."

She snapped her fingers. "Champagne!"

"Coming, your ladyship." He moved to the refrigerator.

Talya was now free to find the most important answer on K. Y. Smith's list. The crate. Where was it? Enough rope had been spun out to permit the crate to be moved to the far part of the room. Talya walked around, her eyes busy. It was not in sight. There was no piece of furniture that could have covered it.

She went back to the bar, and while she puzzled over the situation, she ran her fingers over the entwined naked men and women. Raising her head, she caught the shine from a brass ring-bolt set deep into one of the beams. Careful examination with her eyes and brain showed the outline of the hatch through which the crate had entered, at the end of a rope.

Her bare toes felt a wide crack in the deck planking. Turning her gaze down, she saw that there was a second hatch. It was immediately below the one in the roof, clearly indicated and identical in size. There was a logical conclusion. The crate was somewhere below her. Perhaps in the hold.

Killinger's voice came through her thoughts. "The champagne, your ladyship."

As they toasted each other and drank, her toes followed the edges of the hatch on which she stood.

Her eyes went to the blue shoes with the four-inch heels.

Chapter Sixteen

"The door is unlocked."

João had knocked, and now he entered Count Risponyi's suite. The Count was in a deep chair with a towel across his lap, holding a hand mirror and a small pair of golden scissors. He was trimming his brush moustache. João had expected him to be in a foul mood because they had not gotten the box they had gone after on the *Katja*. Instead, the little man was happy and rather jovial.

Risponyi pointed the golden scissors at João. "I shall tell you a story." The rhythm of the bullfrog croaks and the expression on his face indicated that the Count was laughing, and the way the laughter continued, it seemed uncontrollable. He wiped his eyes and caught his breath. "It is a very funny story."

João sat and lit a cigarette, preparing himself for some dull tale about Calcutta, India. Instead, he heard how the big Chinaman from Australia had destroyed his own encircling movement by using a fictitious French female named Madame Boulanger. When he was finished, they both laughed.

João remembered. "He used the same kind of theft when he stole that twenty tons of pepper from you on the Island of Celebes."

Risponyi's smile vanished. His eyes narrowed and his voice hardened. "This time it will be my turn."

"But how can we get the crate from the junk? Killinger will be prepared. It is an impossibility."

The Count's smile was thin. "It is my fervent hope that

Mr. Killinger believes that." He looked into the mirror as he worked on the moustache. "Supreme confidence leads to carelessness." The thin smile grew fatter. "That is all we will need."

"Have you formulated a plan?"

"*Two* plans, my dear O'Reilly." A small frog chuckle. "Two plans."

João moved closer, hoping to hear more.

Count Risponyi's blueprints had been stamped TOP SECRET and would remain that way until João had received a further security clearance. However, it was time for one small corner to be translated into motion. He pulled forth a fat envelope containing crisp currency. "I want you to buy two pounds of the finest ground beef. Also, you are to purchase one ounce of strychnine." He plucked a hundred-dollar bill from the envelope and handed it to João. Grandly: "You may keep whatever money remains."

João was conscious of having been turned into an errand boy. He hid his resentment. "Might I ask what will be done with the ground beef and strychnine?"

"You will poison Mr. Killinger's very noisy dogs."

Copper and Auric lay comfortably, watching Killinger and lazily wagging their tails.

Talya lay back on one of the couches, provocatively, with her knees high and her skirt fallen partway back. She sipped her champagne.

Killinger had never said the name K. Y. Smith to her. She had never mentioned her last name. They were both aware of this, in the game they played. Unless Killinger put the thought into words, she would ignore it. As a matter of policy, he would not.

The stereo was playing softly what Killinger thought of as Music for Making Love. The old numbers were the best. Arthur Prysock, Sinatra, Matt Monroe.

Talya finished her drink and held the glass to him.

He refilled it. Then his own.

She rolled on the thick cushions, turning her body to him,

her skirt falling back further. "Will you not say some words to accompany the champagne?"

He touched her glass with his, and he said some words.
"Time
walks slowly
as it runs
in circles.

Yet,
Time
never moves.
For
it is always
Now."

Talya drank with her eyes closed. She liked the philosophy she had just heard. She was a woman. The Time was Now. Her father had forced her to think of yesterday and of tomorrow. She had been rehearsed and trained and shaped by K. Y. Smith. She had never been permitted to think that "It is always Now."

She patted the couch next to her, and Killinger sat, leaning against her. His right hand held his glass. His left hand caressed the smoothness of her thigh. Call the texture velvet or silk or satin. It was the best of these, all together. Her skin was both cool and warm. The fragrance that arose from her was fresh as a mountain brook running over worn rocks. She was no longer the daughter of K. Y. Smith. She was an exquisite nymph. Virginal yet worldly.

Talya put her champagne glass on the teak decking. Then she took Killinger's and placed it next to hers. She put her arms around him and her cheek softly against his. It was almost the voice of a young and untouched girl. "Hold me." Two tiny tears fell. She hid them against his shoulder. "Do I feel like a machine?"

He held her tenderly, brushing his cheek against hers and kissing her gently. "No. You are a woman. You feel as a woman should feel."

She pressed her face into his shoulder, eyes closed.

"Sometimes, inside . . ." She fought the new tears. " . . . I am a machine."

His arms enclosed her until she released herself. Her eyes opened slowly. They were soft and dewy. She looked around her as though she had never seen any of this before. The tough tungsten-steel rods of her heart and mind had become young flesh and blood. Her gaze was that of a newly awakened child who had neither problems nor troubles. Like a high-school girl with her first love, Talya kissed him shyly.

Her arms moved around his large chest, making her seem even smaller. She sighed and leaned her cheek against him. In a little girl's voice, from afar, she spoke with a wondrous sweetness. "Please make love to me."

Killinger put his fingers under her chin and lifted it. Her lips were petals of crimson lotus, opening for the morning sun, shining and moist. Her hands fluttered to his cheeks, like butterflies. Her tongue tasted his lips and crept into his mouth. To Killinger, her flavor was exquisite.

Her eyes opened wide and swallowed him in their lustrous depths. She whispered one word: "Now."

Wordlessly, he took her hand and led her to the circular stairway. He descended two steps and turned, that he might see her face on a level. She was living a joyous dream. He kept his eyes on hers as he lifted her hand to his lips, palm up. As his lips caressed the smooth skin, she made a soft animal noise.

They went down the steps to Killinger's master cabin.

João Aranha Mijangos O'Reilly had a small amount of pride.

Cynicism might enable him to justify doing injury to human beings. Animals, especially beautiful dogs like Killinger's, fell into a different category. A man could raise beef cattle, for food. That was what he, himself, had done at one time on the broad Brazilian plains. But a dog was more like a baby that gave love, and, in return, only asked for love. He had dogs of his own, and he missed them.

He would not poison a dog!

From Risponyi's suite, he walked directly to the phone

booth which he had used earlier when he called the Chinaman. He put his money into the coin slot and dialed. After three rings, the phone was picked up.

The blue ice-cube eyes had watched Killinger's junk.

They had seen Talya, through the binoculars, follow Killinger to the staircase which led to below decks. He had watched their love-making closely. He had been pleased that the machine who was his daughter had been so evidently successful. However, he had watched the reaction on her face when Killinger had kissed the palm of her hand.

And he had been concerned. For she had seemed like someone else. Not the daughter he had indoctrinated to be an extension of himself.

The phone at his side had begun to ring.

On the third ring, he picked it up. "Yes."

"João Aranha Mijangos O'Reilly here."

"Precisely where?"

João told him.

"You will be picked up and driven here in a matter of minutes." The yellow hand placed the phone in its cradle.

His belly laughed while the frozen turquoise eyes stared inward, concentrating on his computer. His face was an expressionless mask.

Chapter Seventeen

In Calcutta it was early morning, with dawn hours away.

David Ochterlony's second houseboy answered the phone call from Oxnard, California. He told whoever it was in Oxnard that he would awaken Mr. Ochterlony and tell him about the call.

He was a well-trained servant. His instructions were that he was never to awaken the master of the household unless he had a fresh pot of tea and a cup in hand. So, naturally, he left the receiver off of its hook for many minutes, at four dollars a minute, until the tea was perfect.

Count Vaclav Risponyi waited for the bank's managing director to come on the line. His impatience was controlled for his mind was working on two levels. Top level was his blueprint, and David Ochterlony was an integral part of his Plan Number Two.

Ochterlony sipped his tea to wash away the cobwebs of sleep. He was aware that money was ticking away on the phone. But the cost of communication was none of his affair. He thought about money as any good banker should. Selfishly.

Finally: "Hello. David Ochterlony here."

"Good morning, David. Count Vaclav Risponyi, from Oxnard, California."

"Everyone knows about California." Pause for a sip of tea. "But what is Oxnard? And why did you call at this utterly ridiculous hour?"

Never aggravate your banker. "I shall send you some literature concerning Oxnard." A try at a friendly man-to-man chuckle. "By air, of course." A deep breath before the big question. "Has the report come through on my account? The warehouse receipts and my land holdings?"

Long aggravating wait for the Count while Ochterlony savored his tea. He cleared his throat in Calcutta, and a millisecond later, it was heard in Oxnard. "My pot of wake-up tea is quite good." Risponyi heard the next sip. "About your report. It came in this morning." A dry cackle. "I mean yesterday morning."

A large sharp-toothed steel trap snapped shut on Risponyi's stomach while he awaited the next words.

"First, the warehouse receipts. Exceptionally fluid."

The steel trap still held.

"About your holdings in land. I should like to commend you on your choice of crops." He smiled and nodded at the telephone. "My earlier assessment of your financial liquidity was a vast underestimation."

The trap opened, released Risponyi's insides, and disappeared. He felt Ochterlony's smile on the phone and he returned it. "The papers I signed for you were open-ended. Can I count on an additional $125,000, American?"

"Without question, Count Risponyi."

"Good. If I need it, I will phone."

"Then I will telex it immediately. You will have it within hours."

They hung up. The Count had completed an important part of Plan Number Two. He went back to work on his blueprints.

The two cats slow-blinked at Talya.

The door had been open to Killinger's bedroom and Coco Chanel and Lollipop had wanted their nap in comfort. They lay on the kingsize waterbed, listening to the music and watching the fish in the large tank at the side.

Talya walked down the two steps to the cats and began to scratch them behind their ears and on their tummies. They recognized her as a fellow feline when she cooed at them, and they talked to her. Killinger looked down at the three of them and smiled at the warm picture of three domesticated jungle creatures.

Talya examined the big room appreciatively. She liked the

feeling of all teak, and from where she lay, she could see the open bathtub and shower, carved of teak. She liked the openness and the opportunity for display of bodies. She looked at Killinger and laughed happily, rolling over on her back, reaching for him. "I am the love prisoner of that terrible pirate, Jedediah Killinger."

He came, barefoot, to the bed and lay beside her. She put her arms around him, and he held her close. She had never felt so much herself, so completely relaxed and free from worries and disturbing thoughts. Her dreamy eyes were caught by what seemed a familiar gleam on the ceiling. She focused on it and saw that it was a twin to the brass ring-bolt she had seen on the ceiling of the large living room directly above them.

The sight triggered a conditioned reaction, one which had been drilled into her since childhood. She was her father's machine, and she had been sent to obtain specific information. Talya was again a prisoner of her father's instructions, and her feeling of euphoria was smashed into dust.

Shock waves went through her, and Killinger felt them without knowing their source. As though electrically controlled, the girl in his arms had an automatic response. *Find the crate!!* She fought it briefly, closing her eyes in personal pain. Without sound, without moving her lips, she spoke to herself. "Damn! Damn! Damn! Why must I be my father's daughter . . . when I want to be me?" Her tears were deep inside.

The magnificent machine which had replaced the lovely lady rose from the bed, to the beat of the music. She danced sensuously to the languorous song, moving about the room. She saw no place for the crate. Her movements grew wilder, and as she spun, her feet kicked away the rugs on the decking. Tantalizingly, she undid the coronet braid around her head and started a long spinning, round and round. The last rug to be kicked aside was under the ring-bolt. Her feet felt deep cracks between the tight planking. She looked down and saw another hatch cover, fitted into the decking. The crate was below her, in the bottom hold.

Talya had the answer she was sent for.

Relief dripped into her blood and was carried through her body. Now, for a while, she could be Talya, her own woman. Her smile grew, and Killinger, watching, felt a change and a glow in her.

As she danced, she undid her gown, letting it slide from her. The silk clung like a thousand little hands, departing reluctantly. Not a gossamer wisp, not a thread destroyed the fluid lines of her supple body. Her breasts were luscious fruit, to be enjoyed in small bites. Her arms moved in utter grace. Her long lovely legs carried her with elegance.

Fires of passion had burned away the bad memories. Waves swept from this superb Eurasian girl, waves of love and loving. They broke against Killinger, whispering and teasing and exciting. They created pictures in which his face was buried in her long hair, in which he nibbled at her breasts and stroked her belly, in which her legs were wrapped around him, with her feet high and her toes pointed to the heavens.

She fell across the bed and rolled to him. From the roaring fires of the furnace of desire, Talya's voice spoke with a wondrous sweetness. "Love me . . . love me . . . love me. . . ." A jungle purr hummed low in her leopard's throat. "Now." The purr swelled to a scream. "Now!! . . ."

Talya became many women, moulded into one superb creature.

Killinger loved them all, that night, and he loved them well.

There were two green turbans in the front seat of the Mercedes-Benz 600.

One had acted as a footman and had opened the door for João. They had both been exceedingly polite. João had been impressed. And his feelings were automatically extended to K. Y. Smith when he was taken to the *Valhalla* and met the Chinaman for the second time.

The Australian accent dripped with heavy charm. "It is a pleasure to see you again, Senor Aranha Mijangos O'Reilly." He handed João an unsealed blue envelope with an engraved crest. The center of the crest was a hawk in flight. "Senor O'Reilly, I am a man of my word."

João took the envelope and looked into it. His great surprise could have enveloped the entire yacht *Valhalla*, together with its landing dock. It held a thick wad of green paper.

K. Y. Smith bellowed in laughter. The glee avoided his eyes. "When we spoke, I stated that I would pay you a substantial amount for your time." A theatrical gesture indicated the envelope. "Five thousand dollars." The computer stared at João through eyes of turquoise. "For the purpose of this meeting, your time is worth two thousand and five hundred dollars an hour. Therefore, we shall consult for two hours." He waved a hand and one of his green turbaned geniis placed a large clock with a sweep-second hand before him.

João was truly without words, unable to talk. His eyes watched what his mind could not believe. He held the blue envelope of money in both hands, afraid he would lose it. Money was so important to him.

Kuan Yang knew his man. "If, however, you are unable to spare me two precious hours . . ." Laughter rumbled and spewed forth. ". . . or if you deem my assessment of your worth to be insultingly low, I promise not to be offended if you return the envelope and the money."

João's two hands tightened around the five thousand dollars. "What you have been saying is a compliment of the highest order. For me to return the envelope would be an insult to your courtesy." The envelope went into his pocket. "Sir, believe me. Being in your company is an honor." A hand patted the envelope's resting place.

A yellow finger pressed the start button, and the second hand began its crawl around the clock, carefully counting up to $5,000.

Chapter Eighteen

Talya curled into a ball, her knees against her bare breasts.

She lay on her side, within the shelter of Killinger's arm, her head dreamily on his chest and her eyes closed. She was relaxed and warm and content. Physically, it had been perfect.

But she was unable to control her mind. The machine her father had created awoke, and its wheels began to spin. The shiny black leopard paced back and forth in its cage. Talya was again an extension of K. Y. Smith.

Somewhere below her, the crate was resting. Her father would consider "somewhere" to be incomplete information. Her instructions had been to deliver to the computer a complete series of pictures.

Rubbing against her, Killinger felt the light electric flow of tension move through her silken ivory skin. Subtle though the change was, it existed. As though to keep him from noticing, she kissed him and put his hand over her glorious breasts. She breathed deeply. Her fingers walked down his stomach and held him with light pressures.

The actions were right. Emotion had disappeared.

He asked. "Everything all right?"

"Perfect." She smiled her perfect smile. She rubbed her perfect body against him. She straddled him with her perfect legs. She nibbled him with her perfect teeth.

Perfection was an illusion. It had flown away.

Her fingers traced a meaningless map across his chest. "This is a lovely bedroom. . . ." Wheels spinning and the important question. "What is below us? Underneath?"

Killinger had expected this question from the moment she had come aboard. He was ready with his act. "Why don't I show you?"

"I'd like that."

After they dressed, he took her to the foot of the circular stairs outside his room. He swung back the section of decking that revealed a continuation of the stairs. Talya's eyes and mind photographed a complete picture. He turned on the lights, and they descended to the hold.

Her mental camera made a continual and rhythmic silent clicking. The wide angle lens missed nothing.

He showed her the engine housing, the driveshaft, the auxiliary generator. She listened and made proper responses and seemed terribly interested.

But her eyes stayed on the big safe, imbedded in concrete.

Paolo followed the Rolls-Bentley in his little black car.

Hawkins was driving to the Oxnard Airport. Count Vaclav Risponyi's mind was at the drawing board, putting neat white lines on crisp blue paper. This blueprint under construction was Plan Number One. The car was on its way to the airplane charter office and the pilot, Griff McLellan.

Risponyi had no need of an airplane. He was returning because of a certificate he'd seen on the wall behind Griff McLellan's desk. It was an honorable discharge from the U. S. Navy which stated that Griffith W. McLellan had been a member of an Underwater Demolition Team. He had been what is called a "frogman."

Ability to work underwater was the prime consideration of Plan Number One.

The British Royal Navy had once had a frogman named Vaclav Risponyi. The use of the title Count had been occasional since it had lost its solid base when Russia became the Union of Soviet Socialist Republics. Risponyi liked the respect which was automatically given to the invisible cloak of nobility.

In the beginning, he had to fight his lack of height. One of the ways was his acceptance of all challenges. His long and powerful arms, combined with his speed, made him a deadly opponent. Risponyi had been one of the great rope-climbers in international competition. This little known sport requires coordination and strength. It is a speedy hand-over-hand climb, and the competitors are capable of fantastic feats in the handling of their bodies. In an assault, the Count was fearless, and he was consistently first in reaching the top of the rope netting.

Griff McLellan's attitude had drawn the Count because it had reminded him of some of the many men who had fought and died at his side. It was the fuck-'em-all recklessness of a man who runs barefoot on the naked edge of the sword of life, laughing at death on both sides of the blade.

Hawkins parked in front of the airport office and opened the door for the Count. Risponyi entered the office. McLellan was pouring a glass of rosé wine from a gallon jug. When he saw the Count, he grinned and pulled over a second glass. "How about some cheap wine?"

Risponyi looked at the UDT certificate on the wall. He seemed to move backward in time to his days in the Royal Navy. He sat, put his feet up on the desk, and laughed. "Right ho. To the top."

McLellan filled the Count's glass exactly to the top, so that it was impossible to pick up without spilling. Risponyi's laughter was genuine. This old trick had not been played on him since he had been a frogman. He leaned over and sipped enough to make the glass manageable. Then, a big gulp. "Not bad."

"Especially for two and a half bucks a gallon." McLellan toasted Risponyi and drank.

McLellan was an exerciser. There was a chinning bar next to the closet. Risponyi walked to the bar, wine in his right hand. He reached up from his five-feet-two with his apelike left arm and grasped the bar. He chinned slowly five times. Then he switched the glass to the left hand and chinned five more times, with his right hand. He gestured a toast to the chinning bar and emptied his glass.

McLellan shook his head in amazement. "You're a better man than I am."

Risponyi chuckled. "That's a good way to begin a business relationship, acknowledging the leader." He indicated the UDT certificate. "Once upon a time, I was a frogman in the Royal Navy."

"Great." McLellan swallowed his wine. "We can kill this grape juice and bullshit each other to death." He refilled their glasses.

"Griffith W. McLellan!!" The name cracked like a whip. McLellan raised his head to the sound of command.

"Does money interest you?"

"Always has. Always will."

The monocle appeared from nowhere in twinkles of light. It settled in the Count's eye and shone at Griff McLellan. "I have a high-paying job for you." A short pause for effect. "And I must warn you that it is rather dangerous."

"Beautiful!" McLellan swallowed more wine. "I'm tired of the quiet life."

The sweep-second hand had just spent five thousand dollars.

Punching the proper keys to store João's information, the computer which looked at the world through chill blue eyes felt that the money had been well used. K. Y. Smith had bought himself a lackey.

The Chinaman had made it an integral part of the deal that João would continue to work for the Count. Further, that the Brazilian should keep every penny he received from the little man. Besides, Kuan Yang's financial inducement was unbeatable as well as simple. For every dollar João received from Risponyi, K. Y. Smith would pay him an additional two. So, if he made $10,000 from the Count, the Chinaman would give him $20,000 more—for relaying all information. A total of $30,000. And the $5,000 ticked off by the second hand was to be considered a bonus, over and above all future monies.

Great good humor was audible in the powerful, bellowing laughter. "Senor O'Reilly, we have completed the use of your time. I shall now allow you a small bit of my time so that you may ask questions." The bellows reached a peak. "You cannot afford my rates. Consider it a donation to our cause." There

194

was neither laughter, nor chuckle, nor smile. The non-circuit turquoise eyes gripped João tightly.

Sitting before K. Y. Smith, João was wrapped in a thin and chilly fabric of fear. He forced out one question. "The statue . . . the Chin P'ing Mei . . . why is it worth so much?"

The speech became more Australian with each word. "Does not a precious and ancient jade statue of a beautiful woman have appeal for you?"

João nodded.

"And if this jade statue were on a jewel-encrusted throne, would there not be great value?" K. Y. Smith interrupted himself to throw some words in Chinese over his shoulder at a green turban.

João's attention was undistracted.

The Chinaman's teeth stared at O'Reilly in a smile. "I believe that the words you used in telling about Count Vaclav Risponyi's explanation were . . . uh . . . 'cock-and-bull' . . . when he had claimed that the crate held only a hand-tooled sealskin case with his grandfather's name on it. Also, you stated that he said the case contained something of little worth."

João's nods were in agreement.

The green turban placed an ancient volume before K. Y. Smith. All writing was in Chinese. A yellow finger tapped the book. "In the year 1568, of the Gregorian calendar, this book was written." The chuckle was soft and lewd. "It is mostly concerned with the glorious and universal . . ." Laughter took over briefly. " . . . sport of inventive fornication." Sudden absolute quiet. A flat, hard voice. "The title of the book is *Chin P'ing Mei.*"

João Aranha Mijangos O'Reilly was thoroughly confused.

K. Y. Smith brought his game to a close. "The crate from Hong Kong contains exactly what the good Count Risponyi said it does."

Chapter Nineteen

Talya took the twin stilettos from the shelf behind the bar.

She slipped on the cerulean silk-covered shoes. Then she got on tiptoe to kiss Killinger good-bye before leaving the *Sybaris*. His eyes followed the four-inch heels all the way down the gangplank.

Killinger returned to the master cabin and put on his work-out clothes. He had had a completely full day, with the attempted robbery of the chest and his time spent with Elena and Talya. So long as he exercised regularly, he kept himself close to a physical peak. He began with the one-man Karate work-out, doing the groups of exercises which use the different combinations of Karate movements. These are called *pinan* and *saifa*. They keep the reflexes fast and almost automatic.

He followed the Karate exercises with a short weight-lifting session. He did sets of military presses, building to a top weight of two hundred fifty pounds. Next, his sets of supine presses with four hundred pounds on the barbell. Finally, sets of "cheat curls," f   the biceps, using two hundred pounds.

Killinger was strong, but he was far from the best weightlifter around. He ran, but he wasn't the fastest runner. In Karate, he wasn't a champ. However, as in a decathlon, the final total of points from each event marks the champion. Killinger always ran up a good score.

As his body worked, his mind cleared. He thought out his problems. Actually, they were all in one place. Seven feet below him and about twenty feet nearer the stern. Locked in a safe that was imbedded in concrete. Away from harm.

The low tone of the gong rolled through the junk. A visitor.

João stared at K. Y. Smith in shock.

He had just heard the blue-eyed Aussie say that the crate everybody wanted actually contained a sealskin case with the name of Risponyi's grandfather imprinted on the leather. While he worked on lining up what facts he had heard, and doing it logically, the phone at K. Y. Smith's elbow rang.

On the third ring, a big yellow hand picked it up. "Yes."

This was the way it had been when João had phoned. Same formula. João was not privy to both sides of the conversation. He missed what was being said in what were, to him, long silences.

"Paolo here. I am in a telephone booth at the airport. Count Risponyi is in the office of Griff McLellan, plane charters."

"What are they doing?" The freezing blue eyes ignored João.

"I looked through the window. They were drinking from a gallon of wine with their feet on the desk. They had a framed piece of paper that the Count had taken from the wall. I was too far away to read it all. However, in big letters it said: Griffith W. McLellan ... United States Navy ... and the letters 'U', 'D', and 'T'. They were together as one word, UDT."

"I will be here." The big yellow hand hung up. Cold, empty blue eyes held João in a refrigerator.

João's curiosity was acute. He tried to hide it with a casual note. "Something important?"

Kuan Yang ignored the question. "You will be taken to your hotel." He motioned to a green turban behind him. It was Teffki. "You will drive Senor O'Reilly."

Teffki bowed his head respectfully. "Yes, sir."

Dismissal: "Good day, Senor. I shall hear from you." It was an order, not a question.

Teffki started for the companionway. João followed. He now had seven thousand dollars, in cash. There was much more to be made. One hand patted the pocket with the engraved blue envelope, reassuringly.

Count Risponyi's head was covered with thick white foam.

He sat in a straight-backed chair, wrapped in a large cloth, getting a haircut. A haircut for him consisted of a shave from his Adam's apple to the top of his head, with a small trim for the big brush moustache. His barber was a female, for when he had phoned asking for service in his room, a female had answered. Since she had a low, soft, sexy voice, he had hired her.

While her bosom was almost forty inches, her waist was nearer forty-seven, and her hips continued the outward flare. The Count was unhappy.

Griff McLellan enjoyed the scene from a soft couch where he sat working on a bottle of a good Pinot Noir wine. He rose to answer a knock at the door. It was João. Risponyi indicated that João was all right. McLellan went back to his wine, and João did simple arithmetic, figuring how much money he could get from the little man in the barber chair.

The lady barber finished the shave and blotted Risponyi's head. Its gleam lit up the room. He paid her, and she left, throwing him a farewell smile of badly done silver inlays.

Risponyi stared at the closed door. "It is inconceivable that a woman like that should own the voice of Venus."

Griff McLellan gave the Count a glass of wine. "I'll bet seven pesos that when you were a frogman, without a chick for months, you'd have settled for a beast like that."

Risponyi held up his hand. He shuddered as he drank his wine. "Please." Another sip. "Memories of that sort are better forgotten." Introducing them: "João Aranha Mijangos O'Reilly . . . this is Griffith W. McLellan."

João and McLellan gave each other cold acknowledgements. Neither knew the other's place in this scene.

Risponyi gave partial explanations. "O'Reilly assures me that he is an expert on motors and boats." He looked to João.

João nodded.

"McLellan is a former UDT man. Better known as a frogman."

McLellan toasted to that with the wine glass. He emptied it in a gulp and turned to João with a big, friendly grin. "Sounds like we're gonna work together. How 'bout some wine?"

"A very good idea."

The Count held his glass for McLellan to refill. "We shall be a team." He gave them a quick rundown on his blueprint. Basically, the plans were simple. A surprise attack, combined with a speedy taking of the crate, and a quick withdrawal. Risponyi and McLellan would swim underwater to the junk, climb aboard, using three-pronged throwing hooks on a nylon line, and overpower whoever was aboard. They would have lightweight hooks and pulleys with them for lifting the crate and lowering it to the motorboat which João would run, bringing it alongside on signal.

McLellan wondered aloud: "Who and/or what are the big obstacles?"

Risponyi elaborated. "O'Reilly will destroy the watchdogs by using a slingshot to put pellets of poisoned meat aboard. And a young lady whom you have not yet met will keep Jedediah Killinger III occupied."

At that moment, Elena had a hand raised to knock on Risponyi's door. She heard voices inside. Quickly, she looked to either side, up and down the corridor. Not another person in sight. She put her ear to the door. After all, she'd read about spying in books, and she knew what to do.

Inside, Risponyi turned to João, as he explained: "O'Reilly has met the main problem. A three-hundred pound Chinaman, named K. Y. Smith."

João was quick to interrupt. "But that was just the one time, aboard the *Katja*."

"Of course. To continue, it is impossible to mistake him. His eyes are a turquoise blue, and he speaks with an Australian accent."

McLellan laughed. "He'd sure as hell stand out in a crowd."

Count Vaclav Risponyi made his point with measured firmness. "The blueprint will work—so long as Jedediah Killinger III and K. Y. Smith do not learn of our plans."

João Aranha Mijangos O'Reilly looked at the ceiling, his hand on the engraved blue envelope.

There was a knock at the door.

K. Y. Smith's computer examined Count Risponyi's blueprint.

Paolo's phoned information concerning the UDT certificate was the key. Count Vaclav Risponyi's complete background was contained within the computer's memory banks. His frogman background in the Royal Navy had been printed clearly on the read-out tube. No facts had shown to negate the subtotal which had read "the attack will be made underwater."

Senor O'Reilly would shortly furnish necessary details about the people concerned and the time set for the operation.

When Talya had told her father the location of the crate, the effect on the computer was exactly the same as though she had been plugged in, a switch had been turned on, and each picture her mind had snapped had been thoroughly absorbed and filed accurately. She was part of the machinery.

The blueprint was a pincers movement.

Complete encirclement was planned by the computer.

Chapter Twenty

Katja Mylius O'Reilly held the hammer by its violet silken cord.

She had struck Pangkalanbuun a second time, and his bass roar rumbled across the deck, meeting Killinger when he came to the top of the circular stairway. Both Pangkalanbuun, the devil from Borneo, and Killinger paid homage to the redhaired beauty. Her state of near exhaustion seemed to soften her and make her more fragile.

A small celebration seemed demanded, and Killinger took her to the bar in the living room at the stern of the main deck. While he poured her a Jack Daniel's on the rocks, she told him the good news. Her grandfather had been operated on, and it had been a complete success. However, he would be under heavy sedation and unable to have visitors for almost twenty-four hours.

Killinger had thought that her arrival was well timed. As yet, she knew nothing of the robbery attempts. Before telling her, he needed answers. "Who is the legal owner of the schooner and its contents?"

"My grandfather."

"While he is unconscious, is there someone authorized to act in his place?"

"Oh, yes." She pointed to herself. "Me."

Things might be easier than he had thought. "Is there a legal document?"

She nodded. "One copy is on file with Mylius Shipping Lines. Another with the attorneys. And, I believe, a third with the insurance company." A small bitter laugh. "It states that I am my grandfather's attorney-in-fact. I am empowered to sell the shipping lines." Tired smile. "Are you interested?"

"Not 'til I read the profit and loss statement." He shifted from a smile to deep seriousness and told her the whole story about the crate, attempted robberies, and his moving the crate to the big safe, below.

He left out the parts which concerned Talya and Elena.

She was fascinated. "I wish I knew what this was all about."

"If you give me permission to open the wooden box, we may learn."

Mock seriousness. "As attorney-in-fact, I, Katja Mylius O'Reilly, do hereby give to Jedediah Killinger III permission to open said crate and handle its contents in any way he deems proper." She laughed. "Is that good enough?"

"Perfect."

"Uh . . . one more thing. You must promise to tell me what's inside."

He offered her his hand. "It's a deal."

"Who needs handshakes to seal a deal?" She threw her arms around his neck and kissed him.

Now she was a hungry little girl, pouting and asking, "Have you a sandwich, or something? I haven't eaten all day."

"Let's go down to the kitchen and dig up something good."

She glanced down at her hands. "Where can I wash up?"

He led her to the sink in his master cabin and left her to get the food. After he had chopped and sliced salad and goodies, he was ready to broil double French lamb chops. But she hadn't returned. He went to find her.

He opened the door to his bedroom suite and looked in. The dim light showed him a figure in the middle of his bed. It was curled in a ball, like a baby in the safety of its own crib.

Katja was sound asleep, completely dressed. She hadn't even removed her shoes. The strain had wiped her out.

He unfolded a blanket and threw it over her.

The telephone rang at the side of the bed. Katja didn't budge. Killinger got it before the second ring. He whispered, "Hello."

A woman's voice. "Hello, Jed. It's me, Elena."

Killinger had told Elena that when she called him, there had to be a way of telling him whether she was alone, or with Count Risponyi. Using the name Jed meant that the Count was listening. He played it cool.

"Hi, luv. What's on your mind?"

Risponyi was listening on an extension phone which had a long enough cord for him to walk to the door of his room and watch Elena as she spoke.

Elena glanced at Risponyi, but she spoke to Killinger. "I want to see you."

Still whispering: "I want to see you, too, luv."

"Good. I will be right there."

"Sorry, Elena. Not now."

Her voice rose a note, in anger. "Why you whisper?"

"I'll explain when I see you."

Accusation. "You have a woman there!"

Risponyi mouthed the words: "In the morning."

She nodded to the Count and continued. "How about you feed me an early breakfast and explain this whole thing?"

"We have a date."

"I be there at eight, sharp. You better be alone!" She slammed down the receiver.

It was early morning in Amsterdam, Holland. Mynheer van der Helft sat over his morning coffee reading his notes. He picked up his phone and asked for a number in Oxnard, California. In minutes, his party was on the line.

The international operator had identified van der Helft to Killinger, who took the call in the living room. It had been person-to-person. "What took you so long, Mynheer?"

"I believe I acted with great haste. You requested certain

information, and I have obtained certain facts for you." Sipping coffee and with a sad tone: "Have you any idea of the cost of the many calls I made?" Complaint: "It was necessary to phone all over Asia."

"Any leads in Hong Kong?"

"That is the city in which I started. To learn about Kuan Yang Smith, it was necessary to talk to several people at great length in Singapore." Tired sigh. "For Count Risponyi, it was Calcutta."

"What did you learn?"

"Both gentlemen are far too well known, in the wrong circles. Neither has been convicted of anything criminal." Van der Helft lit a long green cheroot, blowing the smoke at the ceiling. "Believe me, the police of several countries have tried. They are both men of means. However, K. Y. Smith can be termed 'wealthy'."

"Have you dug up any signs of their having worked together? Say, in partnership?"

"Regarding a friendship between these men, I can state, unequivocally, that they have a long history of enmity. There is no record of their having been anything less than head-to-head competitors."

"Mynheer, are you relaxed?"

Testily: "Of course I am relaxed." Calming and a realization that Killinger was leading to something: "Why? What has gone wrong?"

"Nothing. And everything."

"Please do not play games at these telephone rates."

Killinger figured the best way was direct truth. "There has been a second attempted robbery of the crate."

"What does it contain that could cause trouble?"

Killinger told van der Helft every detail to that moment, including Katja Mylius O'Reilly's permission to open the crate.

Of course, he didn't mention the episodes with Elena and Talya. Knowing Killinger, van der Helft would have believed every word.

Van der Helft helped Killinger's decision. "Open that troublesome box immediately. If it is of any importance, phone me." Several nervous puffs on the green cheroot. "Under no conditions are we courting publicity. It would not be to the best interests of The Association for the Improvement of Marine Insurance."

"Understood."

Van der Helft hung up. He took a deep puff of the green cheroot. From his lips a gigantic smoke ring floated upwards. Mynheer contemplated it. No answer came forth.

The fantail of the yacht *Valhalla* lay in absolute darkness.

K. Y. Smith's computer worked best under those conditions. The unblinking blue eyes rested without expression in their pools of liquid hydrogen, throwing deep cold wherever they pointed.

Buttons had been pushed. Keys had been punched. Subtotal after subtotal had come up on the read-out tube. Alternatives had been consistently examined and reexamined for flaws.

The cat's-paw was Plan Number One. Count Risponyi was an efficient operator. As the Chinaman learned the good Count's blueprint from Senor O'Reilly, he would plan meticulously. And the little man from Calcutta would find that his empty paws had been burnt by the fire.

The binoculars had followed Katja Mylius O'Reilly aboard the junk. Unfortunately, there seemed to be no immediate way of learning what had happened between them.

Movement on the dock near the *Sybaris* caught his eye. He turned the telescope to the spot. Three people. Killinger's employees.

Copper and Auric barked big hellos to Marjorie, Kimo, and Samantha. The dogs followed the three to the living room where Killinger was munching sandwiches and drinking beer. He had called to them.

He waved his mug. "Beer, anyone?"

They were a sad-looking group. No answer.

Killinger tried again. "What's the bad news?"

Marjorie was angry. "I'm sure glad I split from that place."

Kimo began pouring beer into the chilled mugs he took from the chest under Ho-Tai's feet. He pulled Ho-Tai's upraised right hand down, and the cold, frothy liquid of German Pilsener poured forth through Ho-Tai's lips, open wide in laughter and good cheer. He passed the mugs around.

Killinger cut the plate of sandwiches into quarters and placed them in the center of the bar. He asked Marjorie: "Why are you glad you split?"

"Everybody's a militant. No one laughs. Blacks and Whites."

"Aren't you militant?" he asked quietly.

Hard: "Was! Not am!" She took a beer mug from Kimo. She waved it. "They're militant about beer!" She picked up a piece of sandwich. "Sandwiches!" She took an angry bite. "Everything!"

Killinger turned to Kimo. "Lousy evening?"

Kimo shook his head. "Lousy? Man, they took the world's heaviest drag and stuck it in this little house. Nobody had a happy word about anything."

Marjorie indicated the junk with a sweep of her arm. "Maybe this floating palace has me twisted. Maybe they're right, and we're wrong."

"Maybe." Killinger smiled. "Then again, you might be right and they're wrong." Marjorie's seriousness had to be broken down somehow. Killinger tried with a line from left field. "Sorry we don't have any prunes up here."

Marjorie repeated the word, first not understanding. "Prunes?" Then, it hit her, and she giggled. All was well.

Samantha, wise to Killinger and his ways, turned her eyes around the big room. Something indefinable hit her. "You got a woman aboard, and we're in the way." She laughed. Where is she?"

"Where else? In my bed."

Samantha and Kimo appreciated that. But Marjorie suddenly stiffened and pretended a yawn. "I'm tired. I'm going to sleep."

"Marjorie, I'd appreciate it if you'd give Samantha a hand.

The lady in question should really be getting up and going home."

Marjorie was stuck and she knew it. She became insufferably haughty. "I do hope that Miss Talya Smith isn't ill."

Killinger laughed. "When you see Miss Smith, you can ask her."

The telescope followed Katja Mylius O'Reilly as she left the *Sybaris* and walked to her own schooner.

The guard saluted her aboard. When she went below, the lights went on.

K. Y. Smith was certain that Killinger had said something to her about the missing crate. A computer read-out indicated clearly that Killinger had told her the complete story.

It didn't require a computer read-out for Smith to believe it was a shame that the crate had been moved to the safe in the hold of the *Sybaris*.

Killinger used a crowbar to open the metal straps, removing the nails.

The safe was open, and the crate was on a dolly under the hanging light. The straps gave easily. They covered a line of screws which Killinger removed without trouble.

The lid lifted easily.

Leather showed, It might have been sealskin. Russian Cyrillic script had been written over the old lock. A map was laid out on the leather in seed pearls, with four rubies and three emeralds as markers.

So far, it matched Count Risponyi's description.

Using a small screwdriver and a pick, he opened the brass lock. The leather was still soft, and the case-trunk opened easily.

It was full of metal that reflected golden lights into his eyes.

Pile after pile of golden coins. One thousand pounds of precious metal in the form of money.

The going price for gold at the U. S. Treasury was about $560 a pound. Or over a half-million dollars. At $35 an ounce.

On the international market, gold was being quoted at about $90 an ounce. That way, at about $1,440 a pound, Killinger was looking at a little less than $1,500,000.

He picked up one of the coins and held it to the light. It was imprinted in the French language. It was a French Napoleon, the famous golden coin minted by Napoleon Bonaparte after the Revolution.

The Napoleon in his hand was dated 1813.

Seventy-two hours ago, the schooner *Katja* had brushed a barge in a storm off California's Pacific Coast.

the
fourth
day . . .

Chapter One

K. Y. Smith tried to project his body to the *Sybaris,* invisibly.

It did not happen. He remained on the fantail of the *Valhalla,* wrapped in darkness. The computer waited for instructions.

The two-way radio at his side crackled and spoke. "Paolo here. Count Risponyi's chauffeur has taken Griffith W. McLellan to his office. Mr. McLellan was staggering and laughing. The chauffeur helped him open the door."

"You may take the remainder of the evening off. Report in at six-thirty."

"Six-thirty. Yes, sir." A moment for thought. "In the morning?"

"Of course." A yellow finger turned off the transmitting button.

Evidently, the good Count had been celebrating with this UDT man. The conclusion was that they had consummated a business arrangement.

His telephone sounded with a muted bell. On the third ring, it was picked up. "Yes."

"Hello, Mr. Smith. This is João Arnaha Mijangos O'Reilly."

"I am listening, Senor." A friendly chuckle to reassure the Brazilian. "You have good news, I am certain."

"Indeed, Mr. Smith. And it is of great importance." A drop in voice volume while presenting a precious jewel. "I have come from a meeting with Count Risponyi." A pause to make his announcement seem of greater worth. "Another man was present. His name is Griffith W. McLellan."

Permit the Brazilian to think his information was both

important and secret. "How interesting. Who is Mr. McLellan?"

"He is an airplane pilot who was an Underwater Demolition man with the United Stated Navy." As though explaining to an uninitiate: "He is a frogman. That means he can operate underwater. Also, Count Risponyi had been a frogman with the British Royal Navy."

"How clever of you to have learned this, Senor O'Reilly." Complete confirmation of information thus far received. Thus, facts fed to the computer were truths. "If you continue in this fashion, you might be worth a small bonus at the conclusion of our relationship."

João felt doubly good at this sign of approbation. "There is yet more, Mr. Smith. Count Risponyi has ordered a girl named Elena to have breakfast with Killinger at eight o'clock this morning. She is to learn where the crate is kept. Later she will have other duties. When I learn them, I shall phone you."

"I expect you to phone much sooner than that. Several times, as a matter of fact."

The iron tone flattened João. "Yes, Mr. Smith."

K. Y. Smith hung up abruptly.

Killinger had put the crate back together.

The screws had been put back into their original holes, and the nails had been similarly replaced. There was no sign tthat the box had been opened without counting the golden Napoleons. Five were missing.

They were in Killinger's pocket. He rolled the dolly back into the safe, closed the door, and spun the lock. All was secure.

Killinger turned off the light.

Sunrise of this fourth morning cleared away the early mists. The sky was clear.

A beam of sunshine had awakened Katja, and she had left the schooner extra early, for she wanted to be at the hospital at eight o'clock. Killinger was on the poop of the junk, playing with the dogs, and he saw her. He called: "Morning! Had your coffee?" He had been waiting for her to show.

She smiled and waved up to him. "Not yet. I hope it's an invitation."

"It is."

Killinger raided Marjorie's desk for a pen, papers, and carbons. Katja accepted morning kisses from the two Vizslas. Lollipop greeted her and then walked away. Coco Chanel rubbed against her legs. They all went into the deck living room where Killinger had a pot of coffee and Danish coffee-cake ready. While she drank her coffee, Killinger wrote a release form for her to sign, in triplicate. He needed a copy to mail to van der Helft and one for his own files. The third copy was for her.

He put them before her for her signature. She signed without reading, between bites of the cake.

He was concerned. "Don't you read what you sign?"

She fluttered her sea-green eyes at him. "But I trust you."

"Then I'll trust you."

Katja patted his knee, leaving her hand there, briefly. Her smile was fun. "Don't."

He gave her a copy of the release. She kissed him on the tip of his nose and left for the hospital, folding the paper as she walked.

Killinger hadn't told her about opening the crate.

Turquoise eyes watched Katja leave the junk.

The telescope saw her stop at the head of the gangway and open her shoulder bag. She folded a paper she was holding and placed it in the bag. After throwing a kiss to Killinger, she left.

Clicking silently, the computer digested the new information and put a read-out on the tube. Papers which needed folding were new. New papers came from Killinger. Katja Mylius O'Reilly was on her way to the hospital. Businesslike procedures on the part of an insurance company's representative required copies for everything.

The read-out said that Killinger wanted an authorization

213

to open the crate, and that the paper which Katja Mylius O'Reilly folded was to be signed by her grandfather, Mylius O'Reilly.

Therefore, said the read-out, the crate would remain sealed until Ejnar Mylius put his name on a form of release.

K. Y. Smith reached for the phone and dialed St. John's Hospital. He asked after his dear friend, Ejnar Mylius, and said that he would like to pay a visit to the hospital room. The floor nurse told him that Mr. Mylius was under heavy sedation, and that no one, absolutely no one, could see him for quite a while.

K. Y. Smith hung up, secure in the knowledge that the secret of the crate was safe for at least another day. He sat in his brilliantly colored silk mandarin robe, wearing a buttoned mandarin cap, and contemplated the new day with optimism. His laugh sounded like the growling of the two fiery red-green dragons embroidered on his robe.

A cough from the transceiver at his side was followed by a distorted voice. "Paolo here. The English chauffeur drove Count Risponyi and Mr. O'Reilly to Mr. McLellan's office. They then went to a small deserted boatyard in a cove of the harbor. They are now standing beside a boat which is covered by canvas."

"Keep your eyes open."

"Yes, sir." The transceiver coughed again at close of transmission.

The computer sang to itself, without words or music.

The boat was seventeen feet long, with a wide beam and an inboard motor. Low, wide, and squat, it gave a feeling of power. The tarpaulin was lashed tight all around. McLellan got to his knees to open the lock. He checked carefully. "Nobody's touched it." João helped him pull back the canvas. Risponyi walked around it judiciously.

McLellan was proud of the craft. "What do ya think, ol' buddy?"

Risponyi nodded and permitted a fractional smile. "Quite good. In fact, rather better than I had expected."

"Dig the low gunwales. Easy to swing up, out of the water, when you're carryin' something."

João walked to the motor and squatted next to it.

McLellan volunteered information. "Motor's in perfect tune."

João rose. "If I am to be responsible for its use, I must check it out."

Risponyi approved. "Please do so while I examine the other equipment."

McLellan moved to a big locker. "You'll like it. Block, tackle, hooks, nylon line." He grinned. "It'll remind you of the rubber suit days of your youth."

Excitement dripped into Risponyi's bloodstream.

Chapter Two

Killinger made a lovely breakfast for Elena.

He put the whole thing into the dumbwaiter which was fitted into a corner of the kitchen. At the push of a button, it would rise on its cable, guided by tracks, to the main deck level. There, a door on one side led to an opening in the living room, for service inside. Another opening faced the deck, for people who might be there. The dumbwaiter held an electric warmer which would keep the ham steak and eggs as well as the toasted and buttered English muffins at the proper temperature. The electric coffee pot was set for "warm" and would stay that way. The grapefruit juice was in ice. A special button would lower the dumbwaiter to the hold, near the safe.

Pangkalanbuun called twice as he was struck two rapid blows. The low aftertone walked the decks of the junk. Killinger looked at the wall-clock. Elena was on time.

He ran up the steps to meet her. She was lovely and fetching and beautiful and exciting, all at once. Risponyi had instructed her to look her best, and she did.

Elena kissed Killinger perfunctorily, like a maiden aunt. "Good morning." She had capped an interior explosion, holding it tight. "Your guest of last night. She is gone?"

Killinger nodded.

"What time did she leave?"

Killinger laughed.

The interior explosion was uncapped. Elena was angry. "Why do you laugh at me?" She pounded his chest with a fist. "Why? Why?"

They had walked into the living room. Killinger held both her hands, as a matter of self-protection. "Tell me, Elena, would you believe anything I said about last night?"

She looked at him, her lower lip stuck out. After a few seconds, she began to smile. Then she laughed. "I do not think I would believe you."

He dropped her hands. "Why ask questions when you don't want answers?"

"You are correct." She threw her arms around his neck and kissed him thoroughly while she rubbed her body against him. "We have all day together." She pressed into him, hard. "Is not that wonderful?"

Killinger took her arms from his neck and stepped back. "What are your instructions?"

"Business right away! You do not ask how I am or how I slept."

He grinned at her. "How do you feel? Did you sleep well?" He pushed the button for the dumbwaiter. "So much for the formalities. Now, again, what are your instructions?"

"I am supposed to seduce you." She laughed. "While you are helpless in my arms and fascinated by my charms, you are supposed to tell me where a wooden crate is."

"A good beginning. And after that?"

"While you lie in bed, recovering from much love, I am supposed to see where doors and windows and things like that are." She took a pad and pencil from her purse. "From time to time, I must go to the bathroom and make sketches of what I have seen." A pout. "Count Risponyi said to meet him at eleven o'clock. So we have only three hours."

"Anything else? Anybody else? Try to remember."

She bit her lip in thought. "There was a Griff McLellan with the Count. He and João O'Reilly were there. All of them talking."

A valuable bit of information. Killinger had skindived with Griff McLellan a few times. He knew that the man had been an UDT type. He assessed the situation.

Meanwhile, Elena had put her hand in his lap. She patted and stroked him, and then tried to open his zipper. He stopped her. "Why do you stop me when your trousers are wearing that funny expression?"

"First things first. Take out your pad and pencil."

He pointed to the ring-bolt above them. "That shiny brass circle is called a ring-bolt. Do a sketch of it."

While she drew, he took the breakfast from the dumbwaiter and laid it out for them. Her pencil strokes had been fast, and she held the sketch up for him to see. Her work was surprisingly good. She wrote while he described what the ring-bolt was for.

Killinger put her fruit juice before her. "Time for breakfast. Later, I will show you two sets of hatch covers, which you will draw. After that, you can make a picture of the crate and where it is."

"I do not understand why you want to help Count Risponyi."

"Don't worry. Everything will be fine."

Killinger looked up to see Marjorie and Samantha going to work in the office on the bow of the junk. He turned to Elena. "Here. Help yourself. And don't leave." He pushed the food tray to her and ran out of the living room.

Marjorie frowned as she looked across the deck of the *Sybaris*. Samantha looked to see what caused the concern. They both saw Elena working over her pad, pencil in hand and food by her side.

Marjorie snarled, "Another one." Headshake in disbelief. "That redhead, last night. Talya Smith in the afternoon. How does he do it?"

"Vitamins," Samantha laughed. "You know that Mrs. O'Reilly was exhausted from being at the hospital all day."

"Maybe! But what about that Talya Smith?" Indicating with her head. "And now that chick."

"Any chick who comes here at eight in the morning with a pencil and pad has gotta be here on business."

A sniff. "What kind of business?"

Killinger ran across the deck from the living room to the office.

"Morning, ladies."

Samantha grinned. Marjorie ignored him.

"Samantha, you better run over to the post office and check the mailbox."

"Right, boss." She knew he wanted to talk to Marjorie, so Samantha left immediately.

"Marjorie, would you get me Professor Breitland, please. His number's on the roller."

Marjorie found the listing and dialed the number. "Professor Breitland, please. Mr. Killinger is calling." She listened to the reply and turned her face up to him. "It's Mrs. Breitland. She says he's gone to class."

Killinger took the phone from her. "Regina? Jed Killinger. I have a favor to ask of Bob." He looked at Marjorie as he spoke. "My secretary will be there in a half-hour. Her name is Marjorie Stafford. She'll have a coin. It's something special. Give it to Bob and have him call me when he returns." He listened, smiled. "Right. And all of my love, too." He hung up.

Killinger gave the address to Marjorie and told her the shortcuts, to save time.

She held out her hand. "The coin."

Killinger placed a Napoleon in her hand. She stared at it. "Gold." She hefted it. "Solid."

He explained, "Professor Breitland is in the Geology Department of the University of California at Santa Barbara. He's also a numismatist. A coin collector." He took her left wrist and turned it so that he could read her watch. "Figure around two hours round trip, with coffee and everything."

Nastily: "I don't want coffee."

He looked at her hard. "Regina Breitland is a lovely lady. I don't care if she asks you to drink coffee or cold clam chowder. You'll drink it. That's an order." No smile.

Uncertainty. "But . . . she may be . . . uh . . ." The problem came into the light, unwillingly. "I mean . . . I'm black. . . ."

"So is Regina Breitland."

Marjorie gave Killinger a long look. She swallowed and smiled apologetically. A laugh. "I don't get to use that l'il ol' '55 T-Bird enough." She started out and stopped and turned to him, holding the Napoleon. "All that trouble for this ol' thing. What's it worth, anyway?"

"Possibly someone's life."

219

Chapter Three

A turquoise eye followed a black girl through a silver telescope.

She crossed the deck of the *Sybaris* with one hand clenched into a fist. The other held her purse. K. Y. Smith paid her no attention. His computer had nothing to say about Marjorie Stafford. The telescope did not pick up a golden glint from the 1813 Napoleon she gripped so tightly.

The big Chinaman dismissed Killinger's secretary as being less than nothing in importance.

He picked up the telephone at his elbow on its third ring. "Yes."

"This is João Aranha Mijangos O'Reilly. I spent the morning with Count Risponyi and Griff McLellan."

As though he hadn't known, Kuan Yang came on with his syrupy tone. "Wonderful, my boy. Wonderful. You must tell me about it."

João did, with little encouragements from the chill-eyed Chinaman. O'Reilly said nothing that Smith didn't already know. He concluded the brief report. "I shall phone you as soon as I know the planned assault time."

"When will you know it?"

"As soon as Elena returns with the information she was sent to obtain."

The smile was in his controlled voice. It did not touch his lips or eyes. "I will be hearing from you." He broke the connection.

The huge yellow man with the Australian accent pointed the telescope at the junk, looking for Elena. It would be

220

interesting to learn whether the girl from Peru would have a success comparable to Talya's.

Elena's clothes marked a small trail across Killinger's bedroom.

There were but four items. One dress. One pair of sheer briefs. Two shoes. They pointed to the teak bathtub where Elena lay having a wonderful time in the warm water.

Killinger entered with a freshly opened bottle of sparkling burgundy and two glasses which he filled. A silent toast to the joys and wonders of making love, and they drank.

Elena held up a giant bar of emerald green soap. "You will make me to lather all over, and I will make you to lather . . ." Evil chuckle. ". . . all over."

"I guess a fellow can't lose on a deal like that."

"Why are you still wearing clothes?"

No answer to that one. Killinger stepped out of his Levi's and shirt and ended up naked.

Her eyes outsparkled the burgundy. "I have never before made love in a teak bathtub."

Three thoughts hit Killinger. First: Approximately 125 calories are used up in a sex act. Second: Fornication is no more tiring than a hundred-yard dash. Third: Today's two-mile run might be a bit slower than usual.

Elena gave a small scream, as a reminder. Killinger laughed and turned up the volume of the stereo speakers.

After a while, she screamed again. And again. And again. And again.

Elena left the junk, walking with a lively bounce and swing.

The frozen eyes ignored her as a woman and considered her as a container of information for Count Risponyi. Within minutes, the good Count would have learned important facts. Within the hour, he would be forced to make a decision and draw the final white lines of his blueprint.

K. Y. Smith had seen the guard come aboard the *Sybaris* and speak with Killinger before Killinger and the two Vizsla dogs left the junk for the morning run on the beach. Talya had been dispatched immediately to play on the beach with him and ask clever questions.

Probabilities were run through the computer. The abacus was used to check simple totals. No final answers. Elena was run through the memory banks and transistors. The read-out showed one question mark.

Killinger's urgency about the Napoleon had gotten to Marjorie. She watched the rear-view mirror to see whether she was being followed. For miles and miles, she seemed to be alone on the highway.

Relaxation came to her when she turned into the Breitland driveway. It was on a three-quarter acre in a nice section of the Santa Barbara suburbs, with a red tile roof and a large courtyard highlighting the early Spanish style. There was a nice feeling of reassurance in seeing black people live decently.

Regina Breitland was a fine lady, and they had coffee and cake together, plus warm woman-to-woman talk. When Marjorie told her how important Killinger had said the Napoleon was, Regina put it into a small wall safe.

When the dial was spun, and the Napoleon locked away, Marjorie let out a deep sigh of relief and asked for a second cup of coffee.

Five-feet-two of agitated nobility paced the room.

Elena's sketches had been put in a line, in consecutive order. The Count narrowed his eyes at each one, trying it for size on the blueprint. The picture of the big safe imbedded in concrete in the hold was the last in the group. Each time he reached it, his monocle jumped from his eye into his hand where it would be automatically polished and repolished. Elena stood behind him, answering the incessant flow of questions until she had been wholly debriefed.

There was a loud ripping sound in Risponyi's head as he tore the blueprint to shreds. He rolled out a new, clean sheet of blue paper. He opened a fresh bottle of white ink and changed the pen's point.

In the original plan, Elena was to be used to lure Killinger from the *Sybaris* during the time of the pincers invasion. This time, Elena would keep Killinger aboard. His presence was necessary for the opening of the safe. He had the combination.

That would make Killinger a witness. Therefore, he would die.

Risponyi's monocle appeared in his eye when he turned to twinkle it at Elena. The Count was forced to admit that she was a deliciously desirable female. Unfortunate. For she, too, would be a witness.

Chapter Four

Talya, in her shocking pink bikini, was impossible to miss.

Copper and Auric had picked up her scent and were wagging their tails and jumping all over her when Killinger arrived. He wondered whether her father had sent her with any special instructions.

Talya pretended to look at a nonexistent wristwatch. "You are exactly three minutes late."

Killinger picked up on their "game." "Business, you know. Unavoidably detained."

Talya knew what it was that had kept Killinger. Elena. She said sweetly, "I hope it went well."

He gambled that she damned well knew, somehow, who went on and off the junk. Smiling, with a broad wink: "Beautiful!"

She smouldered underneath and hid it. "Insurance business?"

He gave her the wide-eyed and innocent stare. "What else?" A grin. "You going to run with me?"

The coolness of icicles: "If you insist."

Exaggerated gallantry: "I insist."

K. Y. Smith's instructions pushed aside her personal feelings. Her smile lacked warmth. "There will be a price."

"I hope I can afford it."

The machine took ascendency over the female leopard. "You must invite me to have a drink with you . . ." She looked at the nonexistent watch on her empty wrist. "A half-hour after we have run."

Killinger was curious about Smith's timing. "You have just been extended a formal invitation." Evidently, the big Chinaman had plans for him. In his roundabout way, Kuan

Yang had arranged for Killinger to be on some sort of a prearranged spot. But that was in the near future. "You set the pace."

Talya plotted for a revenge. If anything had happened between Killinger and Elena, a hard-run would show it. She set as fast a pace as she could manage. He stayed alongside her, easily. At the end, he passed her as though she had been standing.

Killinger thought, as he dove into the ocean, that the magazine article had been correct. "No more tiring than a hundred-yard dash." It was only a matter of staying in condition.

Talya followed him and swam to him. They played and felt one another and touched bodies. She put her wondrously supple legs around him and chewed his lips tenderly. Their fingers crept under fabric and into openings and around flesh. Her mood was suddenly magic. She had flowed from being her father's machine into being her own leopard.

Marjorie was waiting when Copper and Auric brought Killinger home. Her delightfully pleasant morning was shining in her eyes. "Regina is wonderful."

"It's nice when my friends like my friends."

Tentatively: "Will you be needing me tonight?"

"After five o'clock, your time is your own."

"That's groovy. Regina invited me to dinner. She said there'd be 'interesting people' there." She gave a cute little wiggle that shook her fanny and jiggled her breasts. "There are going to be some men she said I'd like to meet."

"There's safety in numbers."

"I don't want to be safe." Thoughtfully. "About her 'interesting people', what are they like?"

Killinger laughed. "A militant like you had better be careful. They're mostly Republicans." He turned to go to his cabin for a shower.

She called after him: "I forgot to give you Regina's message."

He said it for her. "The Professor will phone me when he gets home."

"How did you know that?"

"That's what he always does."

The old Siamese artisan had loved wood as he had loved the human form. In his attention to detail and proportion, his carvings reached the plateau of fine sculpture. He had combined his finest memories and his best dreams when he had created the chain of entwined males and females that went around Killinger's bar. Talya had arrived early, and she re-examined the erotic couplings while she waited.

She tried to imagine a whole week with Jed Killinger in which they worked from one end of the bar and back again. And if they invented something new, she would carve it into the bar herself.

Killinger entered, freshly showered and changed. "Having fun?"

The leopard smiled through. "I am studying my favorite subject."

"Your marks couldn't be any higher."

She moved to him and put her arms around his waist. Her tummy moved tantalizingly against his hard stomach. Through pouty lips the leopard purred, "Flatterer." She kissed him, and her tongue moved languidly into his mouth.

He bit the tip playfully. "What's your pleasure?"

She leaned back and looked up into his eyes. "Jed Killinger."

"On the rocks?"

She rubbed her pelvis into his. "On the waterbed." The leopard had control but briefly. The machine took over. Her father had sent her to the junk on a mission. She unfastened her long gold pendant earrings and put them onto the bar counter.

Killinger stepped behind the bar and put two bottles on the counter: a fine Scotch and a sour mash bourbon. "If you don't like these, I'll try something else."

Talya touched the bottle of Johnny Walker Black Label with her pinkie. "Straight."

"Me, too." He poured some of the Scotch into two short glasses.

Talya gave the earrings a last little push into obscurity.

With a cough, the transceiver awoke. "Paola here. Count Risponyi is coming from his hotel, and he is entering his car."

"Stay with him." End of transmission.

The computer said that the Count would pay a visit to the junk prior to his underwater attack. A good general examines the terrain himself, whenever possible.

After the third ring: "Yes."

"This is João Aranha Mijangos O'Reilly." The blue-eyed Chinaman wished that João's name were shorter. "Count Risponyi left about a minute ago. He is on his way to the *Sybaris*."

"Wonderful, my boy. You are performing a difficult labor with great ease."

João offered an interesting nugget. "Also, the Count instructed Griff and me to stand by. He said we would be under way in an hour."

At last, information of importance. A clue about the time schedule. The computer's transistors began their silent clicking. "Inform me of his next plans, the moment you hear them."

"How will I get away, to call you?"

"Senor O'Reilly, that is a problem you must plan to solve, in advance." The subarctic temperature of his eyes froze his words, giving his voice the chill of death. "If you should fail to phone me at that crucial moment, it would be better that you had disappeared from the face of the earth." Disconnect.

João's fingers felt the noose around his throat.

Chapter Five

Talya's timing had been exquisite.

The leopard within her wanted to throw away the clock, but the machine was in control. Instead of making love, she had made excuses. Suddenly, she was gone.

Now she was sitting close to her father, on the fantail of the *Valhalla*. Large earphones were cupped on either side of her head. These were plugged in to a small, heavy box of battleship gray. Her concern at the moment was the swinging green needle which she was trying to center on its calibrated dial, set between a series of knobs.

Atop the box was a small directional antenna of tube steel. Talya was manipulating the worm gear which controlled the antenna's spin. Finally the green needle pointed straight up. The antenna was precisely on beam.

The chuckle next to her sounded like coal bouncing down a wooden chute on its way to a deep cellar. The big, blue-eyed Australian with the yellow skin spoke softly: "Our cat's-paw arrives on stage."

K. Y. Smith watched Count Vaclav Risponyi march along the dock on his way to the *Sybaris*. The computer had stated that the good Count would arrive, and he had. Moving with Risponyi, the binoculars showed the little man walk up the gangplank and strike the gong. Killinger had come on the deck. There had been a brief conversation, and then the Count followed Killinger.

Talya turned up the dial marked Volume.

The monocle glared at Killinger. The frog voice croaked a noncommittal greeting. "Good morning, Mr. Killinger."

An inclination of the head. "Count Risponyi."

"Would you be so kind as to grant me a few minutes?"

"Of course, Count Risponyi." Killinger indicated the living room. Count Risponyi strode briskly, followed by Killinger and the two Vizsla dogs.

The Count looked up to Killinger. "I have been concerned about my property." He moved to the bar. "Naturally, I speak of the crate and what it contains."

Killinger's voice was deceptively soft. "And what does the crate hold, Count Risponyi?"

"As I have stated, a sealskin case with the name of my grandfather upon it."

"And that is what weighs a half of a ton?"

Controlled impatience. "Past a certain point, what is mine should not properly concern you, Mr. Killinger."

Killinger's smile was genuine. He gave the Count credit for the manner in which he handled the situation. "I do not speak for myself, Count Risponyi. I speak for the insurance company whose representative I am, in this matter."

The monocle glittered a message that the Count was not amused. The frog croak became excessively English. "Mr. Killinger, if you please! I have not come here to make conversation. I hereby demand that I see that crate. And immediately!"

"It can be arranged."

Talya's earrings lay unnoticed behind a bottle on the bar.

A second set of earphones was clipped to K. Y. Smith's skull.

He listened carefully to the conversation between Killinger and Risponyi. When the speakers were no longer audible via the miniature microphones inside the earrings, the binoculars picked them up across the marina's waters. Killinger led the way down the circular stairs.

Time was of the essence. The computer was called on for a series of subtotals and totals. Then the final read-out. Flat statement that when Count Risponyi saw the crate, he would try his best to make Killinger accept a bond in return for the crate and his copy of the bill of lading.

In answer to the specific question: "Would Killinger accept the bond?" the read-out tube ended with an absolute blank. The question was reworded and again submitted. The tube remained blank.

The phone sounded. On the third ring, a big paw lifted the receiver. "Yes."

"Paolo here. Count Risponyi went to the Chinese junk several minutes ago. Then, as you instructed, I drove to the small cove where Mr. Griff McLellan and Senor O'Reilly are now doing certain things."

"What things?"

"Mr. McLellan is putting on an underwater rubber suit, and Senor O'Reilly is working on the motorboat's engine."

"Stay there." The conversation ended.

Kuan Yang Smith's two hundred eighty-seven pounds moved effortlessly as he raised himself from the chair and stood, his six foot one and a half inches militarily erect. He turned gracefully and walked from the fantail.

Killinger had decided on a plan of action.

Van der Helft's phone call had helped establish the competitive relationship between the huge Chinaman and the small Count. By applying small pressures, he believed that he could bring the explosive situation to a head and defuse it before the fire touched the powder.

Kimo's instructions had been clear. The long-haired Japanese boy had gotten the block and tackle belonging to the *Sybaris* and had taken it to the living room. He had hooked the block through the brass ring-bolt which was set into a ceiling beam. After that, he had lifted out the hatch cover from the deck, opening the shaft down to Killinger's bedroom. Then he put a foot into a loop of rope and let himself down to the bedroom by releasing more tackle through the pulley.

Count Risponyi stood before the safe. It was huge and strong and immovable, because its base had been sunk into the concrete ballast of the hull. He shook his head to himself, realizing that Killinger would have to be kept aboard to work the combination. Vibrations from the crate seemed to reach out to him from behind the steel walls of the safe. He closed his eyes.

"Count Risponyi."

It was Killinger's voice. His eyes remained closed. "Yes, Mr. Killinger."

Flatly: "Your gun, please. And slowly."

Without turning, without looking to see whether Killinger was holding a gun on him, the Count reached into his jacket and pulled his Smith & Wesson .38 from its holster. He handed it behind him where it was taken from his fingers.

Risponyi had been prepared to give away a gun. That was the reason for carrying the .38. His tiny Japanese two-shot 7mm hand-tooled gun sat unseen. "Anything else, Mr. Killinger?"

"Yes. Stand away from the safe, and then move beside it."

"Will this do?"

"Back further, where I can see you. And you cannot see me spin the dial for the safe's combination."

Count Risponyi did as he was told. He could not see the front of the safe. However, he did watch Killinger's face as he worked the combination. He learned nothing. Risponyi's gun was stuck into Killinger's waistband. A second gun, obviously Killinger's, lay on the floor in a position where Killinger could grab it in an emergency. It was on the opposite side from where Risponyi stood, in case the little man tried to rush in.

Risponyi was concerned only with the crate. If it became necessary, one 7mm bullet was all that would be needed.

The safe's door swung open. Killinger stepped back. "Count Risponyi, the crate is on a dolly. Would you mind rolling it out?" Killinger was not about to permit the Count to get behind him.

Risponyi did not mind moving the crate. First, he took time to touch and stroke the rough wooden box. Then he pulled it toward him and backed out of the safe, rolling the dolly and its precious cargo. The Count now stood before the crate like a groom before a bride on their wedding night:

adoring and passionate and on the verge of losing control. His passion-glazed eyes opened wide as he looked straight up at the noise above his head.

It was the hatch cover piece of the floor in Killinger's bedroom, and it was lifted and pushed aside.

Perhaps the Count had expected to see K. Y. Smith standing there, machine gun in hand. But it was Kimo, grinning. "How're we doing?"

"Fine. C'mon down, and finish the job."

Kimo lowered himself and the tackle. He landed next to the crate. Risponyi's eyes were filled with love and concern for his beloved. Nothing must happen to the crate.

Killinger stepped back, to stay away from the Count. "Kimo, pass the line around the box, and make it secure."

Risponyi's voice was emotion-charged. "Do be careful."

Kimo worked in silence. Freshly repolished, the monocle carefully observed every move and tying of knot. Killinger stood away and watched from the side. Finally, Kimo completed his task and turned to Killinger. "Okay?"

"Affirmative." Killinger looked up the shaft to the pulley, hitched to the ringbolt. The situation was Go. "All right, Kimo. Up on the deck and do it."

Kimo nodded and ran to the stairway, taking them two at a time until he reached the top and the living room. He took hold of the line which ran through the two sets of pulleys and began hauling in rope. The crate rose a few inches and squealed against the pressure put on the wood. It began to sway back and forth until Risponyi held it steady. As it rose on its way to the living room, his fingertips stuck to the heavy box as though held by the magnet of love.

Suddenly, Risponyi spun about and charged straight at Killinger, head down. Killinger rolled his body to the side as the little man charged past. Killinger turned to ready himself for the next attack. But Risponyi was nowhere in sight. He was racing up the stairs three at a time.

Killinger sped after him, gun in hand.

Chapter Six

Talya sat in the command chair, earphones clamped tight.

The directional antenna's aim at the miniaturized transmitters in the earrings, on a corner of Killinger's bar, had never varied. Binoculars at her eyes covered the *Sybaris*. The telescope was at her side, next to the two telephones and the transceiver.

Her ears monitored what her eyes could not see. A man named Kimo had used a block and tackle to bring the crate from the lower hold. She had seen Count Risponyi fly up the stairs and run in to the living room. Seconds later, Killinger followed. Gun in hand.

Talya pressed the Broadcast button of the transceiver and began to speak. K. Y. Smith sat in the Mercedes-Benz 600, listening, as the black limousine crawled with dignity around the marina to Killinger's dock.

He heard what Talya's eyes and ears perceived.

When Killinger reached the living room, Count Risponyi was aiding Kimo to lower the crate to the deck of the living room. He turned to Killinger with deep apologies. "I thought the crate was going to fall and that my services were needed."

Tears of sincerity stood in his eyes. "Please accept my most sincere apology." His eyes drifted to the crate. "I am afraid I lost self-control."

Killinger accepted with a nod, not trusting himself to speak. He put the gun back into his waistband. Risponyi had been fast. A dangerous man.

Kimo replaced the hatch cover in its place on the deck.

Count Risponyi turned from the crate to face Killinger. His every move was made with measured dignity. The monocle was polished with a silk handkerchief, deliberately, as though time were unimportant. A hand went into the Count's breast pocket and came out with papers. They were separated, and the top one was handed to Killinger. "The bill of lading. You have seen it before."

Killinger nodded.

An unsealed envelope was next passed over. "Mr. Killinger, I trust that the letter will be considered properly phrased."

Killinger slipped a crisp sheet of white from the envelope. As he read, Risponyi said, "You are looking at a performance bond. If I do not live up to its terms, $50,000 is forfeit. The monies will go to either the insurance company or to Mr. Ejnar Mylius, under the terms of the instrument."

It was read without comment.

The Count tried to make his point. "What I am saying is that if it is not a true bill of lading, guaranteeing my ownership, I forfeit the $50,000 which the bank holds."

Killinger looked carefully at the bill of lading. His face showed nothing. He thought that it was a wonderful forgery, as good as the big Chinaman's bill of lading. He wondered: was there a chance that one of the two papers was actually real? Then again, a $50,000 forfeit in order to obtain well over $1,000,000 in gold was a beautiful move.

The Count prodded. "Mr. Killinger, I am prepared to transfer my property from your boat within the hour." A pause. "Your answer, sir. I await it."

Behind Talya, two green trubans were reconstructing the canvas blind. Within the blind, a third green turban checked the .257 Weatherby Magnum rifle and its Unerti 'scope. After he put it on the bipod support, he aimed it at the stern of the *Sybaris*.

Like an interpreter at the U. N., Talya's flow of words

continued easily, converting what she saw and heard into information for her father's computer. Her most recent description had been of Count Risponyi's $50,000 forfeit bond.

K. Y. Smith's tones came to her on the two-way radio. "We have arrived at the dock. I shall now leave the car." A click as he turned off his broadcast unit.

Her binoculars followed Kuan Yang from the limousine to the dock, as he walked to the junk. The Chinaman from Australia moved with the majesty and strength of an immense aircraft carrier. Huge white waves at his bow were almost visible, as were the boiling and churning green waters in his wake.

He carried an attache case of baby python skin.

Pangkalanbuun was struck across his face by the mallet in Smith's hand. The low tone of his roar, which ran across the deck, was not one of rage. It had a strong undertone of respect for a superior devil.

Killinger and Count Risponyi turned to the source of the sound. Killinger was gratified to see Kuan Yang Smith. Count Vaclav Risponyi's breath stuck in his throat. His heart stopped. He was face to face with his enemy.

K. Y. Smith moved, almost daintily, to the living room.

Killinger wondered how these two opponents would act toward each other.

The Chinaman entered and turned his head toward Count Risponyi.

Count Vaclav Risponyi looked up at Kuan Yang Smith.

There was a pause. A brief silence. The big man with the turquoise eyes broke it. A hearty laughter was programmed to come up from within him. It rolled out the door and onto the deck, meeting the gong's fading tone in a middle ground. His eyes, set in dry ice, showed neither friendship nor enmity. They were seemingly blank. "Count Vaclav Risponyi, my dear friend." The laughter grew more hearty. "It is so terribly good to see you."

Count Risponyi's teeth were displayed brilliantly under his brush moustache. "Kuan Yang Smith! It has been too long."

Killinger decided that they were practised and facile actors, with years of experience behind them. They were playing to an audience of one: Jedediah Killinger III.

Count Risponyi's coal black eyes became as cold and remote as the Chinaman's as he watched K. Y. Smith stare at the crate. They were now head to head. Risponyi thought a logical solution would be to form some sort of a partnership with Kuan Yang. Then, later, take the crate from under his nose.

The big yellow-skinned Australian spoke first. "Mr. Killinger, it must seem more than obvious to you that the good Count and I have come here on the same mission." His laughter swept over Risponyi and held him in a bearhug. "While, to a very small extent, we have been business rivals in the past, there were more times we operated as partners. I believe we found pleasure in twin harness." The turquoise eyes beamed at Risponyi.

Risponyi's frog croak spoke softly. "As always, Kuan Yang, you are an astute businessman." His lips smiled, and he proffered his hand. "Let us make this occasion an official partnership."

Killinger, the audience of one, appreciated professionalism. He admired the way these two handled themselves. He noticed that when they shook hands to seal the deal, they held the gesture of friendship overlong. The whitening of the skin while they gripped showed that they held a short contest of strength. Neither man gave. Their hands fell apart.

Smith looked down at the Count. "May I make an offer on behalf of our partnership?"

"Of course, Kuan Yang."

The Chinaman seemed to turn his back on them without motion. His two hundred eighty-seven pounds were interposed between his attache case and the others. He snapped it open and pulled out a packet of new bills of large denomination. The case carried $100,000 in cash. Under the money, and behind a fold of the baby python skin, lay a broken-apart Tukharev machine gun with a skeleton stock and a full supply of ammunition.

Simultaneously, he closed the case and faced Killinger, holding out the money. "Here, sir, is $25,000 in coin of the realm. Count Risponyi and I shall be more than willing to put this up as a good faith bond." K. Y. Smith had been told by Talya, as she listened to the broadcast from her earrings, that Risponyi had already offered $50,000. In playing ignorant and starting too low, it made the bargaining more fun. And there could be a large saving of cash.

Count Risponyi appreciated the gambit, and he knew what would happen next.

Killinger laughed. "Count Risponyi has offered a $50,000 bond."

The Chinaman's hearty, booming laugh welled up. He turned to Risponyi. "$50,000!? A ridiculously inflated figure." He aimed the hearty boom at Killinger. "However, sir, I want you to feel that we are in full truth, and by every definition, men of our word." A sweeping gesture to Killinger and Risponyi. "I shall add another $25,000 in cash to this magnificent bundle of currency."

As he turned to reopen the attache case, the phone rang. Killinger moved to it quickly, which brought him to a different angle. He caught an odd and interesting reflection from some metal in the attache case.

"Killinger here."

Professor Robert Breitland was at the other end of the line. "Hi. Bob Breitland. What's the big rush-rush about this hunk of metal? It's interfering with my lunch." The warmth of his tone belied his words.

"It's causing me more trouble than that."

K. Y. Smith and Count Risponyi listened to Killinger's end of the conversation, to see if anything concerned them.

"But, ol' buddy, it's only a gold Napoleon."

"Quick. Tell me a few facts."

The Professor rattled them off. "It's a five-franc piece, originally minted in France. It's made with one more grain of gold than comparable coins. This has made it extra valuable in the Middle East. Gold Napoleons have been driven out of circulation into hoarding. They bring a small premium."

Killinger peered at his two guests as he spoke. "And that's all?"

"That's all. Soup's getting cold. Talk to you later." They hung up.

Killinger stepped back from the big Chinaman and the little apelike man. He took a Napoleon from his pocket and held it before them. His voice was flat. "Gentlemen, I took the liberty of opening that crate." He indicated it. "Also, I removed some coins." A hard silence. K. Y. Smith and Count Risponyi seemed to have stopped breathing. Their eyes held the Napoleon.

K. Y. Smith's voice was barely audible. "We are listening, sir."

"The phone call I just received was from a friend to whom I had given one of the Napoleons, for his opinion." A long pause.

K. Y. Smith whispered again: "We are still listening, sir."

"He is both a geologist and a numismatist."

Electricity crackled in the room.

Count Vaclav Risponyi's frog croak was no louder than an exhalation of breath. "What was the opinion of . . . uh . . . this expert?"

Killinger nailed them with his information. "That the coin is of gold. Further, at the U. S. Treasury price, the coins in that box have a worth of approximately $500,000." In different terms, for emphasis, "A half of a million American dollars." A smile. "On the international market, according to London's daily gold-fixing, as of today, it is worth over $1,250,000. A million and a quarter American dollars." His smile grew cold. He had them nailed. "Not a bad bargain for a lousy $50,000 bond."

K. Y. Smith's sudden laughter seemed to shake the *Sybaris*, from bow to stern, from port to starboard sides. It swelled so that it seemed to crush everyone in the room. Suddenly, in mid-note, it was chopped off.

Count Risponyi took advantage of the silence to speak quietly, holding out his hand. "Mr. Killinger, if you would trust me a moment. The Napoleon, please."

Killinger tossed him the coin.

Risponyi held the Napoleon between the thumb and forefinger of his two hands, as one would hold a thick piece of cardboard. The muscles of his jaw showed the strain as he slowly, and literally, tore the Napoleon into two pieces.

Killinger was tremendously impressed by this feat of strength. Then he was shocked.

Count Risponyi held the torn Napoleon for Killinger to see clearly.

Kuan Yang's laughter picked up again, in the middle of the same note, where it had been chopped off.

The metal in the center of the Napoleon was soft and silver-gray.

Chapter Seven

Killinger said one word. "Counterfeit."

K. Y. Smith nodded. Count Vaclav Risponyi smiled.

Killinger thought aloud. "Naturally, you both knew all along that the crate contained Napoleons which were actually forgeries."

The little man with the shaven head stared at Killinger. The big man examined empty space.

"I won't be naive and ask what you want with lead." He looked at another Napoleon he had taken from his pocket. "If they were all real, the crate would be holding a bit less than one and a half million dollars. As good gray lead, it's worth less than $100."

Kuan Yang spoke to the ceiling. "Quite true."

Killinger continued. "It is my guess that you want these coins to sell to the poor people in the Orient." He addressed the Count. "Curiosity only. Why is your grandfather's name on the sealskin case?"

Risponyi grinned and popped his monocle into his eye. "Fortunately, my grandfather was a crook. He lived in the Ural Mountains in Russia, where he worked in metals." The Count held a half of the coin he'd just split, admiring it. "The original Vaclav Risponyi slaved for years, making dies of the French five-franc piece, the Napoleon." An aside, as he turned the coin over, proudly. "An exquisite bit of craftsmanship." A self-conscious cough. "I shall continue. He used base metal to create his pieces of art. These, he dipped in gold." Froglike chuckle. "At one time, he had over two thousand pounds of worthless Napoleons. He used some to purchase the title of Count."

Risponyi's laughter exploded. Suddenly it was drowned by the Chinaman's gigantic bellows and roars of amusement. Killinger smiled at these two thieves, thinking how unbelievably they acted.

K. Y. Smith turned off the loud sound. In the silence, he spoke. "Because of the tremendous sentimental value contained in Grandfather Risponyi's craftsmanship, my partner and I would like to purchase these last bits of his life's work." Laughter at full volume. Silence for a pause. "We shall pay cash."

"And if you use them to cheat people?"

The Australian accent spoke in hard syllables. "People cheat themselves." He indicated the crate. "Those coins will be bought by hoarders who will then bury them in dirt. To them, these Napoleons will not be money. They will be only a symbol of wealth." He looked at Risponyi. "The good Count and I shall help them in their happiness. We shall sell them dreams. Napoleons to hide from the world, so the owners can have secret smiles."

Count Risponyi spoke. "Mr. Smith deals in money, in Singapore. I deal in money in Calcutta." A shrug. "It is our business."

"Don't you care whether the money is real or counterfeit?"

Kuan Yang spoke in a deep, long sigh. "Philosophically, there is no true difference. In some civilizations, a man's possessions are measured by sea shells. In others, by oddly carved rocks. In ours, the measure is gold."

Softly, Killinger asked, "What will you pay for that crate full of lead?"

K. Y. Smith roared in good humor. "Mr. Killinger, a

businessman can have but one answer to that question. As little as possible."

The Count was reassuring. "The monies with which we shall make payment are not counterfeit."

Killinger said, "Gentlemen, you must understand my position. Whether or not I approve of your contemplated thefts, there is nothing I can do. I do not own the crate. Nor can I sell it on behalf of the insurance company."

K. Y. Smith asked the obvious question. "Who is empowered to deal with us?"

Killinger held up one finger. "First, Ejnar Mylius. Second, if he is unable, then his granddaughter has power of attorney. You've both met Mrs. Katja Mylius O'Reilly."

As though rehearsed as a team, both Kuan Yang Smith and Count Vaclav Risponyi nodded and spoke together. "Of course."

Risponyi asked. "Where is Mrs. O'Reilly?"

K. Y. Smith answered for Killinger. "At the hospital." His turquoise eyes sheeted Killinger with ice. "Might I suggest that you phone the lady?"

The white-haired Viking sea god had come out of his sedation, and he was aware of his suite, the two nurses, and his granddaughter. His zest for life had returned with his consciousness, and he had started feeble complaints about being forced to stay in bed.

The phone in the room had been connected, and now it rang gently. Katja picked it up on the first subdued sound. "Hello."

It was a man's voice. "May I speak with Mrs. O'Reilly?"

"This is Mrs. O'Reilly." Recognition dawned. "Jed?"

"Right. How is your grandfather?"

"Beautiful."

"Good. And you?"

"A bit tired. But otherwise, fine."

The old Viking's roar came out as a whisper. "Who's that?"

"Full name, Jedediah Killinger III."

242

Ejnar Mylius glared at the doctor and the nurses. "Let me talk to him."

Katja looked a question at the doctor. He smiled and shrugged. Katja held the phone to the Viking's ear. He spoke. "I'm Ejnar Mylius. Who the bloody hell are you?" The old pirate winked a wild blue eye at Katja.

Concealed surprise. "My name's Killinger."

"Katja spoke about you. Insurance, huh?"

Killinger talked across the room, with his hand on the mouthpiece. "It's Ejnar Mylius, himself."

The partners stared at Killinger.

Killinger was tickled by what sounded like a fiery old man. "You might say insurance."

"I've already said it." His laugh was weak, although it indicated what the Viking really was. "What do you want to cheat me out of?"

"I don't want to cheat you out of a thing." Killinger looked at his two interested guests and laughed. "But I may help you cheat someone else. Depending on your conscience."

"Don't worry about my conscience. I don't." His laugh was a bit stronger. "Who are we going to cheat?"

"Two men you know. K. Y. Smith and Count Vaclav Risponyi."

A cough smothered Ejnar Mylius' laugh. "If there are two bastards in the world I'd like to chop off at the knees, those two are the ones."

Killinger spoke across the phone to K. Y. Smith and Risponyi. "He says he'd like to chop you two bastards off at the knees."

Smith's laugh was genuine. "Give my regards to the old pirate."

Killinger spoke to Mylius. "I understand you're a pirate."

"You goddam well better believe it." He coughed. "When I get out of this jail, you make sure and nail everything down."

K. Y. Smith and Count Risponyi hung on every word of Killinger's question. "You had a small, heavy crate aboard the *Katja*. Where'd you get it? And do you own it?"

"I got it in Hong Kong, and I bloody well own it."

"Your two bastards want to buy it."

The Viking Pirate coughed and laughed at once. "Who else would want counterfeit coins, except thieves?"

Killinger spoke to them, across the phone. "I believe he'll sell to you." Into the phone. "I can't handle the deal. Van der Helft would object."

"The sanctimonious son-of-a-bitch!"

The big question. "Will you sell to them?"

"As long as I make a ridiculously high profit."

To K. Y. Smith and Count Risponyi. "He says as long as he makes a ridiculously high profit."

The partners beamed on each other.

Katja's voice was back on the phone. "The doctor says Grandfather must sleep. I'll be over shortly and close the transaction." She hung up.

"Mrs. O'Reilly will be here shortly to close the sale."

While they were waiting, K. Y. Smith could answer things for Killinger. "You knew my grandfather. What kind of man was he?"

Admiringly: "He was one of the great ones." Laughter started softly, in remembrance. It built with thoughts of things past. "Jedediah Killinger the First was one of the most brilliant businessmen of the shipping industry." Happy memories made happy laughter. "Today, he would be called a freebooter and a pirate."

Killinger asked softly, "Would he have dealt in counterfeit coins?"

Gentlest of laughs. "For shame, my boy. You are attempting to make me hang my head." Proudly: "That is something I shall never do." With dignity: "I am one of the last representatives of a broad and colorful era."

Count Risponyi spoke. "I should like to be included in that select group." Thoughtfully: "Mr. Killinger, I had seen your grandfather four times in my life." Laugh. "You have his blood in your veins. You are part buccaneer."

The phone rang. Killinger picked it up. "Jed Killinger."

"Hi. Bob Breitland again." Laugh. "I have a wonderful surprise for you. About the Napoleon."

244

"I know what it is."

"Wanna make a small bet with your friendly Professor on that?"

"Affirmative."

"Uh . . . let's see . . . Can you afford to wager two more Napoleons, exactly like the first one?"

"Go ahead. The price is right."

"The one I saw was a counterfeit."

Killinger laughed. "You owe me."

"Not yet. That's only the beginning."

Killinger felt a strong tension build as both the big Chinaman and the small man with the monocle stared at him, unblinking. He spoke into the phone. "May as well tell me the rest."

Professor Breitland explained carefully. "Around 1880, in Russia, near the Ural Mountains, there was a great deal of mining in an area known as Ruthenia."

"So?"

"Listen, man. This is going to blow your Chinese junk right out of the water. The cheapest metal was so soft as to be unworkable. The color of lead. And a weight like gold. It was called ruthenium, after Ruthenia."

"You sure tell a lousy story. Get to the point."

"Hold on. Here it comes. Counterfeiters used ruthenium occasionally to make phoney gold coins, which they dipped in gold."

"I'm hanging on your every word."

"Some years later the known elements were listed by atomic weights. Ruthenium, in one of its forms was given the atomic number of 78. Its atomic weight was figured at 195.5. Its specific gravity worked out to 21.50."

"You're beginning to lose me."

The Professor was close to making his point. "Those numbers were given a name at the beginning of this century." Speaking extra clearly. "The metal of which my Napoleon was made is now called platinum!!"

Killinger stared at K. Y. Smith and Count Risponyi, his eyes wide and disbelieving. Then understanding crept in.

245

"I said platinum!! And platinum is worth more than gold!!!"

Killinger hung up abruptly.

The silent humming of efficient machinery was heard by no one. K. Y. Smith's computer had answered an important question. The read-out tube spelled it out clearly. "Killinger knows. . . ."

The big Chinaman spoke to Risponyi in Hindustani. The Count muttered a reply in the same language. They rose to their feet at the same time.

Killinger pulled the gun from his waistband and pointed it. "Speak English, and don't move."

He backed slowly to the $2,000,000 worth of platinum Napoleons.

Chapter Eight

Count Risponyi and K. Y. Smith froze in place.

The Chinaman still held the $50,000 in cash that he had taken from his case. He started forward, after a pause, toward Killinger. "Would you mind if I place this money back into its hiding place?"

"Later." Killinger whistled. The two Vizsla dogs trotted to him, grinning. He spoke to them. "Guns." Their tails wagged. He pointed the Smith & Wesson .38 at Risponyi. "Count Risponyi, your gun. If you please."

"But you have already taken it. And, if I may mention the fact, the gun in your hand belongs to me."

A smile. "That was gun number one. I want gun number two."

A shrug. The monocle winked in the light. "I have no other weapon."

Killinger waved the .38, indicating direction. "Take three steps away from Mr. Smith, and stand with your hands hanging down, in front."

Tolerantly, Risponyi obeyed orders. Smith observed closely.

"Auric! Find. Gun." He pointed to the Count.

Auric walked to the small man, tail wagging. When the dog reached Risponyi, his tail kept wagging, and his nose became more active as he circled the Count. Finally, he pressed his nose hard against Risponyi's right wrist and barked once. Then again.

Killinger guessed. "A small one, up your right sleeve." Cold smile. "Shake it out slowly and give it to the dog." The .38 pointed to the middle of the Count's face.

Risponyi moved his right hand carefully. The 7mm two-shot derringer fell into his waiting hand. He looked straight into the muzzle of the .38. Without change of expression, holding the miniature gun between thumb and forefinger, he held it to the dog. Auric mouthed it as gently as though it were a live bird which he would deliver to his master without ruffling a feather. He brought it to Killinger.

Killinger took it and slipped it into his pocket after giving it a brief glance. "Never saw one like it. Was it made to order?"

The Count nodded.

"A handy weapon." Killinger called the other Vizsla. "Copper! Find. Gun." He pointed to the big Chinaman.

Copper walked to Kuan Yang. Before the Vizsla reached him, a Colt .45 appeared in K. Y. Smith's hand. "Your dogs are well trained." He handed the .45 daintily to Copper, whose tail had been wagging. Copper gave it to Killinger. His reward was a pat on the head, and the tail moved faster.

Killinger pointed to K. Y. Smith again. "Copper! Find. Gun." Copper walked to the turquoise-eyed giant, sniffing his way completely around. He returned to Killinger apologetically. He was patted again, and the two dogs were told how good they were. There was no second handgun.

K. Y. Smith spoke again. "Vizsla?"

Killinger nodded.

"My first experience with the breed. Magnificent animals."

Count Risponyi climbed to his high horse, his superiority which had been given him with the title of Count. He was too short to look down his nose. However, with great dignity, he looked up. "I demand to know the reason for your sudden reversal of attitude toward us."

K. Y. Smith's computer gave the Chinaman the answer before Risponyi's last word fell uselessly to the floor.

"I can tell it in one word." Killinger's eyes went from Risponyi to K. Y. Smith, and back. "Platinum." There was a meaningful silence.

Risponyi looked to the Chinaman. Smith looked at empty space.

"Now, let me mention a few facts. There have been two attempts to steal that crate." Killinger pointed to it. "And to do so violently. There have been nonviolent tries, also. Like offers to put up a bond." Chill smile. "For one thousand pounds of platinum. At more than $2,000 a pound on the world market."

Laughter filled the room and sloshed around like waters in a storm. Then, sudden quiet. K. Y. Smith's soft question filled the void. "Is it your intention to call the authorities, Mr. Killinger?"

A question for a question. "Would a quick answer be best?"

Bland smile. "We await your pleasure, sir." Yellow hand holding up the money. "This $50,000 would rest more easily in the attache case." He started forward.

"Don't move." Killinger moved to the bar, gun pointed at his guests. He reached for the baby python-skin case, pulled it to him, and opened it. Wordlessly, he pushed the money aside and felt around for some metal object which had shone at him. He touched it and pulled it out. It was the main section of the Tukharev machine pistol.

Nobody spoke.

Killinger put the fascinating piece of metal death back into the case. He backed further and placed the case on the dumbwaiter. Then he pressed the 'down' button. Slowly, the python case disappeared into the floor.

Talya wore earphones as she sat in her father's chair and listened to what was happening in the living room of the junk. She knew Killinger was in control. No conversation told her that the Russian-made machine pistol had been put on the dumbwaiter and sent down to the hold, so she was certain that K. Y. Smith was in a position to take over at a time of his own choice.

The green turban behind the three-sided canvas blind had

his eye at the 24X 'scope and his finger on the trigger. He awaited instructions to fire.

The binoculars showed Talya little of what was happening in the living room of the *Sybaris*.

K. Y. Smith placed his left hand on his right bicep.

He felt the thin metal cylinder, strapped to his arm. His forefinger brushed the release button through the fabric of his jacket and shirt. He applied no pressure. His left hand moved down his right arm, tracing the strong tubing that went from the thin metal cylinder to a small directional metal nozzle. The tip of the nozzle ended at his palm, on the inside of his wrist, where it was strapped. Four inches of extra tubing was held by a snap-off metal clip. Smith could spray it like a hose.

The gas in the cylinder was compressed to 1,850 pounds per square inch. Pressed against a man's skin, it could blow a hole in an instant and explode compacted muscle tissue. Blown into the air, it would put all who breathed it into a deep, but not permanent, sleep.

Killinger stood against the bar, holding his own gun. He had taken the others from his waistband and pockets and had laid them on the bar top. He saw that the big Chinaman was edging toward him. Killinger's voice was hard. "Don't move any closer, Mr. Smith."

"I have a pain in my chest. It is similar to the pain I had a few months ago, when my physician hospitalized me." The Australian twang grew thicker. Sad explanation. "My heart, you know." A well-acted grimace. "I neglected to take along my pills. Perhaps, sir, a glass of brandy?"

Killinger stepped behind the bar, reaching one-handed for the brandy bottle. He put it on the counter. Then he felt around for a glass. His groping fingers knocked some tumblers from the shelf to the floor. Automatically, he began to bend, lowering his head. His gun held the counter. Briefly, his .38 was away from the Chinaman.

With a speed which would have been spectacular in a smaller man, K. Y. Smith leaped forward as his gigantic yellow hand swept up the guns on the counter top. His other hand worked in coordination to pluck Killinger's .38 from his fingers.

Killinger rose slowly, facing his own gun in someone else's fist.

K. Y. Smith's breathing was regular and even. "In your own words, Mr. Killinger, don't move."

Kuan Yang's left hand moved to the release button which would let the metal cylinder fill the room with gas. His finger found the button and pressed it.

The Chinaman aimed the nozzle at Jedediah Killinger III.

Killinger collapsed and fell slowly to the floor.

Chapter Nine

With the grace of a ballet dancer, Smith spun and filled the large room with gas.

Count Risponyi slid to the deck with the fluid motion of a wet noodle. Copper and Auric dropped to the rug on which they were standing and rolled over.

The Chinaman held his breath as he surveyed the cabin. Satisfied with the success of his surprise move, he turned off the flow of the gas. He permitted himself the luxury of smiling down at his former partner, Count Risponyi. The little man should have been prepared for something like this.

K. Y. Smith moved easily to the door leading to outside and fresh air. After he had filled his lungs with oxygen, he would find the guard and put him to sleep also. After that, he would give Talya instructions to relay to the green turbans. Then, in minutes, the platinum would be his.

Killinger had felt like a fool, standing without a weapon in front of the big Chinaman. His eyes had never left the expressionless and unblinking turquoise eyes. The chill he felt as they seemed to swallow him started at the marrow of his bones. He was aware of the giant's deep and evenly paced breathing.

Killinger's ear caught the soft sound of a strong intake of breath. He saw K. Y. Smith's mouth open wide, as though to shout. Automatically, Killinger realized that the Chinaman was filling his lungs with air. Without questioning the reason, Killinger took in as much air as he could hold. As a true skindiver, a man who did not use tanks of air, he was able to hold his breath up to three minutes.

When the cloud of gas leaped from the big yellow right hand and attacked him, Killinger remembered the unconscious guard who was collapsed in a chair, at the time of the first attempt on the crate.

He pretended to have been gassed, and he folded, behind the bar.

Across the marina, Talya watched her father's exit from the living room. He walked over to the guard. The binoculars picked up Smith's smile when he tapped the guard gently on the shoulder. She saw the guard's mouth open to give a polite answer to a question.

When a cloud appeared from her father's right hand and enveloped the man in uniform, she knew he had been successful. Her father would call shortly and give her a list of things to do.

And she would do them.

K. Y. Smith had always been meticulous about his clothes. His tailors had been the best money could buy. He abhorred wrinkles and stuffed pockets. With a feeling of distaste and a knowledge that the guns were now unnecessary, he emptied his pockets of the hardware and piled them next to the slumbering guard's body.

Killinger lay with his ear to the deck, listening to the Chinaman's footsteps. Surprisingly, for a man so huge, they were quiet. Killinger peeked around the end of the bar. He saw K. Y. Smith's back moving away from him, on the deck. Killinger crawled to the opening in the wall which normally was occupied by the dumbwaiter. He looked across the shaft and saw the guard's collapse when Smith sprayed him. It was with relief that he saw the big man unburden himself of the handguns.

A gust of fresh sea breeze swept across his face, but he couldn't risk taking a breath. Not yet. He didn't know the required concentration of gas to air that would take away its strength. A little more than a minute had passed since he had been sprayed. Probably he could hold his breath for another minute and a half.

He crawled to the dumbwaiter shaft, hoping he would not be heard. Rising partway to his feet, he gave a small hop, taking his hands to the other side. It was not high enough for an honest jump, which he could have made easily. Pulling himself across meant that he would have to hook his fingers onto the runners, then drop his body down the shaft, making certain not to fall, finally pulling himself to the level of the deck and climbing out. All without noise. And without running out of breath.

The green turban behind the .257 Weatherby Magnum had his eye to the Unerti 'scope. He beamed his field of vision back and forth slowly, observing every detail the cross hairs covered. He tensed. He had seen a man moving on his belly through the wall of the large rear room on the deck.

Tense whisper to Talya: "A man moves behind Kuan Yang."

Drifting to the center of Killinger's forehead, the cross hairs pointed a path for a soft-nosed bullet.

Chapter Ten

Killinger made it to the deck with ease.

He filled his lungs with the sea air, returning to his normal breathing. Flat-footed, he moved noiselessly around the circular staircase's opening toward K. Y. Smith. Killinger had no sensation of the cross hairs tracking him constantly as he moved.

Meanwhile the Chinaman had decided that his next move was to get in communication with Talya. This could best be done by telephone, so that it could be a two-way conversation. He would need a chestful of clean air to carry him back into the living room, where the phone sat on a table. After a deep inhalation, he spun around to get to the phone.

And he saw Killinger.

Talya watched the confrontation.

The green turban had difficulty keeping Killinger's head centered in the 'scope. Killinger moved in fits and spurts. Only one shot would be allowed. Success was demanded of it. "At last. The man stands still."

Talya heard the voice behind her.

"Kuan Yang would like him dead."

Talya flowed at high speed to the green turban and the .257 Weatherby Magnum. A fraction of a second before he squeezed the trigger, she kicked the rifle upward. It was knocked from the bipod. But a bullet had been fired. It went high over the marshes, causing no damage.

The green turban had been raised in a part of the world where a woman was of no significance. He swung his fist at Talya for having interfered with him. Lightly, Talya countered the blow with her left forearm, pushing it away from her in a

Karate movement. Her right hand hit the green turban in the throat, her fingers stiff.

The green turban fell, choking and strangling.

K. Y. Smith continued his spin, taking a step backward, moving closer to Killinger. He aimed his right elbow at Killinger's midsection. His right fist was in the palm of his left hand, and he used the twisting motion of the trunk of his body to put his two hundred eighty-seven pounds into the blow. Twenty years of dojo experience went into the Karate move.

Whatever the elbow hit would be completely shattered.

Killinger saw the movement as it began. He slapped his left hand against the rails of the staircase, pushing him away from the elbow faster than he could possibly jump.

The Chinaman's lethal swing went past Killinger. But the two hundred eighty-seven pounds remained in orbit. His left leg came up, the foot aimed at Killinger's head. It was a wheel-kick, called a *mawashigeri,* designed to crush a man's skull.

Killinger used a *gedanbarai.* His left hand, in a fist, came up and under the big man's knee, making the *mawashigeri* impossible to complete.

K. Y. Smith was in motion. He used the momentum to bring his other knee up in a *hizakinkeri,* a genital knee-kick.

Killinger countered with a block, turning and using his thigh to deflect the *hizakinkeri.* His Karate movements had been practised many times, and he performed a graceful series of body motions which could be likened to a well choreographed ballet. His force poured into a *kansetsukeri,* using the outside of his left foot, the *sokuto.*

He kicked K. Y. Smith's right knee-joint on the outside, breaking the Chinaman's leg at the knee.

K. Y. Smith fell to the deck with a body damage that would cause him to limp for as long as he lived.

Talya watched the fight through her binoculars.

They fell, shattered, when her father collapsed.

She screamed once. Then she wept.

It was the first time she had cried since her father had turned her into his machine. The sobs and tears were without end. With each salty drop, a small piece of machinery was washed away. When, finally, she could cry no more, she had become her own woman.

K. Y. Smith lay on the deck, his leg bent awkwardly. Though the pain was excruciating, his face did not acknowledge its existence. He stared up at Jedediah Killinger III without emotion. "You will, of course, call the police?"

"No, Mr. Smith."

"Then you will shoot me?"

"I shall not shoot you." Pause. Small, odd smile, "You are free to leave."

"Mr. Killinger, I fail to understand."

"Kuan Yang Smith . . ." Killinger spoke softly with a distant respect. ". . . if I were to turn you over to the police, my grandfather would never forgive me."

K. Y. Smith's hearty laughter was genuine. Saved by the blood of a pirate, two generations removed. The full, rolling bellow poured over the deck of the *Sybaris* in the huge white-capped waves of a major storm, drowning the mighty pain in his leg.

He tried to stand.

After the many years of his life, Kuan Yang Smith's frozen turquoise eyes finally showed expression.

They closed in pain . . . as he fainted.

Chapter Eleven

Crimson wax sealed the ivory colored envelope.

It was addressed simply Jedediah Killinger III. Turning it over, Killinger's fingers moved to the seal.

"You must agree not to open the letter for six hours." The voice was low and very female.

Killinger laughed and leaned the envelope against the silver champagne bucket, full of shaved ice. The ice was packed loosely around a bottle of *Moët et Chandon champagne, cuvée Rothschild*. On either side of the champagne, two glasses rested on the ice, chilling. Their stems pointed to the crescent birth of the new moon, like the legs of a lovely lady in the act of love.

He turned to Katja Mylius O'Reilly. "Why six hours?"

"Because, my love, that is when my plane leaves for Denmark." Katja was as beautiful and warm and lovely as the evening. Her long red hair was loose. Her eyes, the ever-changing green of the sea. Her flowing green gown held her with the ardor of the ocean embracing a Viking sea goddess.

Killinger popped the champagne and filled their glasses halfway.

Katja offered a toast. "To my grandfather. And to his letter to you." They drank. She put her glass on the teak deck of the *Sybaris* and looked at the stars. Then she looked at the crescent moon and closed her eyes. When she opened them, she was smiling. "I made a wish . . . on the new moon."

Killinger emptied his champagne glass, and she took it from him, placing it on the deck next to hers. They moved to and against each other. Her arms went around him, and he held her close. The sweetness of their kisses sparked wondrous colors into the flames of their passion. The sharp edges of her teeth held his lower lip lightly. Floating down her back, his hands cupped the firm roundnesses of her delightful bottom.

She whispered. "We have so little time."

Killinger led her by the hand to the circular staircase and down the steps . . . .

High above, a huge passenger plane sped across the sky, slowly crawling through the stars. It would fly across the North Pole on its way to Denmark.

Killinger broke the crimson wax seal and opened the envelope. Two items. A letter and a check. He controlled himself and left the check folded, reading the letter which Ejnar Mylius had dictated. It was a letter of thanks. Details in the second and third paragraphs stated that a bank armored truck carried the crate so that the platinum could be weighed properly. The worth had been computed on the basis of that precious metal's price quotes on the international market, per troy ounce.

The troy ounce price was multiplied by 14.583, because that is the number of troy ounces in the avoirdupois pound. In turn, this figure was multiplied by the exact number of pounds and ounces of platinum in the crate from Hong Kong, giving the exact value of the platinum.

$2,053,682.13.

The last two sentences of the third paragraph were the most interesting. They stated that Jedediah Killinger III was entitled to a finder's fee, in an amount equal to five percent of the total.

Killinger unfolded the check. It was made out to him. And the figure clearly printed was $102,684.13.

Exactly four days had passed since the schooner *Katja* had been deeply wounded by a low-floating barge that was drifting in a heavy Pacific storm.

epilogue . . .

On the Fifth Day

Sunrise found the *Sybaris* kitchen full of celebrants.

Killinger had given Marjorie and Samantha and Kimo a big, fat bonus check of a month's wages. In addition, they got a week off, with pay. Everybody was happy.

They had a super breakfast of steak and eggs, with melon and coffee and toast and three kinds of jam.

Kimo and Samantha put their surf boards on top of Kimo's van and headed for a week of living on the sand where the waves gave fast rides. First stop, San Onofre. Samantha kissed Killinger good-bye and hugged him and thanked him. Kimo shook hands. And away they went.

Marjorie put some of her clothes into the robin's-egg-blue '55 T-Bird, wore one of her wilder outfits, and came to Killinger to say good-bye. She stood in front of him, stood up on her toes, put her hands on his shoulders to keep from falling, and spoke a magic word. "Prunes."

They kissed. She hugged him briefly and stepped back.

"I'll see you in a week." Her eyes, which were the color of dark green jade, looked sad.

"Are you sure?"

"Of course! This is my home." Lollipop and Coco Chanel were rubbing against her legs, talking to her. Copper and Auric, on each side of Killinger, looked up at her, grinning and tail-wagging.

"Have you decided where you're going?"

She chewed her lower lip and nodded slowly and thoughtfully. "I'm gonna take a look at where I started my life . . . and at what I used to be . . . and say hello to friends I haven't seen for so long . . . " Her words drifted away with the wind.

Killinger watched the beautiful black girl walk from him. Her five-feet-one was held erect, and a yellow wool tie held her Afro in a gleaming nest.

She turned and threw Killinger a last kiss before she got in her car.

Suddenly, the day seemed empty.

Yesterday's excitement was gone.

K. Y. Smith had been taken by ambulance to St. John's Hospital, where he was given a room next to Ejnar Mylius. There, the two brigands spent their time dredging up old memories and swapping lies.

Count Vaclav Risponyi had taken a plane back to Calcutta. He had asked for the old sealskin case of his grandfather's, and Ejnar Mylius gave it to him. A memento of things past.

João Aranha Mijangos O'Reilly had returned to Brazil, seven thousand dollars richer, but not much wiser.

Elena had rushed off to Hollywood. Her agent had found an acting job for her. She had promised to phone Killinger for that week on the junk which he had promised her . . . when the picture was finished shooting.

Killinger took the Vizsla dogs for their regular morning run on the beach.

His legs moved him forward. But his mind moved back over the last four days. He wondered what the future would bring.

Copper and Auric ran ahead to where a brilliantly red beach umbrella leaned on its side. A pair of female legs peeped out from under. The dogs disappeared under the umbrella.

Killinger ran past and looked at whoever it was with the dogs, without breaking his stride. All he could see was the top of a gigantic floppy hat that covered the girl's head and face and shoulders. He continued to his turn-around. As he remembered, her legs were exquisite. The rest was all hat.

Running back, he faced the girl. The dogs were eating something from her hand. He trotted past, hoping Copper and

Auric would stay with the lady, so he could have a reason to open a conversation. He was jogging at a medium pace.

Copper and Auric exploded, speeding past him. So did a girl in a ridiculous tentlike hunk of headgear. She moved well. Her legs and fanny were not only splendid, they looked familiar.

Talya's hat blew off, and she kept running.

She beat him to the water and waited. Happiness shone through her, everywhere. She was no longer a machine. She was a full and complete woman, belonging to herself. She was her own leopard.

Killinger continued past her and dived into a wave. She followed.

They came together in the waves. They were slammed against one another. They held close.

They kissed with tender passion. She looked into his hazel eyes. "I am free. Next week, I shall re-examine the world. First stop, Paris."

His question was soft. "Until then. . . ?"

Another wave swamped them on its way to the beach. Talya's smile was warm. "I shall live the entire seven days with you. And you will teach me gentleness."

They kissed each other easily, for there was no hurry.

THE RAZONI & JACKSON SERIES

One's black, one's white—they're young and the ballsiest detectives on the city beat! Dynamite—and exclusively from Pinnacle!

by W. B. MURPHY

Order	Book No.	Title	Price
————	P00163-O	CITY IN HEAT, #1	95¢
————	P00194-O	DEAD END STREET, #2	95¢
————	P00267-X	ONE NIGHT STAND, #3	95¢
		and more to come . . .	

THE PETER STYLES MYSTERY SERIES

By Judson Philips

The Award Winning Author and Bestselling Mystery/Suspense Series!

Featuring Peter Styles, a magazine writer. His assignments always seem to lead him into situations where life and death hang in the balance.

_____ P00154-1	THE LAUGHTER TRAP, No. 1	.95
_____ P00160-6	THE TWISTED PEOPLE, No. 2	.95
_____ P00191-6	BLACK GLASS CITY, No. 3	.95
_____ P00209-2	WINGS OF MADNESS, No. 4	.95
_____ P00229-7	HOT SUMMER KILLING, No. 5	.95
_____ P00266-1	THURSDAY'S FOLLY, No. 6	.95

and more to come . . .

Introducing
The Toughest Bastard
on the High Seas!

FOX In an all new naval adventure series

by ADAM HARDY

George Abercrombie Fox is a fighting man who doesn't care how he wins as long as he wins. He's mean, cunning and most vicious when trapped. There's no way to outfox Fox!

Order	Book No.	Title	Price
_____	P00180-0	THE PRESS GANG, No. 1	.95
_____	P00210-6	PRIZE MONEY, No. 2	.95
_____	P00233-5	SAVAGE SIEGE, No. 3	.95

and more to come . . .